SURVIVAL COLONY 9

SURVIVAL COLONY 9

JOSHUA DAVID BELLIN

MARGARET K. MCELDERRY BOOKS
New York London Toronto Sydney New Delhi

MARGARET K. MCELDERRY BOOKS

An imprint of Simon & Schuster Children's Publishing Division
1230 Avenue of the Americas, New York, New York 10020

Margaret K. McElderry Books is a trademark of Simon & Schuster, Inc.
For information about special discounts for bulk purchases, please contact Simon & Schuster Special Sales at 1-866-506-1949 or business@simonandschuster.com.
The Simon & Schuster Speakers Bureau can bring authors to your live event. For more information or to book an event, contact the Simon & Schuster Speakers Bureau at 1-866-248-3049 or visit our website at www.simonspeakers.com.
Book design by Sonia Chaghatzbanian and Irene Metaxatos
The text for this book is set in ITC Stone Sans Std.
Manufactured in the United States of America
10 9 8 7 6 5 4 3 2 1
Library of Congress Cataloging-in-Publication Data
Bellin, Joshua David.
Survival Colony 9 / Joshua Bellin.—First edition.
p. cm.
Summary: Querry Genn, a member of one of the last human survivor groups following global war, is targeted by the monstrous Skaldi, although Querry has no memory of why.
ISBN 978-1-4814-0354-2 (hardcover)
ISBN 978-1-4814-0356-6 (eBook)
[1. Space colonies—Fiction. 2. Memory—Fiction. 3. Monsters—Fiction. 4. Science fiction.] I. Title.
PZ7.B41463Sur 2014
[Fic]—dc23
2013034595

for Ray

ACKNOWLEDGMENTS

I love reading the acknowledgments in other people's books. Seeing all the names reminds me how many hands take part in a production that ends up having only one name on the cover. Now that I have a chance to write my own, I appreciate this more fully.

My agent, Liza Fleissig, gave me not only her expertise but also her unflagging enthusiasm, support, and faith. My editor, Karen Wojtyla, pushed me to build the best world I could and to tease out the deeper themes lurking in that world. Her assistant, Annie Nybo, guided a debut novelist through the process. And the book's cover designer, Sonia Chaghatzbanian, made my head explode (in the best possible way).

Tom Isbell, Amalie Howard, and Susan Kim took me under their wings when I was a bewildered newbie. My fellow debuts in OneFourKidLit and the Fall Fourteeners welcomed and supported me through the prepublication year. Many other friends and writers responded to this book in whole or in part, offered advice, tweeted stuff that made me laugh, and generally kept me sane. Were I to list them all, the acknowledgments would grow longer than the book. So I'll simply say: thank you. You know who you are.

I've been writing most of my life, and I've benefited from great teaching every step of the way. In ninth grade, David

Mayer first encouraged me to think of myself as a writer. Three years later, Earl Cohen gave my paper a D- and made me get serious about writing. Anne Greene, Phyllis Rose, and Geraldine Murphy liked my college writing enough to tell me what worked and what didn't. In graduate school, Romulus Linney taught me how (and why) to end a story. And more recently, Aubrey Hirsch convinced me I still had something to say.

Coworkers have afforded me the space to write and the grace not to look at me funny for doing it. I thank in particular Linda Jordan Platt, Chris Abbott, Janine Molinaro Bayer, Rita Yeasted, Michelle Maher, Ed Stankowski, Mike Young, Howard Ishiyama, and Michele Bisbey. I also thank all the students over the years who challenged me to explore the power of writing with them.

My family has been incredibly supportive, even when it seemed I was congenitally attached to the computer. My parents, Marvin Bellin and Judith Crowley Bellin, never doubted I'd publish a novel. My daughter, Lilly, read my first few tentative pages and gave me the courage to keep writing. My son, Jonah, assured me my ideas were cool. And my wife, Christine Saitz, understood my need to write from the very beginning.

But in the end, the most important people are my readers, past, present, and future. This book is my thank-you.

1

WEST

"Querry."

My dad's voice in the dark.

"Son. Come on. Time to get moving."

His hand on my shoulder, shaking me from sleep.

"Querry. On your feet. Now."

I opened my eyes to more darkness and my dad's shadowy shape filling the tent. I couldn't make out his face, but I could hear his quiet breath. There was no urgency in his voice, there never was, but I knew this was for real.

I swung my legs over the side of the cot and fished for my boots. I could see my dad's silhouette where he'd lifted the tent flap, letting in a pale slice of light.

"Skaldi?" I asked, fumbling with the laces.

He grunted.

"How many?"

He half turned, moonlight carving his angular features from the night. "It only takes one."

"How close?"

"Let's hope we don't find out." He let the flap fall and approached me in the renewed dark. His hands gripped my shoulders, guiding me to my feet. "Ready? Let's get moving." He lifted the heavy canvas and ushered me into the night.

The hollow where we'd camped bustled with activity. Everywhere I looked, men and women in identical gray-brown camouflage uniforms were taking down shelters, packing camp stoves and propane tanks, loading bundles onto the three remaining trucks. The nozzles and tanks of flamethrowers gleamed dully in the hands of the three sentries on the eastern fringe of camp. Nobody spoke, but there were plenty of quiet sounds: the pad of boots on dusty ground, the clink of metal against metal as tin pots, plates, and cups were rolled into packs, the whisper of tents collapsing. Enough moonlight peeked through the shrouded sky to show figures, but not faces. We don't use fires or lanterns unless we have to. Fires draw the ones that are hunting us, and fuel is too precious to waste. But our eyes are sharp, even at night.

Not that there's much to see. In the daylight, just about everything is brown, like us. Land, sky, and water.

"I'll be right back," my dad said. He took a step toward the small knot of trucks lined up on the western edge of camp.

Then it hit me. "West?"

He looked at me sharply, but nodded.

"The Skaldi always come from the west."

"Seems times have changed."

"But—"

He returned to where I stood and held up his right hand, palm facing me, then tapped his forehead with his first two fingers. "Focus." He forked his fingers and pointed straight at me. "Eyes open. Mind sharp. Remember." He nodded emphatically and headed for the trucks. His bad hip made him move unevenly, his right leg seeming about to crumple with each step. He huddled with his officers, giving orders in a quiet but forceful voice.

I knew my job. Working as quickly as possible, I tugged my cot from the tent, released the legs, and folded it in half. Next I yanked the tent stakes out, collapsed the frame, and rolled the tent into a tight bundle. When I hoisted everything onto my back, it was like carrying another body around with me. But we needed every inch of space on the trucks to hold the fuel drums and supplies, the stoves and tools and ammunition, while still leaving room for the people too young to keep up with the rest of us. My dad had been giving me driving lessons for the past month, showing me how to work the heavy, awkward stick, how to put my weight on the squeaky brakes, but that was only in case of an emergency. Realistically, it would be another couple years before he let me take a turn behind the wheel.

If the fuel lasted that long.

If we lasted that long.

I wiggled my shoulders, trying to find a more comfortable fit. Even with the sun down, sweat beaded on my forehead, pooled under my arms. The whole procedure had taken me just over seven minutes, which was good but not great. My dad wanted me to get it down to five. When I first started breaking camp on my own, he would stand there with a stopwatch while I fumbled with all the stakes and straps, his presence making me way clumsier than I would have been if I was practicing alone, and when I finally finished he'd hold out the watch without saying a word. Then the watch stopped working and he kept count instead. Which was even worse, him standing there counting the seconds in his head. Even now that he trusted me to keep my own time, I couldn't break camp without seeing him there, silent and impatient, counting for me.

I made one final check of my area, verified that nothing was missing, nothing left behind. Then, bent under my pack, I hurried to where the trucks were parked and being readied for evacuation.

I double-checked our coordinates. The command truck pointed due west.

I tried not to think about what that meant.

The little kids had already been loaded onto the back of the rear truck, seven of them in all. They were keeping quiet, sitting among the dark mountains of crates under the canvas frame, only their eyes visible in the moonlight. I could tell they were scared, though. Most of the time, in daylight or when there hadn't been an alarm for weeks, you could convince yourself they were just kids, having fun, playing kick the can around camp, getting into arguments, who tagged who or where base was or whatever. But they grew up in a hurry. Kids six, seven years old, kids with gaps in their mouths from lost baby teeth, wouldn't cry even when they had to move out in the middle of the night. That was one of the first jobs my dad gave me, once he decided I was ready for the responsibility. I'd come to their tents and take their hands, lead them in a chain to the trucks, and they wouldn't make a sound. The littlest of the bunch, a five-year-old named Keely, the son of my dad's driver, would peer out at me through uncut bangs, brown and as thick as they say the forests used to be. He'd squeeze my hand so tight I knew he was determined to prove he was brave. I'd squeeze back, glad he was too little to realize I was trying to prove the same thing.

I don't know if Keely knew what we were running from. But he definitely knew we were running.

I joined the other teenagers, clustered by the back of the command truck, talking nervously in low voices, waiting for my dad to give the order to move out. Eight total, counting me, though as usual, Yov hadn't showed up yet. Most had no parents, or only one, and my dad relied on them to get ready on their own.

"What's taking so long?" one girl, Nessa, said in a pinched whisper.

"Maybe it's a false alarm," a boy named Wali whispered back.

"If it's a false alarm, why are you whispering?" Wali's girlfriend, Korah, mimicked his hushed voice. She shook her black hair and made a face. The others giggled nervously, all except Kelmen, a dimwitted giant who always looked like he had no idea what anyone was talking about.

That was when Yov showed up, slouching toward us with his pack slung carelessly over one shoulder. He was the oldest kid in camp, about seventeen, and taller than most of the grown-ups.

"How do we know this isn't some kind of drill?" he said, not bothering to lower his voice. "Did the scouts even report in?"

"The scouts to the east, you mean," I said.

Everyone got really quiet. Yov glared at me.

"Yeah," he said. "That's what I mean."

"Well?" I said. "What do you think?"

"We're supposed to think now?" he sniffed. "Isn't that what daddy's for?" He smirked at me. "Space Boy."

"Shut up," I said.

"And if I don't?"

"Hey!" Keely's father, Araz, leaned out the driver's side window. "Skaldi have ears, you know."

"You sure?" Yov shot back. "Because I was under the impression they followed our lovely stench."

"Wise guy," Araz muttered.

"So did the scouts report in?" Yov called out.

Araz opened his mouth to yell back, but he caught himself and spoke in a tense undertone. "We're leaving, aren't we? Figure it out yourself, genius."

"Yes sir!" Yov tossed him a pretend salute.

Araz looked like he was about to exit the truck. Then, saying something under his breath, he pulled his head back in the window.

Yov put his hands on his hips and turned dramatically to face me. The smirk never left his lips. Korah got my attention, rolled her eyes, and let out a loud, exaggerated sigh. I looked away, feeling my face grow warm.

With Yov, it was easy to forget my dad's orders. With Korah, it was impossible to remember anything.

We waited without saying another word while workers hurriedly loaded the rest of the supplies onto the trucks, hauled up the ramps, and slammed the tailgates. As usual, it took forever for the oldest person in camp to climb into the cab of the rear truck, a crazy old woman clutching a large, bottle-green jar to her chest. I watched my dad move from vehicle to vehicle, making sure all the little kids were on board and the equipment tied down, giving final instructions to the drivers. To save fuel, they wouldn't start the engines until he gave the order. When he was satisfied with the preparations, he came over to us.

"You ready?" he said.

Everyone nodded. Even Yov kept his mouth shut.

"Querry," my dad said, "you forget anything?"

"No," I mumbled. A little wave of giggles and shoves

passed through the group. Yov, I noticed, was grinning broadly. My dad looked me up and down, but for once he didn't pursue it.

"Stay close," he said to all of us. "And stick with the group. No heroics, right?"

We nodded again.

"Good." He signaled and his second-in-command, Aleka, a tall woman with a severe face, joined us at the back of the truck. They consulted quietly for a moment before he hobbled off to make one final check of everything. He looked once over his shoulder as he left, and I tried to stand straight under the burden of my pack.

Aleka eyed us dispassionately. "If we get separated, don't wander," she said. "Lay low and wait for my signal. Querry." I stepped forward. "You're staying with me."

"What for?"

She shot me a look, but didn't answer. "Yov." He gave a lazy nod. "You're in charge tonight. I need you to keep an eye on the others."

"What's so special about him?"

"I need you to watch the others," Aleka said. Her eyes never left his.

For a minute he stared back, and I was sure he was going to give her grief like he'd done with Araz. Korah opened her mouth and seemed about to intervene when Yov let out a laugh. It sounded loud and tinny in the quiet night.

"We clear?" Aleka said.

"Yeah," Yov shrugged. "Whatever."

Aleka took my arm. I could feel my ears burning, Yov's eyes boring into my back. I couldn't get his question out of my mind.

What's so special about him?

"I can walk," I said, trying to shrug away from her.

"I need you to stay close," she said, but she let go of my arm.

My dad leaned out the passenger window of the command truck, looking back at us. Under his long hair his dark eyes glittered, and his face was unsmiling beneath his beard. I'd never seen him smile that I could remember.

He nodded to Aleka, or to me, and his head disappeared into the cab.

With a rattle and cough the trucks started up, filling the air with the oily smell of diesel. The ground shook as, headlights off, the line of trucks rumbled up the hill and out of the hollow. Aleka waved a hand and our group started to march, the two of us in the lead, the rest behind. I heard Yov grumbling under his breath, but I couldn't make out the words.

At the crest of the hill, a trio of bare trees drew twisted shapes against the night sky. Through clouds of dust and exhaust I saw the other walkers, the twenty or so adults who weren't driving or babysitting, trudging up the opposite slope, their packs double the size of ours. Behind them the sentries marched backward, flamethrowers at the ready. In the gray light everyone looked shadowy and leeched of color like old photos, the kind I'd seen people take out of their packs at night and caress with their fingertips, as if they were trying to cast a magic spell to bring the scarred, glossy images back to life.

When we reached the top of the hill I leaned a hand against a tree trunk, its bark as dry and scaly as thorns. The land to our west stretched into darkness. I tried to swallow the lump in my throat, but the knot in my gut wouldn't let it go down.

Did it really matter which way we were heading? East, west, it all looked the same.

I took a step.

Then I heard a sharp hiss of breath from behind me, and I turned to peer back down the hill.

A tall, thin man stood in the swirling smoke we'd left in our wake.

He could have been anyone, with his camouflage uniform and shadowed face. But the way he moved was wrong. All the grown-ups in camp moved with purpose, keeping the drills and rituals intact, never showing hesitation or doubt no matter what they felt. This man moved in a drifting, unsteady way, taking small steps in one direction, then the other, as if he was up to his waist in water. Only his head, turning back and forth like a snake tonguing the air for prey, seemed fixed with intent.

"Skaldi!" someone yelled.

The man in the hollow froze. His nose lifted into the air, more like he'd caught the scent than heard the sound. For a second he stood rooted to the spot, swaying slightly.

Then he dropped to a crouch and sprang up the hill toward us, one hand propelling him across the ground, the other tucked at his side. His face stayed in shadow, but I caught a glint of his teeth, bared and white in the moonlight.

Aleka grabbed my arm and dragged me toward the trucks. The group behind us broke formation and ran in the same direction. Korah shouted above the confusion. Doors slammed and my dad's voice barked orders.

A yellow burst of flame exploded from the rear truck, its heat searing my eyeballs. The next thing I knew, Aleka had thrown me into the back of the command truck, whispering harshly, "Stay down!" Then she disappeared.

I lay still and listened to the chaos outside. When I couldn't take it anymore, I lifted my head to look over the cargo door, but just then Araz hit the gas and all I saw as we blasted into enemy territory were the zigzag trails of flame against a sky without a hint of dawn.

"The colony!" my dad's voice rose for a second before drowning in the trucks' roar. "Protect . . ." Then I heard nothing more.

The colony. HSC-9, Human Survival Colony Number 9.

Survival Colony 9. The only home I can remember.

I just wish I could remember how I got here.

Or who I am.

DUST

Somehow we gave it the slip.

The flamethrowers held it at bay long enough for everyone to scramble out of the hollow and onto the trucks. There wasn't nearly enough room, people hung out the windows and held onto the rails as we bounced and jolted over rough ground. Yov stuck his elbow in my eye, I'm pretty sure not by accident. We must have put twenty miles between us and the creature before slowing down, circling the trucks, and checking for injured or missing. Miraculously, no one had fallen off. The worst anyone got was a scrape from someone else's fingernails or a bruise from one of the fuel drums. My dad did a head count, twice, but of the fifty-one of us, the only people not accounted for were six of our eight scouts.

The little kids hadn't cried once the whole ride.

My dad stayed up the rest of the night in the command truck, talking to Aleka and the other officers. Everyone else found a spot in the remaining trucks or just threw themselves on the ground. But no one really slept. I curled up behind a tire, and for what was left of the night I lay half-awake, hearing boots shuffle past my head and whispers from the other teenagers lying nearby. Every time my eyes flickered open, I saw the shadowy forms of the sentries prowling the outskirts of our makeshift camp. Sometime in the middle of the night I heard Korah reading our one storybook to the little kids, a fable about a mother rabbit and a baby rabbit. "I'll come back for you," she said soothingly. But her voice got all mixed up with the image of the bared teeth of the man in the hollow, and I had the weird thought that the mother rabbit was threatening her baby instead of comforting it. It must have been near morning when I heard two grown-ups arguing, in the hissing whispers people use when they're trying to keep their voices down.

"It was too close this time."

"Do you think they know?"

"Don't be absurd."

"This is new territory. Unmapped territory."

"You're suggesting we go back?"

"I'm suggesting it's not safe."

"It never was."

The next thing I knew, a hand settled on my shoulder

and my eyes fluttered open to see a man crouching beside me. The light stood behind him, and it took me a second to recognize him as my dad.

"We have to talk," he said.

"Did it come back?"

"Not so far."

I dragged myself from behind the truck and sat to face him. He lowered himself carefully, with his good leg, the left, tucked beneath the right. His hair, long and brown and streaked with gray, veiled his face. With a stick, he absently traced patterns in the dirt. Nothing I had to worry about memorizing, like instructions or schematics, just doodles. Swirls of dust rose to coat his already filthy boots.

I surveyed the scene while I waited. The sun hung above the trucks, a brownish smear in the brown sky. People sleepwalked around camp in soiled uniforms. My dad had switched the sentries, but even the fresh ones looked dead on their feet. The little kids were still dozing, their bodies flung everywhere like firewood. I could tell from the low haze on the southern horizon that we'd camped near the river, but other than that, the land was empty of familiar markers, no road or rise or ripple to fix our position.

"Aleka tells me you gave her a hard time last night," my dad said, not looking at me, still drawing his random squiggles.

"What?"

"You heard me."

I ran back over the events of the night before, but I couldn't think of anything that would qualify as "a hard time." I wondered if Yov had been bad-mouthing me.

"Is it true?"

"No way," I said. "She told me to stick with her and I did. She practically threw me in the back of the truck. End of story."

"Because you know I expect you to listen to her the same way you listen to me."

"I did, Dad," I said. "What did she tell you?"

He sighed and lifted his head to look at me. His face was deeply lined, with dirt in the crevices of his cheeks and the hollows beneath his eyes. An old scar trailed across his forehead to the bridge of his nose, so filthy it seemed to have been dyed black.

"Aleka's the best officer I have," he said. "You saw how close we came last night. From now on, we all need to buckle down. No more fun and games."

"Yeah, it's been such a blast till now."

He ignored me. "And we both know you can have trouble focusing. Concentrating on what you need to do." His fingers speared the air between us, the old signal. "You remember what happened six months ago."

"That's the problem, Dad," I said bitterly. "I can't."

His eyes flared briefly at the interruption, but his voice stayed calm. "Next time, if there is a next time, I don't want to have to have this conversation."

That makes two of us, I thought.

"Querry?"

"Yeah," I said. "All right. Fine."

"I can't be worrying about you in addition to everything else."

"All right, Dad," I said. "I get it."

"I hope so." He tossed his stick aside and climbed slowly and painfully to his feet, then held out his hand. "Let's get moving."

I took his hand and stood. We didn't exchange another word. His lecture took me back to the morning, six months ago, when I'd woken to discover two things: I was a member of Survival Colony 9, and my past was gone. I squeezed my eyes shut, recalling that morning, trying to recall what lay beyond it. But as always, I came up empty.

The smudge of a sun beat down on us as we started our first day on the edge of the unknown.

Querry.

That was the first thing I remember him saying that morning six months ago. His bearded face hovering over me in the gray dark. His almost black eyes keen and watchful. And the unfamiliar word on his lips, spoken with an intensity that made me sure I was supposed to know what it meant.

"Querry," he repeated that morning. "How are you feeling?"

I shook my head.

"Let's see if we can get you on your feet," he said.

I threw aside the blanket, found myself clothed in camouflage gear. My body ached, hypersensitive to his touch. But I stood, draped my arm over his shoulder. Together we staggered into the bleak light of a newly risen sun.

And I stared, speechless, at the scene that lay at my feet.

"What . . ." The word felt like a weight on my tongue. "What is this place?"

He looked at me sharply. My head throbbed, my eyes felt like they'd been held to a fire.

"You don't remember," he said.

I shook my head. Everything was fuzzy, blank. I didn't know what I'd expected to see. Just not this.

The world stretched in an endless circle of dust around me, broken only by the shapes of ragged tents and squat, rusted trucks. Both were patterned with camouflage colors. Everything else was a dead reddish-brown, the color of dried blood under fingernails. The sky reared across the waste, a uniform brown so similar to the soil my head spun with the feeling that the solid ground was only a reflection. The heat felt like a blanket wrapped around my hands, my eyes, my throat.

"The Skaldi," he said. "Do you remember?"

The word made me shiver, shiver in a hundred-twenty-plus degree day, but why it did I couldn't have said.

That's when he did a strange thing. At first, when he reached out, I flinched. He gripped my hand, guided my fingers to the back of my head, a few inches above where my skull joined my neck. My fingertips brushed against a lump, hard and sore.

"Querry," he said. "We have to talk."

He told me about the accident that had occurred the night before. The Skaldi attack, the creature in our midst. Me falling off the truck as we were peeling out, the blow to my head. When I still looked at him blankly he gave me a crash course on planetary history. As much of it as he knew, anyway. The wars, the colonies, the Skaldi. How five thousand years of civilization had been wiped out in a few years of madness, how the survivors had barely begun to pick up the pieces when the Skaldi appeared to feed on the few who remained. He sounded annoyed, maybe because this was all news to me. Or maybe because he was so unclear on the details. He'd only been a little kid himself when the wars began, and by the time they were over, hardly anyone was left who remembered.

"Let's take a walk," he said. "Check in on the troops."

He helped me stand. Dust billowed around our legs as we walked. When I looked back I saw clouds of it suspended in the angled rays of the sun like spears.

We approached a tall woman who stood with her back to us, hands on hips, the sharp angles of her elbows accentuating her slenderness. When she heard us she turned, and her eyes, hard and gray as iron, fell on me.

"Aleka," he said. "As you can see, Querry's back on his feet."

She nodded curtly. "Laman," she said. "I'd like to have a few words with you once you're done showing Querry around."

She spun and stalked away.

"What did I . . . ?" I started to say.

"Nothing," he said. "It's just been a bad day for all of us."

We resumed our walk. More faces passed in front of me. A boy with bare, muscled arms and shaggy hair, who looked at me with a smug, superior smile. Wali. The black-haired girl by his side, whose brilliant blue eyes watched me curiously in a way that made my heart pound in my chest. Korah. Grown-ups, all of them confronting me with surly expressions I couldn't understand. Araz. Soon. Kin. A group of little kids who trailed each other in some frenzied game, moving so fast the names he hurled at them didn't seem to stick on any one in particular. A lean, lanky boy who lounged on a crate outside a tent, skinning a stake with his pocketknife. He smiled crookedly and pointed his blade at my chest as we approached.

"Might want to button up," he said. "Wouldn't want to catch cold." His eyebrows rose mockingly. "Space Boy."

I looked down and saw that my uniform top was unbuttoned from my midsection to my belt. I hastily did the remaining buttons, shoved the top into my pants. My escort looked at me, shaking his head slowly.

"This is Yov," he said.

The scraping sound of the knife prickled along my spine.

We moved on. More names, faces. Scouts, officers, drivers. The camp healer, Tyris. The mechanic, Mika. A group of teens. Adem. Nessa. Kelmen. With each introduction my right hand itched to reach out, but none of the uniformed people offered to do the same. And their names and faces, no matter how much I repeated them, became tangled the moment we moved on.

My guide must have seen it in my eyes.

"They're just spooked by what happened," he said. "Give it time."

I nodded. The knot on my skull throbbed.

The days immediately after the accident were the worst. I walked around in a fog, staring at faces without names, thinking I had to get dressed only to discover I already had my clothes on. Every morning the same: his bearded face floating above me, the word on his tongue, the empty world outside. He walked me through camp, showing me the trucks, the supply tent, the latrine. That was nothing but a hole in the ground. He reviewed drills, briefed me on the procedure in case of Skaldi attack. He tried to fill in the larger world, our coordinates, our movements. We hiked south to the riverside, north to the remains of the road that had once carried thousands of cars, then squadrons of military vehicles, then nothing but dust. But for those first few days my brain was like the road, empty of traffic. Only snippets stuck: Yov's knife, Aleka's frown, Korah's eyes. Maybe a week passed before the snippets turned to solids, before the camp started to fall into place, the names, the history, the routines. One morning, I woke with the realization that I could string days together, each day enough unlike the others to tell the difference, and fix the whole sequence in my head to compose a larger span of time. I reached behind me to touch the tender spot on my head, only to find it was gone.

"I remember," I told him that morning. For the first time, when I'd woken to find him hanging over me, it hadn't been either a surprise or a shock.

"Tell me."

"I remember what we did yesterday." The concept of *yesterday* was so new to me it seemed miraculous. "When we reviewed troop formations. And the day before. When Korah helped me set up the tent."

I felt my face grow warm as I said her name, and I knew I remembered her. Our hands had touched once or twice when she instructed me how to lift the frame, tie the stakes. I even thought she'd smiled at me, before Wali showed up to steer her away.

"And . . . ?"

"And . . . the day before. I remember about the Skaldi, what you told me. How they take control of your body. Imitate you. How you can't trust anyone you don't know." I sensed I'd reached the end of what I remembered, so I added, "Or anyone you're not sure you know either."

"You watch them," he said, nodding, his face darkening.

21

"For erratic behavior. Not acting like themselves. If you sus-pect, you alert the commander and have them taken in for the trials." He leaned back on the canvas and metal seat beside my bed. "That's all?"

"That's all."

And that was all. The week rested in my memory, more or less intact. But beyond that, nothing. Not the creature attacking, not the fall from the truck, not the impact with the ground. Not a trace of all the years that had come before. The accident had cut me off from my past as completely as a knife slicing through rope. I could unspool days in my mind, think I was getting closer to the starting point, but then the rope would fall slack. And no matter how much I pulled, all I'd end up with in my hand was the frayed end.

"Give it time," he had said. I clung to that.

But time passed.

And time failed.

That first morning we returned to my tent, as the sun lent a reddish cast to the dun brown sky. I'd begun to feel lightheaded, the bump on my head pulsing to the beat of my heart. He'd reintroduced me to everyone in camp, but I'd confused all the names and faces by now.

He helped me lower myself to my cot. He was about to go when I stopped him. "How old am I?"

"Fourteen," he said. "More or less." He dropped his eyes. "We don't keep such good track of dates. They don't matter much anymore." He reached inside his jacket. "Here."

I took the shard of half-silvered glass. Through splotches and black speckles I saw a shock of sandy blond hair, a forehead sprinkled with red dots, a chin covered with fine fuzz. A face that seemed both lean and lumpy, as if someone had stretched the skin tight over cheekbones and nose and forehead. I stared at it for what seemed hours. Its blue-gray eyes stared back.

I handed the mirror back to him. "Keep it," he said, waving it away.

Finally I asked the question I hadn't wanted to admit I had to ask.

"Who am I?"

"You're my son." He said it as if he was trying to force it through the hole in my memory. "My name is Laman Genn, and I'm the commander of this camp. Survival Colony Nine. Your name is Querry Genn. You're my son."

Your name is Querry Genn. I rolled the words around on my tongue, repeated them inside my head, listened for a response. None came.

"We don't keep much in camp," he said, lowering his eyes again. "Only what we need. I wish I had something to show you. Some proof."

"Proof?"

"Something from when you were growing up," he said. "Boots, a drawing. Some parents keep those things. I don't."

"That's okay." I felt the room spinning, not from dizziness or nausea. It was like everything had come loose from its moorings, like the whole world was floating in space with nothing to hold it down. "I've lost so much," I said.

"How's that?"

"I've lost everything." My hands grasped the air between us. I didn't want to cry in front of him, but I felt the sting in my eyes. "I've lost everything."

"Then you'll just have to win it back." His eyes met mine, and I saw no compromise there. "I'm sorry this happened, Querry. But we don't have the luxury of mourning or regret. Those creatures are out there, the western desert is swarming with them, and if they see a weakness, they'll strike. You've lost a lifetime of training, information we need to fight against them, and you'll have to relearn it in a matter of days. Before they find us again."

"I'll try," I said.

"Try now." He leaned forward, his eyes holding mine. "We talked to Araz earlier today about the loading sequence for an evacuation. What do you remember?"

"Araz?"

"My driver. The loading sequence." And then he said it, his fingers pointing straight at me, his mouth a grim line beneath his unkempt beard. "Focus."

I tried. I struggled to remember. For my sake, his, ours. I pictured Araz, a burly man with a shaved head, leaning on the tailgate of the truck and ticking off supplies on a mental manifest. I closed my eyes and fought to recover the items on his list, information I'd apparently learned at one time, apparently relearned just hours ago.

"I don't remember," I admitted.

He sighed, sat back, chewed the ends of his mustache with teeth that were chipped and discolored. "Well then," he said. "I'd better go over it again."

He began, running down the contents of Araz's list, naming everyone responsible for the loading, rattling off numbers and figures and code. I found myself nodding, his words becoming a steady hum of sound. I studied his mannerisms, the way he narrowed his eyes and averted his head when he paused for thought, the way his bony fingers came together to make a point, steepled then separated, sliced the air in invisible diagrams. Something nagged at me, something important. I didn't care if he'd thrown away my baby boots and drawings, but this I was sure I needed to know.

Finally it came to me. "What happened to my mom?"

He stopped abruptly, hands frozen in mid-motion. "That was a long time ago," he said softly. "This is what matters today."

He stood and went to the door of the tent. Outside, the sounds of the camp filtered through the slit in the heavy canvas. He pulled the flap shut and returned to my cot, and his eyes flashed like hot embers on a dying fire. "You have to understand something, Querry," he said in a fierce undertone. "Everything around you is a relic from a world that's disappeared. The trucks, the tents, the weapons. The uniform on your back is the uniform one of them wore, half a century ago, when their armies marched in the millions to destroy each other. They damn near succeeded. They sucked the place dry, bombed it to pieces, and left us with . . . this." His gesture took in everything, the endless emptiness of the world outside. "Then, when there weren't enough of them left to kill each other, the Skaldi came and tried to finish the job. Some might say they've already won. But from where I'm sitting, they're exactly fifty-one survivors short of their goal."

He leaned in closer, fixing me with his eyes. "The past is gone, Querry. We're still here. The only things you need to remember are the things that will help us stay alive. I haven't lost anyone in a very long time. And I don't intend to start now."

I dropped my eyes and nodded, understanding.

"All right," he said. "Now focus. Again."

And it began, my reeducation into the life of Survival Colony 9. It continued through six months of drills, attacks, escapes. It continued through Korah's smile, Aleka's stony gaze, Yov's sneer. It continued through days I hoped I would remember my past, nights I began to doubt I ever would. In six short months, I tried to relearn a lifetime, and he was always there to remind me when I forgot.

But through the entire six months, I never forgot that first morning. I never forgot how I watched his hands, his eyes, how I formed his words silently on my tongue. How I tried to focus on what the colony had suffered, what it needed from me. How I tried not to let all I'd lost flicker across my mind.

POST

The missing scouts returned the second morning after the attack in the hollow.

Most of them, anyway. They'd found the remains of our camp, figured out from the scorch marks and tire tracks what had happened, and tramped across the desert to our new hideout. They'd met nothing along the way.

But one of the scouting teams, a man named Danis and a woman named Petra, never reported back. My dad tried raising them on the walkie-talkie, but all he got was static. Not that this was unusual. All he got most of the time was static.

What was unusual, though, was for Petra to lag behind. She was our best scout, the one we always counted on to keep us on alert. She wasn't the best at taking orders, she pretty much did her own thing, but my dad overlooked that in her case.

Her absence settled over the camp, heavy as a stone. No one said anything, but I could see in their eyes what they were thinking.

No chance she'd gotten lost. She might still be scouting, trying to draw them off our trail. But it might be that the one in the hollow had finished with that body and jumped to hers.

So we had to be careful if she did return. She might not be herself.

That's the worst thing about them. Besides what they can do to you, I mean. They make you suspicious, paranoid. It's not so bad when they attack the whole camp. At least then you know what you're up against. More often, though, they show up in the body of someone you used to know, a scout or some other straggler. They insinuate themselves into the colony, wait for nightfall, for someone to stray off by himself. Then they take that body and leave the other behind. Tyris figures they use up a body in days, weeks at most. But even when you find the remains of their last victim, you're never sure who's infected. My dad told me about this one guy, years ago, when he was second-in-command of Survival Colony 9. The guy had a mannerism, or a tic: the left side of his face would jerk up in a sort of half-smile. When the Skaldi took him, it copied that quirk so perfectly no one knew it wasn't him. It fooled everyone except my dad, who insisted they drag the guy in for the trials. My dad's predecessor nearly became the creature's final kill before it got fed to the flamethrowers.

"I can still see it," my dad said to me. "The head was the last thing to go. And I'll swear it still had that half-smile on its face."

Leeches, he calls them. Soul-suckers. Others call them a whole lot worse.

No one knows how they do what they do. How they mimic the people they infect, why they use up bodies so fast. You'd think after a half-century of being hunted by them we'd have a better idea of what we're up against, but the sad truth is, we're no closer than we ever were. No one knows how many of them there are, why they tend to attack singly, why their attacks have always come from the west. I've heard that the cities, what's left of them, are overrun by Skaldi, and that's why the colonies fled to the desert fifty years ago. But it's all rumor. No one's ever seen Skaldi outside the bodies they steal, or at least no one's ever lived to tell the tale. No one even knows how they got their name. They've always been called Skaldi, and I don't think anyone's ever figured out where the word came from.

And no one knows where *they* came from, either. The first anyone heard of them was after the wars, when the survival colonies had newly come into existence. Once the colonists realized the Skaldi were among them, their task— rebuilding civilization—turned into something a lot less lofty: staying alive. Everyone has a theory of Skaldi origins.

Radiation, evolution, outer space. But no one knows.

All anyone knows is that they're here.

When the missing scouts straggled into camp, I was still in bed. Not sleeping, just lying there, running over lists in my head. Trying to fill in the blanks. I knew I should be up, I knew I needed to set an example. I also knew that with my dad a fine line existed between toleration and fury. But it was one of my few moments to be completely by myself, and I wasn't willing to lose it.

This morning, though, it wasn't going to happen. The scouts were too beat to go back out, and we needed to investigate our new surroundings. We'd never been this far west, not that I could remember, and Korah confirmed what my memory couldn't. We'd seen no signs of Skaldi at our new camp, but that was like saying we'd seen no signs of air. Some things you don't need to see.

So while the scouts dozed in the tents, me and the rest of the teens went out on recon. In the company of grown-ups, of course. Not that it's all that dangerous in the daytime. The Skaldi mostly come out at night. Aside from the obvious advantage darkness gives them, Tyris thinks the light hurts their skin and eyes. Something about what they do to the bodies they steal makes their flesh burn easily, she thinks. But she and Soon took along flamethrowers just in case, and Aleka carried one of our four functioning walkie-talkies. Before we left, she sat us down for a lecture.

"We have no idea what's in this sector," she said. "If anyone steps out of line, Laman will hear of it."

"I'm quaking in my boots," Yov muttered. Aleka glared but said nothing.

Tyris and Soon went up ahead with the main body of teenagers, and I pretty much stuck with Aleka. At first I expected an environment totally unlike anything I'd seen—canyons, prairies, I didn't know what—but it turned out the land didn't look so different from what we were used to, except the east-west road had vanished into the dust. Bombed, probably. The desert undulated a little like waves, but other than that it was as bare and blank as ever. Once the tents and trucks disappeared into the heat haze, I had the feeling I always got out in the field, like I was a thousand miles from where I'd begun. I'd turn around and in the time it took to turn back, I'd need to use the sun to orient myself. Every once in a while I'd see Wali or Korah glance back, as if they were checking up on me. Wali wasn't so bad, I'd gotten used to him looking at me coolly, like I was inside a jar. With Korah it was different. My heart jumped every time her dazzling blue eyes swung my way. And then Wali would put his arm around her shoulders or slide his hand down her forearm, and I'd watch the muscles flex beneath his shirt and I'd look somewhere else before he got any ideas.

My dad had called this a recon operation, and there was something to that. Not only did we need to keep an eye out for Skaldi, but we needed to map this new terrain, to avoid the places so littered with drill pits and sinkholes you could vanish into the land, others so strewn with mines you could blow yourself into the sky. But like all our operations, this one's unstated purpose was to hunt for food. The land farther east yielded just enough to keep us constantly hungry: tough roots that could be gnawed, tree bark that could be boiled into a watery soup, the occasional desert bloom. Termites afforded a rare delicacy, if by *delicacy* you meant anything that carried an ounce of protein. We came across their mounds every so often and battered them apart with gun butts to get at the swarming creatures inside. They tasted terrible, like everything else, but they were numerous and easy to catch and there was no telling when you'd have another chance at a meal that size. When you found them your stomach went to war with your head. Your stomach always won, even if your head wasn't happy about it.

We'd been stumbling around in the sun and dust for a couple hours, not finding anything except the distortion heat makes on the horizon, when Wali swore he saw something up ahead, a shape the color of the dust creeping on all fours. We froze, and Aleka scouted ahead with our one pair of working binoculars. I crept to her side.

"Skaldi?"

She strained into the distance, and for a second I thought I saw her go rigid. Then she relaxed. "False alarm."

Yov's laugh broke the desert stillness. "When's the last time you heard of Skaldi crawling around like babies?"

"Laman told me they don't always try to imitate you," Wali said. "It depends on what they want your body for."

"Laman told you," Yov sniffed.

"He said if they're only using it for locomotion they don't take care of it. They let it get broken, dirty." For once, he looked embarrassed. "Dirtier than usual, I mean."

"You sound like Space Boy," Yov said. "Laman this, Laman that." He turned to me, smiling cruelly. "That right, Space Boy? Daddy write the gospel?"

"Then what do you think it was?" Wali demanded.

"How should I know?" Yov said. "Could be an elephant that didn't get the news the world ended. Or a figment of your overactive imagination."

Wali balled his fists and seemed ready to go for Yov, but Korah pulled him away. Her whispered words thrilled me even more than if I'd actually heard what she said. Yov smirked at the two of them, looking about as concerned as he would have if a beetle had dive-bombed his face.

It was getting dangerously close to midday, and Aleka had just about decided we were wasting our time when Yov reported spotting shapes that looked like trees farther to the west. At first I figured he was still messing with Wali, or maybe he'd gotten sick from the heat and seen something that wasn't there. But when Aleka trained her binoculars in the direction he pointed, she made out what looked like a row of stakes on a ripple in the land you might call a hill. A mile distant, possibly more. But she decided it was worth checking out. "Carefully," she said. We pulled our caps lower on our heads and plodded forward, raising trails of dust that eddied around our legs before sinking back as if they'd never been there at all.

In less than an hour we drew close enough to see that the shapes weren't trees but the remains of buildings, perched on the only elevation for miles. Aleka called a halt at the base of the hill, and she and Soon conferred for a minute. He thought the structures might be the ruins of a survival colony, one of the earlier ones that had started rebuilding before the Skaldi killed them off or forced them to run. But Aleka said no survival colony would have built houses that large. And she was right, they dominated the landscape, a cluster of them standing stark against the lowering sky. Our boots struck clumps of something black, the remains of a road.

We climbed to the crest and surveyed what was left. The buildings the road had once led to consisted of nothing but shells, uprights and crossbeams without roofs or floors, cracked patios and walkways surrounded by acres of emptiness. Beside some of them, deep rectangular holes had been carved into the ground, holes now filled with hills and valleys of dust like subterranean sand dunes. Those used to be swimming pools, Aleka speculated. Whatever had leveled this place had made a crater in the center, and she pointed out how the shockwave had flattened the buildings in a circle outward from that point. But we found plenty of usable stone from collapsed walls, plus broken stretches of metal fence

with tall, sharp points in a perimeter around the entire compound. Aleka suggested, haltingly, that this must have been a
gated community, built by rich people far from the cities for
protection. All I could think was, they'd thrown away a lot of
money to construct their own cemetery.

Yov voiced my thought. "What were they trying to keep
out?" he scoffed. "Dust?"

"Laman will want to know about this," Aleka said.

She called base on her walkie-talkie. After a few minutes
of silence followed by a few minutes of crackly talk, to which
she gave short replies like "seems to be" and "nothing obvious," she announced, "They're coming."

We sat in the shadows of the houses to wait. The sun
had climbed to midday, and looking out over the land was
like squinting through rippling ribbons of heat. I squeezed
my empty stomach to keep it from growling. No one talked.

A half hour later I saw the trucks inching across the plain,
clouds of dust billowing behind them. My dad must have
been impressed by what Aleka told him if he was willing to
relocate camp so shortly after we'd moved. He'd told me a
hundred times: fuel was like blood. Only more precious.

The trucks crawled up the hill, coughing and wheezing,
pulled up on bare dirt, and stopped with a squeal. My dad,
moving faster than I'd seen him move in weeks, jumped
down from the cab. He took a long look at the place, hands
on hips, nodding slowly. Then he turned to us.

"Who found it?" He directed his question at Aleka, but

I could tell he hoped the answer was me.

"Yov," she said. "The kid's got eyes like a hawk."

My dad stepped over to Yov and reached up to pat him awkwardly on the shoulder. Yov had a calm look on his face, like he was saying, "Hey, just doing my job," but I knew I'd be hearing about this later. From both of them.

"Good work," my dad said.

Sure enough, Yov looked sidelong at me and smirked.

"We'll have to double-check," my dad said. "Aleka, have your team sweep the perimeter. Querry," he said, signaling, "get over here."

While Aleka and the others fanned out to circle the compound, I accompanied him to the interior, near the crater. For an hour he had me get down on my hands and knees to peer in the dust for signs of Skaldi. He'd taught me how to detect their presence, but it's not easy. When they leave a body behind, there's nothing much to see. Emptied, like a sack of skin.

He kept up a running commentary as I crawled around in the dirt searching for evidence. "It doesn't have to be much," he reminded me. "Scraps, flakes. Teeth. Anything they might have left behind."

"What about this?" I lifted a long, thin strip of some translucent material from the floor of a ruined house.

He scrutinized it. "I don't think so. Bring it back, though. I'll have Tyris take a look at it."

Eventually we came to the very lip of the crater. He

considered sending me down inside, but the walls fell away steeply and the rock looked precarious. He made me hunt around the edge anyway.

"Seems clean," I told him when I was done.

"Check again," he said.

I dropped to the dust and searched once more for signs I couldn't see.

We strolled back to the others when he was satisfied with my inspection. "Something about this place," he said. "Familiar. Like I've heard someone talk about it before."

He shook his head, remembering, not remembering. He'd told me stories about what cities used to look like, with shining towers of steel and legions of cars streaming down the avenues. But he'd never seen one himself, not that he could remember. Only the old woman had, and the holes in her memory gaped as wide as the cracks in the houses that were left.

When we returned to the others, I could feel the anticipation in the air. No one budged, but all eyes zeroed in on him.

"Aleka," he said. "Report."

"No sign," she said. "And Laman—there's food."

The magic word shivered through the crowd. His face remained composed, but I saw his eyes light up. "Where?"

Aleka led the two of us to the structure farthest from the nucleus of camp, a windowless square of gray cinderblock overlooking the hill's eastern edge. My dad said it looked like a bomb shelter, but even if bombs had been flying or

Skaldi breathing down our necks, there was nowhere near enough room for our whole camp. Probably it had belonged to a single family in the time before. It seemed to be the only building in the compound with working locks, two in fact, one in front and one on a trapdoor that led to a basement level. But the doors stood open, the deadbolts sprung. A flight of rickety wooden stairs led below. And in a corner of the basement, on the packed dirt floor, sat a pyramid of wooden cases filled with rusty metal cans.

"You're sure it's edible?" my dad asked, holding one of the cans up in the glow of Aleka's flashlight.

"According to Tyris, properly canned goods have an effective shelf life of forever," she answered. "But Laman . . ."

He lowered the can. "I'm listening."

"It might be best to take what we can carry and go. I'm not . . . comfortable here. We're exposed. There's only one way out. If they were to block the road—"

"Not their typical behavior," he said. "And you told me the perimeter's clean."

"So far as we can ascertain," she said. "But this room—I suspect it's been looted." She shone her flashlight on the floor, revealing parallel tracks where cases had been dragged. "We may not be the only colony to have visited this place."

"And the ones who beat us to it are plainly gone," he replied. "Driven away by Skaldi, most likely. Leaving nothing but food the Skaldi won't return for."

"Unless they return for us."

My dad stared. "You believe they laid a trap?"

"I'm merely suggesting we be cautious," Aleka returned, her face showing not the slightest quaver under his dark eyes' scrutiny. "The provisions are what we need. Let's transfer what we can to the trucks and go."

He shook his head. "These are Skaldi we're talking about, Aleka. They don't strategize. They just feed."

"Are you willing to take that chance?"

My dad's face reddened and he opened his mouth to respond, but then he seemed to become aware of me. "Querry," he said softly, "would you mind stepping outside?"

I waited by the door for ten minutes. The sound of their conversation drifted from within, their voices low and calm. The words escaped me. When they emerged, my dad first, Aleka following, I could read nothing in their eyes.

But I knew he'd won.

We walked back to the group waiting by the trucks. If anything, the delay had made them even more anxious for my dad's command.

"All right, people," he said. "You know what to do."

Instantly, everyone sprang into action. Workers started unloading the trucks, moving stoves and propane tanks and flamethrowers down wooden planks and into the basement of one of the houses. Or what used to be the basement, because the first floor was gone. While we worked, Tyris inspected the cans in the bomb shelter, checking for dents and bulges. When she'd given the all-clear, everyone over the age of ten made a chain from the shelter and passed the crates to the supply post. Under Aleka's orders, we got to work with shovels and crowbars digging up sections of fence and replanting them in twin arcs closer to the building my dad had selected as head-quarters, a house marginally more intact than most, only miss-ing its second floor and with a gaping hole where one-third of its front used to be. The sun showed no mercy, the heat pouring out of the sky and emanating from the cracked, baked ground. Some people draped their jackets over their heads or rolled up their shirt sleeves and pant legs, but it made no dif-ference. Sweat drenched my back and my neck felt like it was on fire when my dad finally came over, sized up our work, and told Aleka we could knock off for the day.

I collapsed in the burning shade and surveyed our new home. It didn't look like much, in fact it looked like a fort whose army had already surrendered to the enemy. The transplanted fence leaned crazily, anchored by nothing more solid than dirt. The buildings could have been mistaken for piles of rubble. But the adults made approving noises as they studied it, so I guess it was no worse than the bombed-out places they'd seen before.

My dad took the opportunity to deliver a speech, or as much of one as he ever made.

"This is a secure place," he said to everyone who lay there, sick and dizzy with the heat. Aleka kept quiet, but she stared hard at him as he spoke. "There's food, shelter, clear sightlines to the plain. We have to be prepared to defend it."

41

"To the bitter end," Yov groaned. I guess three hours on anyone's good side was about all he could handle.

Night was coming by the time my dad had made all the minor adjustments to our defenses he always made. While he and Aleka roamed the compound, repositioning lookouts and tinkering with the location of the trucks, Tyris and a couple other adults doled out small rations of the food she'd decided was safest to eat. The meal consisted of slices of some dark purple vegetable and a lumpy white paste, all of it tasting sour and metallic. Thanks to my dad, there was only enough of it to make my mouth water for more. But for once, my stomach groaned with a noise that wasn't pure emptiness.

As the temperature dropped the few merciful degrees night afforded us, everyone in camp who wasn't on sentry duty settled down to sleep. I watched people hunt around to make sure everything they'd had with them at our last encampment was still there, every button of their uniforms, every nail or utensil or photograph they'd stuffed in their packs. Next they freed their feet from their patched, splitting boots, stripped off their belts and sweat-stained uniform jackets, and hung everything on the fence posts to air out until morning. Most dropped off to sleep instantly, with the conditioning that comes from never knowing when you might need to wake up. Four of the adults, though, stayed up into the night, bent over pieces of tin they'd flattened into wiggly mirrors, to complete their bedtime rituals.

I'd been watching the four perform the same acts for six months. But I still couldn't watch without a knot forming in my stomach.

Two of them shaved or plucked hair from their heads, their arms, their eyebrows, then collected the trimmed hair in jars and tucked the containers into the deepest pouches of their packs. The other two cut or chewed their fingernails to the nub and stashed the clippings in similar containers. The next time we made a trip to the river, they'd empty the jars and watch the sluggish water carry dead bits of their bodies away. Korah had told me of one guy in the colony, years ago, who'd kept his entire body wrapped like a mummy, only his eyes showing through the bandages. What ever happened to him she didn't say.

But it was no secret why some people went to such extremes to keep anything from falling off their bodies. No one knows how the Skaldi track us, but the best we can guess is that they use our smell. Our sweat, our blood. I've seen people suck cuts until the bleeding stops, so they don't have to use a bandage. I've even heard people say that anything you touch, anything that falls off you, can lead them to us. Clothes. Crumbs. Hair. Fingernails. Skin. I asked my dad about it, and all he said was, "Some people don't know when it's time to move on." He told me it was pointless to trim your nails and hair, because you shed your skin all the time and there's not a thing you can do about it. He said if a single hair was all it took to fill the Skaldi's nostrils, we'd all have been dead long before now.

43

Still, he must have half-believed the theories himself, because he always told us not to leave anything behind. He insisted we dig the latrine pits extra deep and cover them extra well. And he went ballistic one time when Wali, who'd just started shaving, had the bright idea to burn the trimmings in a rusty, dented mess tin.

"Are you out of your mind?" my dad yelled that time, his face so close to Wali's he could have bit him. His own chin lay buried beneath a dirty, tangled beard, his matted hair trailed to his shoulders. The camp stank, thick and sweet from Wali's fire.

"Do you have any idea what this smells like?" my dad demanded, shoving the tin under Wali's nose.

Wali's mouth moved in the word *no*, but no sound came out.

"It smells like you," my dad said. "Like supper. Like another body for them to chew up and spit out."

He threw the tin at Wali's feet, scattering sparks.

"You want to kill yourself, be my guest," he said. "But I'll be damned if you kill anyone in my camp."

"I'm sorry, Laman," Wali managed to say.

"Clean this mess up," my dad cut him off. "And get with the program."

He left Wali on his knees, putting out the fire with dirt and his own shaky hands.

Korah stooped to help him. I heard her say, "He's just trying to protect us" before I turned away and left them to work it out themselves.

I've often wondered what we smell like to the Skaldi. Living in camp, washing as little as we do, and then in muddy water with a film of oil on top, we don't smell so great to each other. People talk with faces averted to avoid getting a whiff of each other's breath.

But to Skaldi, I guess we smell good enough, or maybe bad enough, to eat.

By the time the diehards were done grooming, full night had arrived, the moon riding high and casting a net of shadows over camp. In the pale light, the place looked even emptier than before, the homes seeming as threadbare and precarious as the matchstick houses the little kids built. Me and the other teens had set up against a low wall that framed one of the structures. My own bedtime preparations weren't much, taking off my boots and rinsing my mouth and swallowing the dirty water. All I felt like doing after a day of work was lying there and staring at the sky until sleep came.

But I knew I had to fulfill one more ritual, just for me, before the day was done.

I heard the crunch of his boots and turned to see his shadowy shape, outlined in bronze. His belt and holster were strapped on, his uniform jacket buttoned to the top. I don't know if he ever took them off. He came around the wall and sat on a stone that'd come loose, leaving a gap like a missing tooth. He rested his hands on his knees and drew a deep, grunting breath. I stopped preparing my bed and waited for him to begin.

"This place," he said, taking it all in with a nod. "You kids did all right."

I didn't say anything.

"How'd it go today?" he said. "Any change?"

"You mean . . . ?"

He raised an eyebrow. "Yeah."

"About the same, Dad. No real change."

"You sure, now."

"Pretty sure."

He fiddled with something in his hand, tucked it in his jacket. When his eyes met mine his expression had hardened. "It's been six months. Lot of things have happened since then. All that time, I'd have thought. . . ."

"It doesn't work like that," I said. "It just gets further away."

He acted as if he didn't hear me. "The memory exercises Tyris taught you. You've been using them?"

Truth was, I barely remembered the memory exercises. "They don't seem to work very well."

I got ready for him to blow up at that, but he didn't. He just sat there, scratching his beard absently. When he spoke again his voice was deadly calm.

"I don't know how long we're going to be here," he said. "If it was up to Aleka, we'd already be gone."

"She thinks we're sitting ducks."

He sniffed. "We talked that through."

"Maybe she's right."

Again I braced for an explosion that never came. "I'll worry about when it's time to move on," he said. "But while we're here, you have a chance to focus on what happened. Really focus. You might not get another chance like this for a long time."

"Is that why we're here?"

"That's why *you're* here," he said. "And I don't want you to waste it."

"I'll do my best."

"Do better," he said. "Remember what's at stake."

He rose with an effort, stood beside me and laid a hand on my shoulder, like he'd done with Yov. Through the thick cloth of my uniform I felt his hand clench as if to pull the memory out of me.

Then he released my shoulder and left. I watched his dark shape limp toward headquarters until he was lost from sight.

I spread out my bedroll and lay perfectly still, arms under my head, staring into the moonlit dark. The frames of houses glowed skeletal above me. Every night since I'd recovered from my accident it had been the same. Though he told me to forget the past, he insisted I try to remember the accident itself. For the good of the colony, he said. I couldn't see what good it would do for me to remember how I lost my memory, but I knew better than to say that to him.

I felt eyes on me and turned to find that Yov had lifted

himself on an elbow and was staring at me across the row of sleeping bodies, a taunting smile on his lips. I wondered if he'd heard the whole conversation. I got the feeling he'd heard others like it on other nights.

"Daddy tuck you in real tight, Space Boy?" he said. "He tell you the big bad monsters won't come back to get you?"

I looked away, tried to focus.

"Boo!" he hissed. And wouldn't you know it, I flinched.

His laughter trailed off until there was only silence.

The empty houses leaned over me like sentinels. I shut my eyes, tried to trace the lost memory in the pulsing darkness beneath my eyelids. But it was like looking down a dark tunnel with a twist in it, seeing solid rock then, just beyond, nothing. What came into my mind instead were Aleka's words: *Are you willing to take that chance?* If my dad had chosen to keep us here on the off chance that staying put would help me remember the attack, was that worth what we risked? Worth waiting here, in unknown territory, for someone or something to find us?

I knew sleep would be a long time coming. Another night of questions that had no answers lay ahead of me, without the company of a single sound or soul.

4

RUST

The next morning, we found tracks leading from the bomb shelter.

Human tracks. Not that that meant much. Skaldi make human tracks with whatever body they happen to steal.

But whoever or whatever had made these tracks hadn't wanted to be identified by boot size or markings, because they'd gone barefoot. The prints got smudged and vanished into the dust about twenty paces from the shelter, so there was no way to tell where they'd come from or gone to. Maybe Petra could have figured it out. But none of the other scouts could.

The sentries swore they'd seen no one. Since my dad hadn't posted any of them at the emptied shelter, that made sense. Still, he took the whole group into his headquarters with Aleka and the other officers, leaving one officer to stand watch at the front door. I got as close as the guard would let me, but I heard nothing.

Korah stood nearby, her upper lip in her teeth. Somehow, on her, that didn't look bad at all.

"Why would anyone go back?" I asked her.

She jumped as if she'd just come out of a trance. Then she smiled. "They must have been hoping to filch extra rations."

I was about to ask her who in camp was stupid enough not to know we'd cleaned the place out, but then I remembered who I was talking to. "He's checking them, isn't he?" I said. "To see if they're infected?"

She shot me a look, and I thought I saw a flash of fear in her eyes. But before I could say anything else, Wali swaggered over. I swear the guy had a homing device on me. He took Korah's arm, flexed every muscle in his body, and walked away.

An hour later the sentries came out, their shaken expressions making me glad I wasn't them. A smear of blood crossed one of the men's cheeks.

My dad appeared at their rear. His face revealed nothing.

"Let's go, people," he said. "Show's over. Time to get to work."

"Laman," Aleka said. "Quarantine procedures."

Everyone froze. My dad had told me about quarantine. It meant subjecting every person in camp to the trials, no exceptions. Risky, because the results weren't always reliable. False positive, you torch one of your friends. False negative, you relax your guard. Normally, he'd told me, you put quarantine into effect only when you had a very good reason to suspect a breach.

"Laman?" Aleka repeated.

My dad must not have thought this was one of those occasions, because he didn't even bother to respond.

"Querry," he called. "Seems like you've got time on your hands. How about helping us out over here?"

We left Aleka standing there, a frown on her thin lips.

I spent the rest of the morning shoveling.

The location of our new camp might not have made us more vulnerable to Skaldi. I guess it depended on who you asked. But there was no doubt it made us vulnerable to a different kind of enemy: dust. Perched on the highest spot for miles, with only our flimsy fence as a windbreak, it had gotten pummeled by a dust storm that blew through overnight. I guess my dad should have foreseen that possibility the day we arrived, what with dust choking the empty swimming pools and painting miniature sand dunes up walls and foundations. Maybe he had, but he'd decided that was worth the risk, too. When daybreak revealed the dust piled on everything, coating our trucks, our equipment, our clothes, I'm not sure everyone agreed.

The strange thing for me was that I'd hardly noticed the dust accumulating while I lay half-awake those long hours before dawn. I'd heard the wind blow and felt the tickle on my cheek. But when I joined the work detail and discovered our supplies buried, I couldn't believe it had all materialized in a single night. I guess it was something like the snowstorms the old woman had told me about, from the time when there still was snow. Overnight squalls that blanketed the world in white. People dreamed about it, she said. Prayed for it. Kids pressed their faces against frosty windowpanes and stared through the steam of their own breath at the sparkling shroud. Why they were so excited about seeing their world erased I don't know.

But then, this was the woman who wouldn't tell anyone in camp her own name, so I'm not sure I believed her until I waded through the brown powder that had obliterated everything we owned in a single night.

The shoveling took forever. We didn't have nearly enough tools to go around, and the ones we did have were in lousy shape. Shovels, picks, crowbars with broken handles, blades bent and brittle. The adults hogged what we had, so we teens dropped to our knees and did the best we could with our bare hands. Over and over, I scooped the ground into my raw palms, carried it up the stairs, dumped it someplace else. It didn't take a genius to figure out that meant we'd be doing the same thing tomorrow morning, and the next day, and the next. Yov vented his frustration by shouldering me out of the way whenever we crossed paths. He was the last guy I would have asked about our nighttime prowler, but my dad stood watch through the whole operation, so I wouldn't have had a chance even if I'd wanted to.

We managed to clean out the basement before the sun got high. We also moved our equipment around, transferring it to the corner that seemed best protected from the wind. But the area of the compound just east of the central crater, where we'd set up our sleeping quarters, still swam under a sea of dust.

"We could shift the trucks," one of the officers suggested. "Create a windbreak."

To my surprise, my dad agreed. If it had been a matter of moving the trucks more than a couple hundred yards, I'm sure he would have said no.

The drivers jumped into the trucks and started the engines. Two motors churned to life, two puffs of black smoke chugged from tailpipes. Two of the three trucks crept forward. Aleka and my dad stood in front to direct the drivers where to pull in.

That's when I noticed that the command truck, the one my dad always rode in, hadn't moved. It hadn't even started. Araz sat hunched over in the cab, doing something I couldn't see. His head bobbed out of sight for a second, rose back into view. He rolled down the window and gestured for my dad.

"We've got trouble, Laman," he said.

He lowered his bulk from the cab as my dad limped over. The two of them poked around under the hood for a couple minutes, then Araz swore. I strained to hear the rest of their hushed conversation, but I couldn't make anything out. Araz kept pointing at the truck, then at my dad, his face contorted and his lips moving nonstop. Finally he slammed the hood down and stomped away, wiping greasy hands on his already filthy pants.

"Get back here, Araz," my dad called.

Araz kept on walking. My dad was left standing by the truck, his face calm but his eyes stormy. In a minute the hollow clatter of propane tanks echoed from the storage basement. Aleka slipped away, I guess to stop Araz before he blew something up.

I took a step toward the truck. "Dad?"

"Where's Mika?" he said, talking not to me but to the group, or maybe to himself.

Korah's mom, the black hair she shared with her daughter cut short over her ears, separated herself from the crowd and approached him.

"Distributor cap," he said, and she winced.

"Everything checked out fine last week," she said.

"It's cracked," he said. "Can it be replaced?" He corrected himself. "Fixed?"

"I'll see what I can do," she said.

She lifted the hood and quickly confirmed the diagnosis. Heat, dust, rough terrain, or just age, she couldn't tell. Whether it could be fixed she refused to say. But there was nothing like a replacement part, unless somewhere out in the desert we stumbled across an abandoned auto supply store that hadn't been smashed to pieces or ransacked by colonies past. The trucks were old, no one knew how old. Soldiers had probably driven them to the wars that swept away the old world. There'd been three times as many when he was a boy, my dad had told me, enough for everyone to ride in with room to spare. But one by one they'd died, lost working parts, developed flat tires that couldn't be patched, and one by one they'd been left to litter the landscape. We'd circled past one a couple months ago, found it axle-deep in dust like it was being devoured by the hungry land.

People in camp exchanged nervous glances. With three trucks, we could barely squeak by. If we'd had only two the night the Skaldi attacked us, not all of us would be standing here.

And after two, one. And after one . . . what?

The thought of sabotage jumped into my head. I tried to catch people's eyes, but no one would look at me. If a vandal had left any tracks, the dust storm had erased them. The idea that someone would actually disable one of our last vehicles made my stomach twist, but I wondered if the thought had passed through anyone else's mind too.

A crowd watched in stony silence as Mika got to work. She rechecked under the hood, crawled beneath the chassis with a flashlight in her teeth, as if she might spot some miracle hidden from view that would cancel out the one thing that was obviously wrong. Araz wandered over to take a look at her progress once he'd finished beating up on propane tanks.

"Give it a rest, Mika," he said laconically, leaning against the hood. "I've been over all that."

She pulled herself from under the truck. "Unless you're here to help," she said, "why don't you go find something else to do?"

Araz kicked a tire. "Such as?"

"Be creative, Araz." She ducked back under the truck, her tools banging away. "Take a nap. Torture puppies. Just get the hell out of my hair."

Araz spat on the ground and sauntered off, hands in his pockets. My dad watched him go and, for once, said nothing.

But he wasn't letting the rest of us off the hook that easy.

"What are we waiting for, people?" he said to the group of loiterers who stood there listening to the muffled clatter of Mika's tools. "Let's move."

He pulled the sentries to patrol the compound, assigned a couple teens to keep an eye on the little kids. While Korah stayed with her mom to work on the truck, Aleka and a couple officers gathered the rest of us and we trooped back to the sleeping quarters. She told us to empty our rucksacks and lay the contents on the ground. If the truck couldn't be fixed, we'd need room to carry more supplies in our packs. Yov grumbled, but he hauled out his pack along with me and the other teens. The grown-ups simply stood there in stunned silence.

"Everything?" one of them said at last.

"Everything," Aleka said flatly.

I watched as people stooped over their packs and shakily began removing items. For the first time ever, I was glad not to have anything from my past.

Because frankly, it was pathetic. I'd always assumed everyone carried pretty much the same supplies I did: rope, blankets, bandages, utensils, cot, tent, all the stuff our colony needed to survive. And they did carry those things, but that wasn't all. The desert, it seems, wasn't as empty as I'd thought. It constantly spit up discards from the time before. And now here it lay, junk someone else hadn't had the time or heart to bury, scavenged on the road by one of the adults from Survival Colony 9 and hoarded for a day, a decade, a lifetime.

It was only the grown-ups. Yov and the other teens' packs were as clean as mine.

One man pulled out a framed painting of a tall, slim tower with a light on top, standing by the kind of coastline I could hardly believe had ever existed: dark blue water, lush green trees, pale pink and purple clouds. The glass had chipped away and the frame was splintered and cockeyed, but the guy stared at the image as if mesmerized. Someone else had a pair of sunglasses with one lens missing, another had a pair with the frames completely empty. Practically everyone had palm-size flat screens that had once been phones, but now their batteries and the networks that used to carry their signals and the people who used to receive their calls were all dead. One guy even had a computer that opened like a book, its screen as blank as the phones. A woman produced our only picture book, the one about the mother and baby bunny, its spine cracked and its last few thick cardboard pages torn out, so it was anyone's guess if the mother bunny ever came back or not. Another woman unwrapped a dirty rag from a foot-long stick with a fake gold ball on top of it. An old flag, possibly, though too faded and shredded by now to know which country someone had waved it for. A man had scavenged a dirty pink shoe, nubby on top and with cracked leather on the sole and toe, that didn't look like it would fit anyone with a normal-size foot. A woman had found a plastic baby doll head, dotted with holes where I guess it used to have hair, and when she pulled it from her pack and laid it on the ground, miniature eyelids closed over empty sockets with a tiny click. Then there was the ceramic handle of what might once have been a mug. A hinged, cracked plastic case. A small paper pouch with a picture of a lumpy orange vegetable growing from a twisting green vine. The scarred remains of a piece of thick rubber, with two raised letters on it: *M-E.*

And that was just the beginning. It was unbelievable, the stuff that came out of those packs and lay spoiled and rotten in the desert dust.

And it was all worthless. The mug handle you could maybe use as a weapon or a scraper. The doll's head would have been a water container if not for the holes. A few other odds and ends might be salvageable. But everything else was an obvious, total loss.

"What about these?" an officer said, snatching a collection jar from one of the camp's chief crazies. Its owner stiffened, eyeing the clouded jar half-full of his own hair and clippings.

Aleka cocked her head. "I'll have to double-check with Laman."

"Take your time." Yov smiled as she headed off to find my dad. "It'll give me and Space Boy a chance to catch up." He nudged me with an elbow. "Now, where were we?"

An uneasy murmur passed through the grown-ups once Aleka was gone. My dad had never made a stink about people's jars in the past, so long as their owners didn't slack off in their other duties. It was weird, considering that the few people who used them washed away what they'd collected every time they had a chance, but they clung to those containers like they actually held their bodies. The craziest of the bunch, the old woman who'd told me about snowstorms though she wouldn't tell anyone her own name, didn't use a jar herself. But she still carried her dead husband's, a jug-size container filled to overflowing with black hair despite the fact that the hair on her head had long since turned white. He'd died twenty years ago, Korah told me, but she wouldn't give it up. She held it, cradled it, rubbed its side, mumbled to it all day long. What she would do if it ever broke I had no idea.

This time, though, my dad wasn't going to yield.

"Jars we keep," he said when he returned with Aleka. "But not for hair and fingernails. Those are potential drinking vessels, storage containers. Empty them and set them aside."

"And the rest?" she said.

"We've got important things to carry," he said. "Food, weapons, medical supplies. I can't have people weighing themselves down with junk."

"We could wait a day or two," she tried. "Give them time to adjust."

"We might not have a day or two," he said, and walked off.

Aleka took a deep breath, squared her shoulders, and turned her unsparing gaze on the crowd.

"You heard the man," she said. "Collection jars are to be emptied for future use. As for the rest, anything not directly necessary to the survival of the colony is to be placed in a pile of disposables."

"Necessary according to who?" the man with the painting of the light tower challenged her.

"According to me," she countered. "I'll be inspecting the results in one hour." When no one budged, she repeated, "One hour." Then she left, striding rapidly in the direction my dad had gone.

"If anyone tries to mess with my comic book collection," Yov said loudly, "I'll kill them."

For once, no one laughed.

I double-checked to make sure nothing in my own pack

would fail Aleka's test, then shoved it all back inside. Meanwhile, the people who were supposed to be our elders sat there, surrounded not only by camp supplies but by four or five treasured but totally worthless things. As the minutes passed by and no one made a move to separate the essentials from the trash, I could see in their faces that they weren't going to be able to do it. They put their hands on the items lying in front of them, moved and rearranged piles, held objects in each palm as if weighing them, threw furtive glances at their neighbors, and all the while their faces got more panicky and desperate. The collection jar fanatics sat frozen, eyes darting around as if cages had sprung up out of the dust, trapping them inside. But they weren't the only ones. The man with the picture of the light tower hugged it to his chest like a child he needed to defend against a horde of ravenous Skaldi.

And it dawned on me why.

Everything was important to them. Jars, paintings, sunglasses, baby doll heads. Not just because of what it was. Not even mostly because of that.

Because it was all they had.

I rose from the ground. People sitting paralyzed among their small piles of junk watched me leave.

"Where you going, Space Boy?" Yov called out lazily. "To ask daddy if you can keep your model train set?"

This time, Kelmen did laugh, a mindless bark that barely sounded human.

But I didn't listen. I scanned the compound until I located

my dad, standing with Aleka outside our makeshift fence on the crest of the hill. As I approached, I could hear their voices, see her gesturing toward the bomb shelter and the trucks, him shaking his head slowly but insistently. Watching him there, oblivious to the pain he was causing, made anger bubble in my chest. It wasn't fair, I decided. The more I thought about it, the more certain I felt.

Maybe, I thought, only someone who's lost everything knows he has no right to tell others to throw everything away.

"Hey, Dad," I said. "Can we talk?"

"Not a good time," he said without looking at me. "Can it wait?"

In my dad's language, that's not a question but an order.

"No," I said. "It's important. To the colony's survival."

He turned to face me, his expression keen and wary. Whether he really thought I had something worthwhile to say or was simply on the lookout for another of my brain freezes, I couldn't tell. Only now that I found him staring at me with his dark, penetrating eyes, I felt my confidence start to crawl down my throat and look for a hiding place in my stomach.

"I'm waiting," he said.

"Okay." I tried to put the words together the way they'd shaped themselves in my mind. "It's about people's stuff. The jars and things. I was thinking, when we were sorting, I was thinking. . . ."

He held up his first two fingers, tapped his forehead. "Clock's running, Querry."

"Maybe I should go," Aleka said.

"No," he said. "Querry's got something important to say, you should hear it too." He lifted an eyebrow. "It is important, isn't it, son?"

"Yeah," I said. "It is." I took a breath and said in a rush, "I don't think it's fair to make people throw away their stuff. Even if it looks like junk to you. It doesn't look like junk to them."

He snorted. "Which is exactly why someone like me has to make the call."

"But," and I could feel my thoughts getting tangled again, "what if they're right? I mean, wouldn't they know their own things better than you?"

His face showed nothing but contempt for that idea. "It's time people in this camp learned the difference between *need* and *want*," he said. "The difference between necessities and luxuries."

"That's just it," I said, because his word reminded me of what I wanted to say. "They're not luxuries."

"Ballet slippers aren't luxuries?"

"Not to them."

"When we're fighting a war."

"*Life* isn't a luxury," I said. "And if you take away the ballet slippers, you might be taking away their life."

He looked at me piercingly. Aleka, I saw out of the corner

of my eye, watched me too, her face as stern and unrevealing as ever. I wondered what ballet slippers were, heard the distant ring of Mika's tools against the underbelly of the truck, felt the hot wind blow.

"Aleka," my dad said at last, "would you check on the others? Tell them," and his eyes never left mine, "that we'll make a thorough inventory of camp equipment before returning to personal items."

"Gladly," she said. She left, but not before leveling one last, appraising look at me.

My dad put a hand on my arm. "I need to check the lookouts." He let go and we circled the outskirts of camp, him limping and me following a half-step behind.

Nothing much had changed that I could tell. He'd posted sentries in the upper-story windows of a couple houses that still had upper stories. He pointed them out to me, because I wouldn't have seen them on my own. He also told me he'd moved the two drivable trucks once more, west of our sleeping quarters, closer to the trail that led down the hill. It was obvious, he said, nodding at the dust that had accumulated against the foundations in the last couple hours, that the vehicles weren't serving much purpose as windbreaks, and so he'd decided to put them where we could get to them and get out as quickly as possible.

"Last time was too close for comfort," he said. "The next time we're forced to evacuate, it's got to be fast. No time to pack, no time to look around for anything missing."

I knew what he was getting at, but I decided to play along. "Wouldn't it be better to have everything loaded on the trucks?"

"The fuel's already there," he said. "The rest of the heavy equipment we can load on a moment's notice. But that plus the little ones will take up all the room we have. Everything else will have to be shipped by hand."

"Which means we can't take personal stuff too," I finished his thought.

He nodded, his mouth set in a line beneath his mustache. "That's the predicament. I've allowed people to carry that garbage for so long, I know it's hard for them to let go. I wish I'd done away with it from the start. Before people started to depend on it. Before they got attached."

"Why didn't you?"

He raked his teeth over his upper lip, let out a breath. "Guess I was being sentimental," he said. "Trying to protect them. To give them hope."

"And now you're taking it away?"

He didn't answer at first. His brow lowered, and I thought he was going to let me have it. But when he spoke his voice carried its usual tone of certainty and command.

"Some will see it that way," he said. "Some, maybe, who don't like following my orders. Some who might be willing to tear this colony apart if they think that's the only way for them to end up on top."

"Like Araz," I said.

65

He shrugged. "Araz I've got no quarrel with. But I can't be responsible for how people feel. They'll have to find the hope they're offered. Find it where it truly lies."

"What if there's none to find?"

His eyes narrowed. "Come again?"

"You still don't get it," I said. "You take away their stuff, you're taking away who they are. Listen to Mika, banging away on a truck she knows can't be fixed. You take away the things that let them know who they are when they wake up each morning, it won't matter who's in charge. You take those things away from them," I drew a deep breath, "it's over."

For a second longer his eyes cornered mine. Then, moving faster than I thought he could, he grabbed my arms and squeezed. Hard, so hard it hurt. His face loomed in front of me, his breath sour, his eyes on fire. I tried to twist away, but he clasped me in a grip like a steel trap.

"It's not over," he hissed. "You hear me? You don't say that, you don't even think it. When you start thinking that way, you end up like . . ."

My arms burned. "Like who?"

"Like them," he said, tossing his head. I couldn't tell if he meant the people in camp or someone, something, out there in the dying world.

As suddenly as he'd grabbed me, he let go.

"Life isn't a luxury, Querry," he said. "You've learned that much. But despair is. A luxury and a waste. You think those trinkets they carry around are what's keeping them alive. I think they're just a more subtle form of despair. A form that'll kill them as surely as any monster we have to face."

He pointed toward the tallest of the houses, a full three stories. A sentry's outline filled the frame of the top-floor window.

"That's what's going to keep us alive," he said. "Focus. Caution. Sharp eyes. Concentrating on what can be saved, not crying over what we have to let go. You want hope, you fix your mind on those things. Not on magic and day-dreams."

With that, he left me to return to his sentries, his officers, his broken-down truck and secret schemes.

When he was gone I hugged my arms, felt the blood pounding in them, closed my hands over the place I could still feel his fingers. I waited until my heart had settled, then went back to the others. I found the man with the light tower shaking Aleka's hand, over and over, thanking her for what he didn't know was only a reprieve.

That night, for the first time in the past six months, my dad didn't show up for our bedtime interrogation. I fell asleep to the sound of Mika's tools clattering away in the darkness.

WASTE

I woke up sweating.

Heart pounding. Hands clenched to my chest. Like always, my first thought was that it was a Skaldi attack. But there was no sign of movement from any of the bodies sleeping around me, no noise in the night. Mika must have finally given up and gone to bed. I held my breath to make sure. Dead silence. Whoever came up with that expression sure had it right. When just about everything's dead, there's nothing but silence.

It wasn't an attack that had woken me up. It was a dream, only a dream. But I couldn't remember it.

I sat and rested my head in my hands. My palms felt clammy against my forehead. But no matter how hard I concentrated, whatever I'd dreamed had vanished as completely as the rest of my memory.

And that's the way it always was. I don't remember my dreams. Ever. You're supposed to remember what you're dreaming if you wake up in the middle of one, but for me it felt like a wall slid into place the second I woke. A wall between me and my own mind. I'd clutch at the hazy shapes I sensed on the other side of the wall, but they'd slip through my hands like dust and shadows.

Even so, I was sure I was having dreams. Bad ones. Nothing else could explain why, when I wrenched myself from sleep on nights like this, my gut felt twisted in knots and my pulse raced wildly.

A panic reaction, Tyris called it. A night terror. The kind of dream that happens in deep sleep, when you're not supposed to be dreaming. Dreams that scare you to death while they're playing in your mind, but that you can't call back once they're gone.

My dad filled me in on some of the details. He told me he'd seen me thrashing around on my cot. Clawing at the air. He said he'd even heard me screaming. I didn't thank him for that piece of information.

"It might be related to the head trauma," Tyris said.

And that's all she could say. Though she was officially our camp healer, she didn't have any medicine, any real way to treat anyone. She had bandages, needles and thread for stitching, maybe enough plaster to make a cast. According to her, there'd been a time when people who got sick were taken care of better than anyone, with buildings to live in, workers to stand by their side, machines to feed them drugs and oxygen. Story was her own parents had been working in a building like that when it got bombed. But these days, people who got sick mostly recovered on their own. Or they didn't, and the colonies dug a grave deep enough that the Skaldi couldn't find it. And then they moved on, in case the Skaldi did.

I got my legs under me, stood, almost fell. This was the worst episode yet. The times before, my heart would slow to normal in a minute and all that would be left was a slight tightness in the pit of my stomach. Tonight I felt dizzy, drained. Like I wasn't totally there, like some part of me was back in the depths of the dream I couldn't remember.

I wondered what had triggered it. The truck? The stalker at the bomb shelter? The feeling I'd had since the attack in the hollow that something was wrong, something more than usual? Or the fact that Aleka seemed to feel the same way?

Maybe it was my latest argument with my dad. His anger when he thought I was giving up. Maybe this time, if I really focused, I could give him what he wanted at last.

But I couldn't. The dream had evaporated, and the effort to concentrate made my stomach clench and my head throb. I knew that if I remained where I was, I'd spend the rest of the night staring at the moon-blurred sky, waiting for sleep that wasn't about to come.

I stepped around bodies and made my way across the compound. Moving helped a little. The nausea subsided and my thoughts came into better alignment with the outside world. The trucks squatted in their new location, their black bodies like the shells of some long-dead creature. The light had gone out in the house my dad had designated as headquarters, so even he must have been sleeping. I knew I couldn't get far without running into Wali, who was on guard duty tonight. Thinking about him reminded me of Korah, and thinking about what the two of them probably did when they were alone in the dark didn't help my stomach either. So I stopped at one of the nearby houses, one with an empty swimming pool. I lowered myself carefully by the edge, dangled my legs into the hole, and listened to the silence. The crater in the compound's center yawned like a lake of darkness.

I decided to try one of Tyris's memory exercises. She'd taught them to me in the week after the accident, and though they'd done nothing to restore my past, they did help pass the time. Her favorite was to have me isolate a memory from as far back as I could, a pleasant memory. I'd almost laughed when she said that. "A memory where you felt safe," she amended. I shut my eyes now and remembered the first time my dad took me out in the field after my accident. I'd been cooped up in my tent much of the time before that, and it was something just to get out and move around. He drew troop formations in the dust with a stick, X's for us and O's for them, wiped the diagrams out, made me redraw them from memory. He showed me a tattered field guide he'd picked up somewhere along the way, which described how to determine your position if you had a compass, how to plot points on the horizon if you didn't. It gave me an odd thrill to realize I was one of only a handful of people in camp who knew how to read, though he said nothing about how I'd learned. He tested me on the book's concepts, and it turned out I was pretty good at putting theory to practice. My mind seemed to expand with the open air. There'd been no signs of Skaldi in the days after my accident, so we stayed out well into dusk. When the light got too bad to do any more work, he clapped me on the back and we headed for the mess tent.

That's when he saw a ball one of the little kids had dropped, a tightly wound bundle of twine. He leaned over to pick it up, weighed it in his hand. Then he looked at me, an almost impish gleam in his eyes.

"It's been a while since I've had a catch," he said. "You game?"

He tossed me the ball, and my left hand shot out without hesitation to snatch it from midair. When I threw it back he slid smoothly to his right to pick it off, his bad hip bracing easily for the return throw. We tossed back and forth for the few minutes the dying day left us, snagging flies, backhands, short-hops. My arms and eyes seemed to remember what to do, and thoughts of the creatures pursuing us receded like the last shadows on the dusty ground.

The next day I hunted for the ball, but it was gone.

I leaned back, kicked my legs in the pool, let the memory

seep into me. I wasn't sure what the point of the exercise was, but for once I felt glad I'd done what Tyris asked.

The sound of footsteps behind me was so soft I almost mistook it for the beating of my own heart.

I turned my head to see a dark figure come gliding across the sleeping area toward me. It moved swiftly but cautiously, following the trail I'd taken, avoiding bodies and the rubble of buildings. My memory of that long-ago catch shredded as I jumped up to confront it, realizing I had nothing to confront it with. If it was the prowler from the night before, I had no idea what to say. If it was Skaldi, the best thing for me to do was shout, sound an alarm, hope someone woke up before it took too many of us. If it was Skaldi I was dead anyway, so attracting its attention didn't make any difference. But my throat caught as if it was stuffed with dust, and no sound emerged as the shape closed in on me.

Then I saw the long black hair streaming behind it, and I let out a grateful breath. It was Korah.

She came to my side, peered into my face. Every time I looked at her I marveled at how she alone had avoided being wilted by sun and dust. Her complexion was neither too burned nor too pale, her hair fell past her shoulders free of snarls. Even in the moon-dappled dark, her eyes glowed so blue they seemed transparent, like you could see through them if you stared long enough. Which, for obvious reasons, I wasn't about to do.

"Can't sleep?" she said.

I mumbled something noncommittal.

"Neither can I," she said. "I stayed up half the night working on the truck with my mom, but it's dead. Not a chance of bringing it back. Laman's pretty set on paring down supplies, huh?"

"You could say that."

She sighed. "Maybe it's best if we move on. Wali says this place freaks him out. I can't decide whether I agree with him or not. It seems safe to me. Or as safe as any place we're likely to find."

"Even with someone poking around the bomb shelter?"

"Still on that, huh?" She smiled. "People get restless sometimes, Querry. Especially at night. Like they just have to get up and move around. Like"—she spread her arms and made a face—"me."

She sat by the poolside, and I joined her. Under the usual smells of grime and sweat, her body gave off a husky aroma that twisted my stomach back into the knot that had just started to loosen.

"So what do you think of this place?" she said.

"I'm hardly the guy to ask," I said. "No basis for comparison."

She barely nodded, as if she wasn't really listening. "I keep thinking this is the kind of place the Skaldi first came," she said. "Cities, towns. My mom told me. I guess they figured it'd be easier to blend in where there were more people. Plus it gave them a more plentiful food supply." She shook her head as if to wipe the memory away. "I don't want to think about those things. But I can't help it."

I watched her, tried to think of something to say. What are you supposed to say when someone else's girlfriend shows up in the middle of the night to talk about monsters?

"I keep wondering if they're us," she went on in a strange, tight voice. "When they take us, I mean. If they can copy our look, our voice, does that make them us? Do they think like us? Feel like us? Or is it all just counterfeit?" Her shoulders rippled. "I've really got to stop thinking about this."

She took a deep breath, let it out in a *whoosh*. She picked up a stone from beside the pool and dropped it to the bottom, where it landed with a soft *poof* on the pile of dust. I stole a glimpse at her arm, slim but sleek with muscle.

"Did you ever wonder what the world was like before?" she asked.

"Before when?"

"Before now," she said. "Before the wars, the warming. Before people destroyed it."

"What does Wali say?" I asked, and instantly regretted it.

"He won't talk about it." I thought I heard a note of anger in her voice. "He says it's a waste of time to think about how we got here. He says we're here now, and that's all that matters."

"Sounds familiar."

"Laman." She smiled, then sobered. "He won't talk about it either."

"Except to curse the fools who wrecked the place."

She laughed. It was a deep, melodious sound, and it startled me. You don't hear laughs, real laughs, much in camp.

I imitated his gruff voice. "Big cities, fast cars, instant gratification! It was like living in an amusement park!"

Korah laughed again. Then she asked, "What's an amusement park?"

"I don't know." I felt a smile steal across my lips. "I don't think he knows either."

We fell silent, swinging our legs in the empty swimming pool.

"All the other grown-ups talk about it," she interrupted the quiet. "Even though they never saw it."

"The old woman did."

"But the rest of them," she said. "The ones born after the wars. It's like they have this obsession with it. And no one even knows if any of it's true."

I shrugged.

"My mom's one of the worst offenders," Korah said. "She's not even forty, but she talks about it like she lived there all her life. Like she'd go back there in a second if she could."

The anger had returned to her voice. She brushed hair from her eyes, swung her legs so violently her heels smacked the edge of the pool. They gave off a series of dull echoes, immediately stifled in the dust below.

"The old woman told me she used to wake to the songs of birds," I said quietly.

"Birds." Korah took a deep breath, closed her eyes. When they opened again, their blue struck me like something precious I hadn't seen in years. "Now all we have are bugs." She crossed her eyes, stuck out her tongue. It didn't work. Still beautiful. "Dinner."

"Mostly they're arachnids," I said, then realized what a geeky thing it was to say. In the six short months I could remember, most of the animals I'd seen had been long-legged brown spiders that spun cone-shaped webs in the ground, scorpions black as the beetles they ate. Neither of them particularly dangerous. They could give you a bad stomachache is all. I'd seen them scurry out from inside my boots in the morning, looking for a new place to hide. "I saw a snake once," I added. "I cornered it and tried to catch it."

"Ooh," she said. "A gourmet meal."

"It got away," I said. "Pretty anti-climactic."

"What did the old woman say about the birds?"

"She tried to describe their songs," I said. "But she couldn't really remember."

"She told me about trees," Korah said. "Green trees that changed color once a year and became a rainbow of red and orange and gold. Then the colors would all turn brown and fall off the branches."

"Trees that lost their needles," I said.

"Not needles," she said. "Leaves."

"How'd they get them back?"

She shook her head, and I was left to imagine trees that

could die and come back to life every year.

We sat in silence for a long time. I heard the wind whining through the empty rooms, and I knew we'd be up first thing moving dirt again, like a colony of giant ants.

"The old woman told me it was beautiful," Korah said. "But I don't think she really wanted to remember. Not like the others. Maybe she didn't want to be reminded of what was gone."

I turned to look at her. She held her head high, and she watched me with the look of determination I'd gotten so used to seeing in camp. But in the second before I dropped my gaze, I thought I saw tears glistening in her incredible blue eyes.

"I'd give anything to get my memory back," I said.

"That's what you think." Her voice was gentle, but her words cut through me. "But that's because you haven't seen what I've seen."

I felt my heart thudding. "What have you seen?"

"I've never told anyone this," she said. "Not Wali, not my mom. Not anyone. They wouldn't understand. My mom says I have to get used to horror if I want to be an officer someday." I saw the proud tilt of her head. "I want to be an officer. I plan to be an officer. But horror is just horror. It doesn't make you strong. It only makes you dead inside."

She turned from me to talk into the night. I watched her profile behind the curve of her hair, caught her words as they formed and fell from her perfect lips.

"It was four years ago," she said. "I had just turned twelve. Some people don't keep track of dates, but I do. I was out training when I saw the officers come into camp with something wrapped in a blanket. Laman was there, and Petra, and Tyris, and a couple of others. My mom was working on the trucks, my dad was out scouting. I figured I'd tag along and see what was up."

She smiled humorlessly. "I was pretty stealthy even then. No one saw me. I watched them deposit the thing in Laman's tent, and I got close enough to see through a rip in the fabric. They were unwrapping a body. Except it wasn't a body, not completely. They must have caught the creature just as it got inside. Before it had a chance to take control. It was half-human, with arms and legs and a head. But the rest of it was . . ."

I couldn't stop myself from staring at her. "What?"

"A horror." She turned back to me, her eyes entirely dry. "It had taken over the man's face, and it was like a mouth, except the wrong way. Up and down instead of side to side. Like it had torn him open from forehead to chin and then tried to knit him back together before they killed it. The whole body was like that, from his face down his chest. It was burned, parts of it had melted. The hands mostly. Those parts were red and scaly, but the rest of it was gray. A color nothing like anybody's skin. The color your skin would be if you drained it of all color."

I tried to imagine that grotesque skin, but all I could see

79

were Korah's bronzed cheeks, her dazzling eyes.

"And there was no blood," she said. "Tyris poked around inside it for a good half hour, but there was no blood. It was like he was completely hollow." An involuntary shudder ran through her. "My mom told me the first survivors tried to use guns against them, but their bodies kept moving no matter how many times they'd been shot. Like there was nothing inside them a bullet could kill. That's when they discovered you had to burn them."

I'd been told that too. My dad had pounded it into me.

"The next day we held his funeral," Korah said. "I stood by the grave, and no one knew I'd seen him before they wrapped him back up in his shroud. I went up to the body and put a dried cactus flower where his hands would have been. My mom made me. I even kissed him through the cloth. I remember how scratchy it felt in my mouth." Her blue eyes burned through me. "That man was my father. The Skaldi had ambushed him out in the field, and his partner had killed it before it could complete the takeover. That's what I'd seen that afternoon in Laman's tent."

I didn't know what to say, so I whispered, "I'm sorry."

She didn't respond, didn't acknowledge that I'd spoken a word. "It was Petra who killed it," she said. "I've never known whether to thank her or not. And now it's probably too late."

I realized I was staring straight at her. I also realized she was staring right back. My heart was a hammer trying to pound a hole in the wall of my chest. She rested on a single hand, her legs tucked underneath her, and for an unbeliev-able second I thought she had dropped her shoulder and was leaning toward me. Our faces came so close I could see every line and groove in her full lips. Up close, I could tell that they were ever so slightly chapped.

Then her face fell away and she freed her legs to stand.

My eyes rose to find Wali fifty yards behind her, in the space between houses. Moonlight shadowed his features, but fury radiated from his rigid posture and clenched fists.

"I've got to be getting back," she said. "You'll be all right out here?"

I nodded rapidly, keeping my head lowered.

She stood above me. She took a step toward Wali then turned back, and I raised my eyes once more to hers. A steady breeze lifted her hair, surrounding me with her scent.

"The old woman told me it was like everyone had gone crazy," she said. "Like the whole world was determined to commit suicide. Like," and her voice caught, "seeing what they'd done made them so sick they wanted to die."

I stared at her, unable to speak.

"You're lucky, Querry," she said. "My mom always tells me I have to remember. But sometimes all I want to do is forget."

I watched her walk to where Wali stood, watched him grip her hand and pull her roughly toward the sleeping quar-ters, watched them vanish like wraiths into the darkness. I stared for long minutes at the spot where they'd disappeared, but she didn't return. I knew she wouldn't. I had the strange feeling she belonged to the dream I couldn't remember, and when tomorrow came everything she'd said to me tonight would be gone with the rest of it.

I wished I could erase her memory of whatever had come between her and Wali this night. I wished I could erase her memory of four years ago. I also wished I could bring back my own memory of what lay beyond that long lost game of catch, the days and years before the accident, the entire train of memories that tied me to my life.

But I knew it didn't work that way. You either remember or you forget, that's all. You don't get to choose.

6

THIRST

The next day brought rain.

Hard, scalding rain. My head had barely hit the bunched piece of canvas I used as a pillow when the drops began pelting straight down, hard as pebbles. I felt ragged from my sleepless night and shaken by what I could and couldn't remember of it, but I sprang up instantly and headed for the supplies. My memory might be full of holes, my feeling about this place might be getting worse by the minute, but I knew rain was one thing you didn't waste.

In the six months I could remember, this was only the second rainstorm, and like the first it arrived without warning, without what the old woman called thunder and lightning, and it fell, as she put it, in buckets. The grown-ups who'd seen these sudden storms three or four times a year reported that they were always the same: they came out of nowhere and saturated the land, turned dust to brown slop and the sluggish river to a raging torrent, then retreated as if they'd been scared away by their own ferocity. As soon as they were gone the sun resumed its work, baking the land, leeching the veins of water that formed in the ground's cracks, crinkling the river like a scrap of paper in a fire. An hour later you'd hardly know it had rained at all.

As long as the deluge lasted, though, we did everything we could to capture it. The river was unreliable: we couldn't count on being able to travel there because our own movements depended on whether there were Skaldi in the area. Plus its water was filthy, sludge brown, and smelled like sulfur and petroleum, the kind of water you wouldn't dream of drinking without boiling it first. The water that fell from the sky couldn't exactly be called clean either, it had a gritty quality that caught in your teeth and throat. But it was clean enough that you could hold up a jar full of rainwater and see the particles slowly swirling. Plus whatever happened in the clouds took some of the stink away, so you could stand to drink it without plugging your nose. My dad never talked about the rain, but I knew he was constantly on the lookout for it.

This morning, the moment he heard the first fat, sizzling drops smacking the dry ground, he came charging out of headquarters, limping around like someone trying to put out a fire, shouting orders.

"Let's go, people!" he boomed. "No time like the present. Move, move, move!"

Everyone threw off blankets, pulled on boots, and ran for the supply basement. I was one of the first to get there, and I grabbed a tin pot from the soiled, rusty pile. Other people fought over jars, cups, mess tins, anything they could get their hands on to collect the water. Those who failed to secure a container took off their boots and set them up in the rain, or spread out tents and rucksacks to soak up every last precious drop. We rolled empty fuel drums out into the cloudburst and stood with our arms held up to the skies, hot rain burning our skin more than cooling it, filling one vessel after another and dumping the water into the drums. Everyone worked, even the littlest kids filled cups or caps with rainwater, and people who had nothing at all to fill filled their hands or else lay on their backs with their mouths open and filled their mouths, again and again, spitting a mouthful of water at a time into the barrels. Within minutes everyone was drenched, but we didn't let up. We knew that, once the rain exhausted itself and we fell, equally exhausted, into bed, we'd look out over the parched land and curse ourselves for losing far more than we'd managed to save.

I found myself standing right next to Korah at one of the fuel drums. Her black hair hung in a shiny sheet to her shoulders. Even if there'd been anything to say, we were both way too busy to meet each other's eyes.

My dad circulated through camp while we worked,

urging us on, his shouts as steady as the rainfall, his hair and beard plastered to his face. His limp seemed less noticeable in the rain, as if the water lubricated him, and his eyes glowed with passion, even excitement. He still didn't crack a smile, but the lines around his eyes softened a little at the sight of the whole camp bristling with purpose, the teams laboring in unison to fill and ferry containers to the fuel drums. As the rain picked up, falling in a downpour so solid I could barely see Korah's fluid form beside me, his voice rose with it, until he was hollering encouragement over the raindrops' roar.

"That's right!" he shouted. "Don't let up, people! We can do it!"

And we doubled our already impossible pace, water pouring off our hair and shoulders in such wild cascades I couldn't tell what we were dumping into the drums and what was spilling in on its own.

But it lasted no more than a couple hours. One minute I was working blind, scooping and hauling and pouring, the sounds of rain and shouting and bodies all mixed together in one steady buzz of noise, and the next I recoiled from Korah in her skintight top the way people do when they almost bump into each other. It ended so abruptly and completely I couldn't believe it. I turned my face to the sky and waited for the next wave, but all that struck my nose and cheeks and forehead was sun.

My dad's voice died with the rain, and like everyone else he looked up. His brow contracted, his eyes darkened. Fifty faces turned to him. He squinted into the sun for a second as it seared away the last wisps of vapor that hung in the air. Then he was all business.

"All right, people," he said. "That's that. See if you can find any sources we've missed, then report back to me."

We slogged through quicksand up to our boot tops in search of traces we'd overlooked, but I could tell right away we'd been too thorough for that. What hadn't dried already had turned to mud pudding, and that was hardening fast under the sun's punishment. A few measly puddles glistened darkly in the bottom of the crater, but I knew that by the time we climbed down there, if we could climb down there, they'd be gone. Wali looked ready to try, until Aleka laid a hand on his arm. Korah, for once, said nothing, none of the usual chiding or teasing words she reserved just for him. In fact, she didn't even look at him as he craned his neck to judge the crater's depth. We found a couple basements where the water hadn't drained through cracks in the foundation, and Aleka sent us downstairs to scoop what we could, but it wasn't anything to brag about.

"Next thing you know she'll be telling us to take a leak and collect that too," Yov grumbled as we trudged down the stairs. For once, I couldn't argue with him.

By the time we'd finished searching, the clothes on my back had stiffened and the heat from the ground bled through my boots. I looked around at the faces in camp. Everyone had their mouths half open, panting in the mid-morning sun like underwater creatures that had realized a second too late what a bad idea it was to come up for air.

We trooped back to headquarters, and Aleka told my dad what he already knew. His hair had dried and hung on his shoulders in thick, matted tangles. He moved stiffly, his limp having returned in full force. He told us to sit, and people did, slowly, as if their bodies had hardened as much as the ground. The stone I sat on, the dust beneath my feet, radiated heat like a griddle.

"Good work, people," he said. "The shifts ran right on schedule. A real team effort."

Everyone looked at their hands, their neighbors, anywhere but at him.

"This'll pay off," he promised. "Aleka, when did the barrels run dry?"

"Five weeks ago," she reported.

"So we've been boiling river water for over a month," he announced. "We can take a break from that now. Get our strength back until the next rainfall."

What he didn't mention was that the last rainfall had been months ago, and that the rain that time had fallen a full day and part of a night. We got six barrels out of it, and we'd drained those six barrels, if Aleka's numbers checked out, in roughly two months. We'd collected at most a half-barrel of half-clean water today. Which meant we'd be right back to gagging on river water in less than a week. If we skimped.

I stole glances at the people around me, and saw nothing but sullen stares. Araz sat with the scout Kin, the driver hulking and pensive, his partner diminutive and alert, eyes flicking around the circle. To my surprise, Wali had chosen a seat next to Yov. The older teen whispered something in his ear, and I watched as a smile slowly spread across Wali's face. I risked a sidelong glance at Korah, but she looked directly at my dad, her head held regally and her hair magically softened to its customary shine by the sun.

And I knew we were in trouble for real. I didn't know why or how, but I knew.

"Take an hour to rest," my dad's voice intruded. "Then we need to get back to sorting personal items."

The grown-ups stared numbly as they realized that yesterday's triage order had only been delayed, not revoked. But everyone seemed too exhausted to put up a fight. People rose and wandered off, seeking solitude or shade. My dad and Aleka, along with the other officers, clustered as usual.

The only thing I felt like doing was collapsing into bed, but I forced myself to head over to the supply building. In my exhaustion, a fuzzy plan had formed to consolidate items to save space. The rational part of my mind doubted that would do much good, eventually I knew we'd have to separate what we could carry from what we couldn't. I knew, too, that it would be my dad, not me, who made the call. But maybe, I thought, I could save some little thing.

As I skirted the crater, I saw Yov and the other teenagers

lounging in the shade of a crumpled building. Most had thrown themselves on the ground, but Korah sat apart, her legs pulled up on a half-toppled wall. Yov leaned against what was left of the house, resting casually on an elbow, his white-blond hair barely mussed from the rain. I was about to pass him by when he raised his voice.

"Has anyone noticed," he said, "that the whole camp's been falling to pieces ever since Laman decided to take his little vacation here?"

My heart skipped a beat, but I kept moving.

"Yeah," Wali said. "It's like he's got some thing about Crater Estates he's not telling us."

"You guys found this dump," a kid named Daren said to Yov.

"But didn't go all touchy-feely on it," Yov retorted. "Hey Space Boy!" he called out. "What do you think? Daddy pick a cozy resort?"

I turned back to him. "What do you want him to do? Make it rain?"

I thought it was a pretty good line, but no one laughed. Korah gazed pointedly away from both me and Yov.

"Typical," Yov yawned. "You're missing the big picture, Space Boy. How old is Laman, anyway?"

"About fifty," I said guardedly. Because truthfully, I didn't know.

"And how long's he been running this show?"

"What's your point, Yov?"

"Yes," said Korah, swinging her legs from the wall and standing. "What is your point, Yov?"

He grinned, showing oversize, yellow-brown teeth. "Who says I have to have a point? I'm just trying to establish some numbers here."

He took a step away from the collapsed building and faced me and Korah. He stood nearly a foot taller than either of us, his neck and shoulders wired with muscle. The others seemed like they were still just lying around, eyes half-closed and bland looks on their faces, but I could sense their interest perking up. A few had raised themselves on their elbows or leaned forward, hugging their knees. Wali stared intently at the three of us. Yov's expression hadn't changed from his customary look of bored superiority, but something about his cool smile made me realize he wasn't just messing with me like always.

"You couldn't do the numbers if your life depended on it," Korah said quietly. "So again, what's your point?"

Yov held up his hands. "I'm merely suggesting," he said, "that we've got a broken-down truck, two missing scouts, some shoeless dude creeping around camp, and a couple days worth of muddy pisswater. And instead of going into lockdown and quarantine, Laman's worried about who's packing too many tinker toys. I'm merely calling attention to certain, let us say, kinks in the plan." He let out a sniffing laugh. "If, that is, the plan involves staying alive long enough to partake of our supply of muddy pisswater."

"You think you could do better?" Korah said.

"Hey," Yov replied. "I told you, I'm just pointing things out. I'm not as smart as you and Space Boy here. I can't put two and two together on my own."

"I could tell Laman about this," she said.

"Go ahead," he said, shrugging. "You won't be telling him anything he doesn't already know."

With that, he leaned back against the wall and closed his eyes, like he'd just been hanging out catching some sun all along. The others relaxed as well, but Wali stood and said something to Yov too soft for me to hear, and Yov smiled wickedly, his eyes still closed, his head nodding in satisfaction.

I walked off. My steps felt strange against the packed dust, as if my soles weren't making contact with the ground. I heard Korah calling my name, but it was like her voice traveled out of last night's forgotten dream. In a second she caught up with me.

"You taking a break?" she said.

I shrugged.

"Don't worry about Yov," she said. "He talks a good game, but he's too afraid of Laman to pull anything."

"It's not just him," I said.

She looked at me sharply. "Who is it, then?"

"It's—" I didn't know what to say, so I said the first thing that came into my mind. "What did you tell Wali?"

She didn't answer right away, but her eyes narrowed. "Not that it's any of your business, but I told him you and I talked. I am allowed to talk to people, aren't I?"

"That's not it." It was hard enough getting my thoughts straight with her near, much less with her near to anger. "I have to tell my dad."

"About Yov?" she said. "Or about Wali?"

"About both of them."

"You don't need to do that," she said, the same softly threatening tone she'd used with Yov tingeing her voice.

"Wali's angry at you," I said. "Because of me. Because of what he saw last night."

She laughed, but not the thrilling laugh from our poolside talk. This time it was a scornful laugh that made my stomach clench with fear.

"Wali and I can take care of ourselves, thank you," she said. "And I think he'd know if he had to worry about competition."

My face burned. For the first time ever, her beautiful features seemed to twist under an ugly mask.

Then she shook her head, and her face softened. "I'm sorry," she said, her eyes returning to their usual blue, the way they say the sky used to clear after a rainstorm. "But you don't need to worry about me and Wali. If he is angry with me, it has nothing to do with you. And he's certainly not dumb enough to take his anger out on me by running to Yov."

"I'm not worried," I said. If those crystal blue eyes could see through me, they'd have known in a second I was lying.

"This is nothing new," she said. "Every time something

93

goes wrong, some jerk starts whining about the camp's leadership. But they always stop. You know why?"

I shook my head.

"Because no one *really* wants to take Laman's place," she said. "They want to make it difficult for him, but they don't want the difficulty themselves. You'll see. A couple of days from now, when things are back to normal, Yov will shut his fat trap and everyone will realize he was full of it all along."

She reached out and laid a hand on my arm. Her fingers slid down to my wrist, leaving an electric trail the whole way. I stood there unable to convince myself, unable to believe her. But for the sake of feeling her touch and looking in her eyes a second longer, I pretended I did.

"Korah," I said. "Has my dad ever ordered quarantine?"

She showed no surprise at the question. "Twice. The day of my father's funeral. In case the Skaldi had jumped bodies before Petra burned it. And the day after the attack that left you . . ."

She didn't need to finish the thought.

"So you've been tested?"

She nodded.

"And me."

"Everyone," she said. "Except the little ones."

"And?"

"Nothing. Everyone was just"—she smiled—"who they are."

And who was that? I thought, but didn't say.

"I don't blame Laman for what happened to my father," she said, giving my hand a last squeeze before letting go. "Those things just happen, you know? We have to be stronger than them if we want to win." She smiled and walked off, her black hair swinging. "See you later, Querry."

Evening had fallen.

The work of sorting was finally done. People had muttered under their breath the whole time, their hands trembling as they moved their most prized possessions to the pile marked for oblivion. They'd wrestled with themselves, and they'd lost. And when their stash of personal belongings had dwindled to practically nothing, they stared at what was left with a dazed expression, as if they'd been meaning to say something but couldn't quite call it back. Their lips quivered, their eyes darted over the wreckage. When they finally rose to prepare for the night, their legs wobbled like someone walking a tightrope for the first time. Someone who wasn't sure they had the strength or the courage to make it to the other side.

All this time, Yov and Wali circulated among the grownups, Yov making his usual snide comments, Wali tagging along behind. Whenever one of the officers showed up, the two of them stopped making the rounds and went back to pretending they were packing their own stuff, but as soon as the officer left they went right back at it. Wali laughed louder than anyone as Yov tested his latest one-liners.

"That is certainly a priceless work of art," Yov said to the light tower man, holding up his painting and tilting it to catch the reddish rays of the setting sun. "Tell you what, I'll trade you a moldy button for it."

At that point Korah sidled up to him and whispered something so low all I heard was the menacing vibration in her voice.

"Well, excuse me," he said loudly. "If the artist here can't handle the truth, that's not my problem."

People froze at their tasks, anger and betrayal suffusing their features. Wali stifled a laugh. Korah looked ready to slug him, but she merely stamped off. When she was gone, Yov spread his hands and addressed his audience.

"Now that the princess has retired . . ." He pointed to the miniscule pile of salvageable items. "Not there, people!" he bellowed. "On the trash heap! Move, move, move!"

His taunting laugh and the copycat laugh of his newest disciple echoed in the quiet dusk.

I watched for as long as I could stand, then slunk away from the sleeping area and looked out over the semidarkness. The dusty air seized my throat like always. The buildings seemed brittle as bones. I felt like I was floating above the ground as I made my way to headquarters. I glanced over my shoulder to see if Korah had followed, but she was nowhere to be seen.

I found my dad alone outside the command building, seated on a hunk of fallen stone, his bad leg held out straight.

He seemed to be preoccupied with something in his hands. When I neared I saw it was his gun. He'd opened the chamber to inspect it closely, but as soon as he saw me he snapped it shut and stashed it in its holster.

"Hey, Dad," I said.

"Querry," he said. "Don't tell me there's more bad news on the home front."

His eyes seemed to twinkle in the near dark.

"There's something I need to tell you."

"Actually, I'm glad you showed up," he said. "I've been meaning to give you this."

At first I thought he meant the gun, but then he reached inside his jacket and pulled out a small object. I took it and saw that it was a red-handled pocketknife, the kind with folding blades. It had rusted with age, but all the different gadgets seemed to be intact. On the plastic handle someone had etched a single word in sloppy letters, as if they'd been carved with another knife. It read "Matay."

I looked at him. "What happened to getting rid of personal possessions?"

He met my gaze, unsmiling. "Possessions essential to the survival of the colony are exempted, remember?"

"Who's Matay?"

"One of the lost," he said. "I thought it was time you had it."

He held out a hand, and I helped him clamber to his feet. I saw him wince as his bad hip took his weight.

"Got a minute?" he said. "There's something I need to show you."

I tucked the knife into my jacket and followed him.

We made our way across the compound to the tallest building, the one he'd pointed out to me the evening before. It looked over the eastern slope of the hillside, perfect for scouting the plain below. When I glanced at the top-story window, though, I saw that it stood empty. "Shouldn't the sentry be posted by now?"

"Change of plans," he said, and we entered the building together.

The front hallway glowed dimly from the light of a huge arched window, its glass long gone. I followed as he heaved himself awkwardly up the stairs to the second floor. It seemed like it took all his effort to step up with his good left leg, pull himself by the banister to plant his right foot beside it, then repeat the process. I found myself itching to move faster, but I kept myself in check. At the second-floor landing we turned down a hallway that still had a carpet underneath the coating of dust. Countless footsteps going in both directions had stirred the red-brown film, showing glimpses of light blue beneath.

At the end of the hall, two of the officers stood guard beside a wooden door, their hands on their holsters. They nodded at my dad as he opened the door and started up another, narrower flight of stairs. It was practically pitch-black in the stairwell, and there was no railing. I had to help him on his way up.

We emerged into a room that had been turned into an arsenal.

The room was small and square, with windows facing in three directions and some form of patterned paper peeling in long strips off the walls. The paper, a faded pink, had probably been rusty red at one time. The corners of the room nearest the door had been piled with more weapons than I'd realized the camp possessed: pistols, knives, bayonets, even a couple bows and quivers full of arrows. Boxes of ammunition were stacked neatly beside the firearms, and a canvas folding chair had been placed where you could see out all three windows. The only weapons I didn't see were the flamethrowers, which I knew remained below.

"You preparing for a war?" I said.

His eyes were impossible to read in the dim light leaking through the windows. "I'm preparing for any contingency that might arise."

"Who's the enemy?"

"You tell me."

"Guns don't work against Skaldi," I said. "Neither do arrows, so far as I know."

"No," he said. "They don't."

He walked to the east-facing window, gestured for me to join him. I looked out over a darkened plain. It could have been swarming with a hundred Skaldi or the ranks of an approaching force, and I wouldn't have been able to tell. The north- and south-facing windows, I realized, provided sightlines not to the plain but to the compound below.

"There was a time," he said softly, "when we thought we might find some place not infested by Skaldi. Some island, some fortress they couldn't penetrate. But we had to give up that dream. All the supposedly safe places would last a week before we'd wake up and discover our closest friends were strangers."

He spoke not to me but to the night, as if he was still looking for that place.

"Then there was the plan of combining all the survival colonies into one," he said. "Something that could resist the Skaldi, even defeat them for good. You want to guess what happened to that one?"

"I have a pretty good idea."

"That's right." He nodded. "It made us more vulnerable, not less. We had to give up the dream of saving the species to save ourselves."

"Didn't people realize they'd be stronger if they worked together?" It sounded incredibly lame the moment I said it.

"You don't remember," he said, "but there was a time we joined another colony. Took them in, actually. Maybe twenty people. And within days everyone was at everyone else's throat. The ones we took in were the worst of all." He sighed. "People don't change, Querry. We're the descendants of the madmen who destroyed the planet. Why should we be any different?"

He pointed to the wall beside the south-facing window. I squinted in the darkness and saw hatch marks scratched into the wallpaper, sets of four upright slashes crossed by a fifth diagonal. They'd been carved with a blade, and the pale wall showed through the tattered pink paper like teeth. I realized the marks stretched halfway around the room. I lost count at two hundred.

"It's what gave me the idea to transfer the weapons here," he said. "Whoever made their last stand in this room had a pretty good run of luck, wouldn't you say?"

"Until their luck ran out," I added.

"True enough," he said. "But at least they went down swinging."

He touched his fingers to the wall, pressing a strip of paper back in place. It dropped the instant he let go.

I knew what I had to do. If Yov meant to undermine or overthrow him, I had to tell him everything. I couldn't waste time. If Wali was part of it, if suspicion of what me and Korah had been doing last night had driven him to Yov's camp, I couldn't spare him, either. Even if it was a false alarm, even if I'd somehow misunderstood, it was better to risk the laughter of Yov and his gang, the scorn and anger of Korah, than to take a chance. If I didn't act now and something terrible happened, I'd be the one responsible.

"Dad," I said. "I need to talk to you."

His night-black eyes gleamed as he turned to me.

"Yov and Wali," I said. "The two of them are—plotting, planning something. And not just them. Kelmen's involved too, I think. . . ."

His eyebrows lifted, barely distinguishable in the dark. "Kelmen?"

I felt my face flush. "Well, maybe not Kelmen. But others—more of the teens. Maybe some grown-ups too. Araz. Kin. I don't know how many."

"You're sure of this." It wasn't a question.

"Pretty sure."

"And your evidence?"

I thought over what I could say, what I could tell him. All the things that didn't sit right. Yov's performance at the sorting, the powwow he'd held after the rainstorm. Wali spying on me and Korah one day, hanging on Yov's every word the next. The grown-ups' anger at the things my dad was forcing them to let go, the dry tinder that could easily be lit by the spark of Yov's deceit. The maybe-sabotaged truck. The footprints by the shelter. The quarantine that hadn't happened, should have happened, needed to happen. The Skaldi that had driven us here in the first place, that had come from a direction they never came from, pushing us into territory we'd never traveled before . . .

Then I looked at him. He didn't smile, but the corners of his lips pinched in something like amusement or pity. I glanced around at the armory he'd built for himself. And I knew he already knew.

"Your time is coming, Querry," he said. "But for now, let's let me handle things."

"Yes sir."

"And keep the knife close," he said. "For luck."

He made one last review of the room, then led me back down the stairs, along the dusty corridor to the front hall. He nodded a good night and disappeared across the compound, limping toward headquarters.

The camp lay silent around me. Yov and his supporters had vanished like a bad dream. I took the knife out, turned it in my hands. The name had faded with the dark, but I could feel the gashes when I ran my fingertips over the smooth plastic. I opened one of the blades and imagined myself using it against . . . what? Knives don't work against Skaldi any better than guns.

Focus, I told myself. *Focus*. My dad was on top of things. He'd caught wind of the camp's unrest and he'd moved the weapons someplace safe. The compound had been secured, the Skaldi thrown off our trail. If he'd decided not to impose quarantine, that was because he was confident there'd been no infection. Wali and Korah would make up. The grown-ups would come around. All I had to do was follow orders.

I snapped the blade back into its handle, stashed the knife in my pocket, and walked off to begin my preparations for bed.

7

TEST

Petra came back the next day.

We were out working when we saw her. We'd woken once more to find dust piled to our doorstep, and my dad had gotten fed up and decided there were better things we could do than shovel ourselves out of a hole day after day. So he had us in the yard before the sun got high, tying tents to fence posts in what I sensed was a last-ditch effort to keep us from getting swallowed by the desert.

Like most last-ditch efforts, it didn't work very well. The wind whipped the tents out of our hands, the twine split and left itchy fibers in our fingertips. The dust didn't seem to think much of our barrier, finding any opening it could to sneak through. People grumbled even more than usual. The ones I was most worried about, Yov and Wali and Araz, kept their thoughts to themselves, probably because my dad supervised the whole operation. And Korah I didn't see. I overheard Mika say she wasn't feeling well.

We'd finished tying the first tent to the posts and stepped back to inspect our work when the sentry on the western outskirts of camp gave a whistle. Everyone froze, then ran in a body to look out over the plain. Way off in the distance, indistinct through the heat, a small figure inched across the desert. My dad lifted his binoculars and scrutinized the figure for a minute, his brow lowered behind the lenses. Then he dropped the binoculars and said to Aleka, "Get the others."

In ten minutes I could tell that the figure trudging up the hill was Petra: short and stocky, with nearly black skin and shaved head. Sleeves rolled past her elbows, as always. Businesslike. She moved like the Petra I remembered, setting each foot down sturdily, nothing like the drifting intruder from five nights ago. My dad watched her approach without saying another word.

She cleared the crest of the hill and marched straight toward him. Though she kept up a steady pace, her shoulders slumped and her head bobbed with each step. Of all the people in camp, Petra went the furthest to hide her trail, further even than the collection jar crazies. No eyebrows, no eyelashes even. I didn't want to think about how she'd gotten rid of those. As a result, she was constantly blinking to keep the dust and grit out of her eyes.

Aleka stepped in front of her before she reached my dad.

Two of the officers flanked her. One held a flamethrower at the ready. Petra glared at him, blinking furiously. Her round face was plastered with dust, another of her camouflage techniques. She said it kept her scent down.

"This is as far as you go, Petra," Aleka said.

Petra's bloodshot eyes shone through her dusty mask. "Do you think I'd just stroll into camp," she said, "if I was one of them?"

"I'm taking no chances," my dad said. "Hold her."

The officer with the flamethrower kept it trained on her, while the other stepped behind her and locked her arms. Her muscles tightened, and I sensed the people around her bracing for a fight. Without thinking, my hand went to the knife in my pocket, feeling its solid shape through the cloth.

But then, to my surprise, Petra relaxed and let the officers lead her away. As they walked her off, my dad turned and said to Araz, "Get them back to work." His gaze shifted to me for a second. Then he and Aleka followed the officers and their captive.

I started across camp with the work group, keeping an eye on Araz. The big man was dizzy with the heat, his steps slow and sloppy, and I knew there was no way he was paying attention to his crew. When we passed by a truck-size chunk of wall that had somehow withstood the collapse of the house it had once belonged to, I ducked out of sight, peering around the edge to see if I'd been missed. But our new supervisor's head drooped nearly to his chest while he walked, and everyone else trailed mechanically after him. I glanced over my shoulder one last time as I angled toward headquarters, but even Yov seemed too focused on putting one foot in front of the other to notice I was gone.

Picking my way around the debris of broken buildings, I sidled up to the shell my dad had chosen as headquarters. It stood back from the crest of the hill, surrounded by other buildings, which I guess made it more secure than most. But it was a wreck like the rest. Its top story had been sliced in half, leaving jagged shards of brick and wood in a diagonal like a crooked smile. The front door frame stood empty, and canvas draperies hung over the three side windows to shield the interior from sun and wind. My heart hammered in my throat, but it was easy enough to hook a finger under the canvas that covered the middle window and lift it just enough to peek inside.

The room lay in shadow. It took my eyes a second to adjust, and while they did, swirls and motes of dust danced in front of me.

Then I saw my dad and Aleka standing before Petra. She rested on a slab that might have been a table once, except its legs were missing. The officers crouched at her sides, holding her wrists. The flamethrower leaned against the far wall. The rest of the room was empty of furniture or supplies, but the ground next to the tabletop held a collection of metal objects I couldn't remember ever having seen. Petra breathed steadily through her nose and stared straight at my dad, her dark eyes like bloodstains in her dust-caked face.

"Next," he said.

At his command, one of the officers held onto both of Petra's wrists while the other took one of the metal implements from the floor. He clamped it onto the tip of her right index finger and tugged. Hard, hard enough to make her grit her teeth. He did the same to all the fingers on both hands, then nodded at my dad. When I looked closely at Petra's hands, I saw the blood that had leaked from her torn fingertips.

"Now the teeth," my dad said.

Petra shut her mouth in a firm line.

Aleka said, "Petra." My dad gave her a sharp look.

"I swear I'll bite them off," Petra growled through closed lips.

"Which will only prove you're one of them," my dad said. "So be my guest."

"Petra . . ." Aleka repeated. Her face showed nothing, but her voice sounded uncharacteristically soft, even pleading.

Petra let out a breath. She looked at my dad with a hard expression, whether of disgust or respect I couldn't tell.

"Seems you won't be satisfied till you've taken your share of blood, Laman." Then she tilted her head back. "Just the teeth," she said. "And be careful." She opened her mouth wide.

The officer holding her arms leaned his full weight on her. The other squatted by her head, picked up another of the metal instruments, and reached into her mouth. I couldn't see well with all the bodies in the way, but it seemed he was wiggling and pulling her teeth. Once or twice Petra's eyes tightened with pain, but she kept her mouth open, breathing sharply through her nose. The officer did the top row, then the bottom, then stood and nodded at my dad.

"She's clean," he said.

The other officer let go of Petra. She sat, rubbing her wrists where she'd been held. Blood coated her teeth and lips. "As if this proves anything," she said.

"There are other tests," my dad said softly.

"So I'm supposed to be grateful?" She held her fingers in her mouth, sucked hard until the blood stopped welling. Aleka held a hand out to her, but Petra shrugged it away, threw her legs over the side of the tabletop, and stood on her own.

"You can poke and pry into my flesh all you want, Laman," she said. "But that won't stop them from coming."

"I'll do what's necessary to keep my camp safe," he said.

Petra snorted. "You have no idea. Living large up here in Hilltop Manor, spying on us mere mortals from the clouds. You think they're playing by our rules? They don't play by any rules but their own."

"Let me get you some water, Petra," Aleka said.

Petra ignored her. "We were jumped," she said to my dad. "Danis and me. It came out of nowhere. By the time I knew what was happening it had already taken him."

"Even superwomen sleep."

Petra's eyes smoldered. "I don't sleep," she said acidly. "But you keep believing that if it makes you feel like the big man. If it makes you feel like you're in control."

"I've already gotten an earful of that from Aleka," my dad said. "So why don't you spare me the analysis."

"Fine," Petra said. "I'll make it real simple for you." She took a step toward my dad, and I saw the officers tense. But she didn't threaten him, kept her hands at her sides. Her bloody teeth flashed, her anger seeming to have changed into something else, something harsh and cold as a blade.

"It's no accident we're here," she said, her voice barely above a whisper. "The one you ran from was a messenger. A scout. I searched as far west as I could go, and they've left us only one way to run. They're herding us, Laman. Putting us exactly where they want us, so they can recover what they lost."

"Ridiculous," he said. But she didn't stop.

"I've been in the field all my life, and this is the first time I've seen them moving like this. Focused, targeted. Not like they're just taking anyone they can. More like they're on a mission." Her eyes held his without blinking. "They're closing in on us, Laman. They know."

Something about the way she said *know* made my blood run cold.

"You have no proof of that," my dad said. But for the first time ever, I thought I heard a note of doubt in his voice.

"I have all the proof I need," Petra said. "I have eyes. I had a partner."

"We've got a few tricks of our own," he said, still in that falsely confident voice.

"Those won't help you," Petra said. "They won't help any of us. Danis was lucky. He went quick."

She reached for something at her belt, a small bag or purse I hadn't noticed before. She untied it, dropped it at my dad's feet.

"I found this," she said. "Better start planning the burial."

"Dear God," Aleka breathed.

"That won't help you either," Petra said, her voice breaking. She blinked, licked blood from her dry, peeling lips. "There's not much left," she said. "Like I told you, he went quick."

All of them stared at the bag on the floor. No one moved to pick it up.

"You all enjoy your party," Petra said. "Now where's the mess in this hellhole? I'm getting something to eat."

Without waiting for an answer, she stamped toward the vacant doorway and left.

I flattened myself against the wall as she stormed out, her head lowered and her lips moving without a word I could hear. Once she got clear of the house her posture broke down, her shoulders slumping once again and her steps dragging. I waited until she wandered out of sight, then lifted the canvas to peer inside.

No one had budged. It seemed no one had spoken. Aleka and the two officers stood facing my dad, the bag that contained all that was left of the lost scout lying untouched at his feet. He wasn't looking at it, though. Or at them. His head was turned to the side, his eyes veiled.

"What if it's true?" Aleka broke the silence. "What if the one that attacked our camp was—a decoy? A scout? What if they're looking for . . . ?"

My dad said nothing.

"Laman?"

Slowly, like someone waking from sleep, he raised his eyes to hers. "The one that attacked our camp did nothing we haven't seen before. If Petra's report was true, we would have observed a difference in its behavior. The Skaldi don't scout, Aleka."

"The evidence is beginning to suggest they do."

"The evidence," he said, "suggests that what happened to Danis was either a fluke or a mistake on his part. Or on Petra's."

"Petra's a good soldier."

"Everyone makes mistakes."

"Except you?"

"Don't start, Aleka," he warned.

"We should have been under quarantine from the day we arrived," she said. "And I don't see how we have any option but to do so now. If there's one of them among us—"

"I'd know it."

"I don't understand, Laman," she said, and again the pleading note troubled her voice. "What is it about this place that makes you go against everything you know, every instinct you've ever had? What more evidence will it take for you to *do* something?"

Her hands had formed into fists as she spoke. Now her eyes strayed to the flamethrower against the wall. His eyes followed. When they met again, I knew what both of them were thinking.

"I could have you locked up for insubordination," he said quietly.

"If you'll submit to the trials," she said, "you'll hear no more from me."

"I'm the one who orders the trials," he said. "On any member of my camp I choose."

She faced him squarely, her expression showing neither apology nor fear.

"I know what I am," he said. "And I know what it takes to win this war. If we start turning on each other at every whisper and rumor, we'll never make it. We fight the only way we know how. We fight with our courage, our will, our faith in the colony and each other. We fight until we find—" He stopped abruptly and pivoted to the window.

I ducked out of sight, but not before his fierce eyes locked on mine.

I flung myself against the wall, heart pounding so hard I thought it would explode from my chest. I had no idea what I'd done to give myself away, unless Aleka's suggestion that my dad was the thing we were fleeing from had forced a gasp from my lips. My first impulse was to run, but then I thought, what was the point? Where would I go? I had put myself here. Maybe, without knowing it, I had wanted this all along.

I pushed myself from the building and turned to face him.

My dad rounded the corner, Aleka right at his back. His eyes blazed, and he swung his bad hip so violently it looked like it was about to tear off. Aleka's face was composed, but not compassionate. If he was a meteor, she was a stone.

If either of them was Skaldi, they were playing their parts to perfection.

They stopped right in front of me. I opened my mouth to get the first word in, but his voice trampled mine into the dust.

"You see enough?" he said furiously. "Feel like you're up on the latest news?"

"Hold on," I began, but he kept right on going.

"I told you to stay out of this," he fumed. "But you never listen. You never learn."

"Dad—"

"You want to be a man, Querry?" he said. "Want to make the big decisions around here? Want to tell me what to do when my scouts get waylaid and my officers lose their nerve?"

I shook my head, not answering him, not knowing where to begin.

"You want to prove yourself, you start by following my orders," he said. "Otherwise, we're all going to end up like this."

He whipped Petra's bag at my feet. It landed with a smack that made me sick to my stomach. I looked over his shoulder at Aleka, but her face remained impassive.

"I just wanted to know," I said.

"To know what?"

"To *know*," I repeated, hearing the echo of Petra's voice in my own. "To not be so—in the dark. You say you want me to remember, but you only want me to remember what you say."

If I thought that would impress him, I was wrong. "There are some things you're better off not knowing," he said. "That's why I'm here. To make the decisions you're not ready to make."

He'd said the same thing about people's belongings, and I was tired of hearing it.

"I'm not a child," I said. "I don't need you to make decisions for me."

"No," he said. "I can see what excellent decisions you make all on your own."

His breathing came out in ragged bursts, his face was flushed with red spots. He looked at me like he wished I'd never been born. Or at least, never been born to him.

And in that instant I knew how he felt, because I felt pretty much the same way.

"I'm through," I said. "I tried to warn you last night, but you wouldn't listen. Aleka's right. You might not be one of them, but you're sure as hell helping them get whatever it is they want."

His hand lashed out at me so fast I had no chance to stop it. It caught me across the jaw, an open-handed blow that made my teeth ring. Before he could repeat it Aleka grabbed his arm and pulled him away from me. He didn't struggle, just stood there panting, his body wreathed in the dust he'd kicked up.

"You've chosen your side," he breathed. "Now get out of my sight."

I turned and left, ending the conversation, ending more than that. My face burned, my eyes stung. I didn't look back.

I spent the rest of the day dodging him and everyone else in camp. Word must have leaked that I'd spied on the interrogation, because Yov made a few cracks about me getting in hot water with daddy. His friends, Wali in particular, fell into their usual hysterics, but I tuned them out. Korah was still nowhere to be seen. Yov said nothing about my dad hitting me, so that part of the story must not have reached his ears.

Night found us with a flimsy screen of tents edging the central compound and a camp full of blisters and sore backs.

None of the officers had made more than a token appearance since afternoon, when one of them came out to check on the progress of the windbreak. He stayed no more than a minute and gave no more than a brusque nod before returning to the command building, where my dad and Aleka were holed up with the other officers. What they were doing in there, what accusations or transformations were taking place, I had no idea. And this time, I had no desire to eavesdrop.

When night fell I found myself unable to sleep and unwilling to fake it. So I took a wide tour of the compound, starting by the barrier of tents. They flapped and snapped in the strong nighttime breeze. From there I roamed to the eastern edge of the hill and looked out over the invisible land. It was like standing on the brink of an enormous pit, infinitely bigger than the crater at my back.

"That's where he died," a voice said.

I jumped, then saw Petra sitting on a shattered wall not ten feet from me, her eyes fixed on the pool of darkness at our feet.

"Danis?"

She grunted.

"I'm sorry about what happened."

She kept silent for a long time, her dark profile rimmed by the weak moonlight. Then she said, "Laman tell you how they get inside?"

"I wish."

"They enter through your mouth," she said softly, as if

talking to herself. "You've got to keep your teeth clamped real tight. Any opening. Anywhere you let down your guard. They find a way in."

"You saw it?"

"It was too fast," she spoke to the night. "All I saw was the body after it was done. After it hollowed him out. Turned him into an empty shell with nothing but dust and sand blowing around inside."

Finally she faced me, and I saw the trails running silvery down her cheeks. "I watched his skin peel back, and I knew it was coming for me. I ran. I didn't wait to see if it followed."

"That's enough, Petra," a voice spoke from behind us.

I turned to see Aleka. She took a couple long strides and reached for the scout, but Petra jumped from the wall and backed away.

"Don't touch me," she said dully, and vanished into the night.

Aleka watched her go, then cast her eyes on me. The moon turned her face pale and still as a statue's. The only thing that moved was her close-cropped hair, which ruffled slightly in the breeze.

"You all right?" she said.

I shrugged.

"She'll come around," she said. "It's always toughest right after."

I thought about Korah's secret, buried for years. When would she come around?

Aleka followed me to the sleeping area. She said nothing more, and I wasn't about to start any small talk. I kept my eyes on the darkened hulk of the command building, where a single lantern glowed yellow through the downstairs curtain. When I reached my spot, she stopped on the other side of the crumbled wall. For a second I thought she was going to leave, but then she said, "Mind if I come in?"

I almost laughed because, really, there wasn't much of an *out*. The thought that I might be inviting a Skaldi to the feast flickered through my mind, but I figured if there really was one loose in camp, there was nothing I could do about it. So I said, "Fine with me."

She came around the wall and sat where my dad had sat the first night here. Seeing her in his old place made my heart lurch, with what I wasn't sure.

"So how are you doing?" she asked.

"All right." Then, more out of habit than anything, I asked, "How's my dad?"

"All right," she said, a tiny smile crossing her lips. It changed her face ever so slightly, made her seem less hard and remote.

"He feels bad about what happened," she went on. "He's been under a lot of stress lately, and—well, he wanted to make sure you were okay."

"So he sent you."

"He's worried about you, Querry."

"What, that I'll tell everyone about Petra?"

"That was standard operating procedure," she said, the hardness returning to her voice. "No commander likes to subject their people to the trials. But they do it for their colony's safety."

I laughed. "Except when they decide not to."

Her face had settled back into stone. She braced her hands on her thighs as if she was about to stand, but then she spoke again. "Do you know how he injured his leg?"

I shook my head. He'd never told me the story. I'd assumed it was old age.

"He was trying to save a child," she said. "From the Skaldi. He took a bullet in the hip. A wild shot from one of his own. It's still there, from what I understand."

I didn't know what to say to that. So I said, "So?"

"So he knows he can't protect you like he used to. He knows the time is coming when he won't be able to protect you at all."

I brooded on that for a minute. It seemed like the kind of thing a grown-up would say.

"Do you think it's true?" I said.

"Do I think what's true?"

"What Petra said. About the Skaldi. About them being in the driver's seat." I paused, not sure how much to admit I'd overheard. "About them *knowing*."

Her eyes widened, and for a second I thought she might reveal the secret she and my dad shared. But then the veil settled back over her features. "I can't say," she murmured quietly, almost to herself. "But I know it's adding to Laman's burdens. That and Yov's little revolution." She seemed to enjoy my look of shock, or maybe she was happy to change the subject. "That's not news, Querry. It's gotten worse recently, but it's something Laman's been dealing with for a long time."

"What does Yov have against him, anyway?"

"Yov lost his father to the Skaldi years ago," she said. "When he was only a child. He's been angry ever since. Laman's tried time and again to reach out to him, but . . ."

"But what?"

"But grief can twist people's souls," she said simply. "And sometimes we take our anger out on the ones we owe the most."

I wondered if Aleka had ever had a child herself, one she'd lost. I'd never thought of her that way, all hardness and sharp angles, but she sure seemed to have the parenting speech down. "And do you think . . ." I could barely bring myself to say it. "Do you think my dad's one of them?"

"I'm sorry I suggested that, Querry," she said. "I wouldn't have if I'd known you were listening."

"But do you think it's true?"

She didn't answer at once. Her eyes searched mine, as if the answer to my own question was hidden there.

"I don't know," she said at last. "But I do know this is what they do to us. Make us doubt, make us disbelieve. In that respect Petra's right about their power: they kill the colony from the inside, lead us to do their work. I've believed in Laman since . . ." She shook her head. "I don't want to stop believing in him now."

"Neither do I." Saying it surprised me, but as soon as I said it, I knew it was true.

We sat in silence. I replayed the memory of my dad's hand coming at me out of nowhere, wishing I could dodge it, knowing I couldn't. The image got tangled with Korah's questions from two nights before: *If they can copy our look, our voice, does that make them us? Do they think like us? Feel like us? Or is it all just counterfeit?* I'd know if he was one of them, wouldn't I? His eyes sure had looked like my dad's eyes. His hand sure had felt like a human hand. My jaw could attest to that.

He was my dad. How could I not know if he harbored a monster inside?

"So what do you think he'll do?" I asked.

"Laman?"

I nodded.

The wisp of a smile played around her lips again. "He always has a plan. And sometimes that's the problem." Then she added, "He could use your help."

"*My* help?"

"Is that so strange?"

"I'm the guy who can't remember," I said. "The guy who can't *focus*." I said it the way my dad always did, like the word left a foul taste in his mouth. "And he made it pretty clear this morning he doesn't want me getting in the way."

She said nothing for a long time. I had a chance to really study her face, to notice how thin it was, bony almost, how deep the hollows sank around her moon-gray eyes. You get used to seeing pinched faces in camp, so used to it you forget that's not how people are supposed to look. But with Aleka it seemed that more than starvation had whittled away her flesh, bringing out her sharp jaw, her high cheeks, her broad forehead. Her face might be a stone, I thought, but even stones get worn down in time.

After a minute she stood.

"He failed, you know," she said. "To save the child."

That was the first time I'd heard one of his officers talk about my dad failing at anything.

"You're becoming a man, Querry," she said. "If you want others to accept that, I think it's time you started accepting it yourself." She nodded a good night, and I watched her walk off into the shadows.

8
TWIST

We buried Danis at dawn.

Everyone filed downhill, hiked a mile into the baked land to the spot my dad had chosen for the gravesite, then stood in formation on the plain where two workers with bent shovels had prepared a small but deep hole. There would be no marker, nothing to prove any part of him lay beneath, nothing to attract the attention of the ones that had taken his life. There would be nothing but the flat and barren land, and in time, if we'd done our job well enough, even we would forget where we'd left the lost scout's remains.

I hadn't really known Danis. Even before the Skaldi took him he'd been like a ghost around camp, flitting between solid objects, his frequent disappearances and reappearances so unremarkable you never knew when he was gone. I couldn't remember him saying more than a handful of words to anyone, and those not to their face but to their shoes. Maybe that was what made him a good scout: he called so little attention to himself he was practically invisible. The only person he seemed the slightest bit comfortable with was Petra, who I'd sometimes seen ribbing him while he stood there with a big goofy smile on his face. Watching the two of them go out on patrol, him gangly and awkward and her squat and no-nonsense, a real mismatch, formed the clearest image I had of the man who had lost his life trying to safeguard our camp.

So I'd be lying if I said I missed him, or even mourned him. But I felt terrible for the life he'd lost, and all for something that might be gone tomorrow.

The ceremony was brief. The sun had risen, and we couldn't afford to stand around, unprotected from its rays and from whatever might be watching us. We lowered what was left of him into the ground and stood there, uncertain what to do next, squinting against the light and heat.

My dad gave another of his famous short speeches. I hadn't seen him since our argument the day before, but he showed no evidence it was still on his mind. I'd checked myself in the shard of mirror he'd given me six months ago, and to my relief, no mark had appeared to commemorate his hand's encounter with my jaw.

"Danis's life and death remind us what we're fighting against, what we're fighting for," he said. "We honor his memory, his years of service. He believed in the future, in the life of our colony. The best way we can remember him is by standing together to guard what he died to preserve."

People in the crowd bowed their heads. I'd have given anything to hear their thoughts.

"Does anyone have something they'd like to say?" my dad asked.

Silence held, lengthened. I looked over at Petra, whose eyes had closed and whose cracked lips moved wordlessly.

Finally Aleka spoke.

"He was a good soldier," she said.

At my dad's signal, one of the officers stepped forward with a raised pistol. Though fanatically strict about not wasting ammunition, my dad had allowed this one gun to be fired in the scout's memory.

The officer held the gun aloft and pulled the trigger. A click sounded, but no explosion. He lowered it, glanced at it, and for a moment seemed about to raise it and try again. Then he changed his mind and, putting the safety back on, returned the gun to its holster.

The workers with the mangled shovels began to fill in the hole. The rest of us turned for the march back to camp.

That was how we buried Danis.

When we got back to camp everyone did their best to act as if nothing had happened. Routines resumed. Some people returned to shoveling dust, others to rearranging canvas windbreaks. The little kids played amid the ruins like always. Some new game they'd invented, something having to do with treasures and robbers, though like all their games it degenerated into pointless chasing and catching in the end. I saw five-year-old Keely trailing hopelessly behind the bigger kids, but I didn't head over to help him out. Soon a work detail would have to start digging a hole to bury the possessions we wouldn't be carrying with us when we left. I could tell by the way people shied from the officers that no one looked forward to being chosen for that assignment.

But my dad surprised me by calling the whole camp together for a meeting. In the six months I could remember, he'd never done that before.

We sat in front of headquarters on the remains of walls and foundations. People fanned themselves with hats or dirty strips of cloth. The compound formed a semicircle of houses around an open space, half of which had been swallowed by the crater. Now my dad stood at the center of the remaining space, his legs spread and his hands locked behind his back, keen eyes looking out at us on our makeshift bleachers. The sun never seemed to bother him. His expression was hard to read, brooding as usual but with an edge of something else, anger or excitement or alertness. He looked, to tell the truth, the way Petra had the day before when they'd led her off to the trials. Like he was expecting a fight. Maybe like he was hoping for one. My hand went to my jaw, which throbbed as if it remembered his blow.

"Is everyone here?" His voice broke the silence. "Good."

I noticed that the officers sat by themselves in a clump, rather than standing beside him as usual. Aleka leaned against a building whose top had been sliced clean off. Her arms were crossed, her attention directed, like everyone's, at my dad.

"Look, people," he said. "We've had some setbacks. There's no point denying it. First the truck, and then worse, a friend and companion. Two losses, each difficult in its own way."

"You forgot about our prized collectibles," Yov muttered under his breath. He sat hunched over, staring at the ground. None of his followers responded to his latest piece of wit.

"But setbacks aren't defeats," my dad resumed, not looking Yov's way. "Setbacks can be opportunities. Signs that it's time to change. If we're sharp enough to read the signs."

He licked his lips, his eyes flicking around the circle. A low wind had risen. It blew hot against my skin, moaned softly through the empty rooms.

"I've read the signs," my dad went on, "and I believe they're telling us something. Something we haven't wanted to admit. Something even I haven't wanted to admit. But something I think it's time we did."

"Cut to the chase," Yov groused.

If my dad heard this second interruption, he didn't show it. "We've been running for years," he said. "Running from our enemy. Maybe," and I swore he was looking right at me when he said this, "running from ourselves. We've gotten so used to running, we've never stopped to ask if there's another way. But maybe it's time we asked that question. Maybe it's time we found another way."

"Excuse me, Laman?" Petra spoke up from the crowd. I hadn't noticed her before, but there she was, looking edgy and agitated, blinking up a storm. "Is there a point to all this? Because I'm kind of on a tight schedule here."

A few titters rose around the circle, mostly from Yov's gang. Yov himself frowned and voiced something I couldn't hear. I guess he didn't appreciate anyone stealing his best lines.

My dad, though, glared at Petra with mingled annoyance and gratification. If he'd been waiting for a fight, it looked like somebody had finally picked one.

"As a matter of fact, Petra," he said, "I was just getting to that. But if you've got more important things to do than assist in the survival of this colony, don't let me stop you." He raised an eyebrow in challenge.

Petra, to my surprise, kept her mouth shut. And sat back down. She even stopped blinking for a moment.

All eyes turned back to my dad. I had the feeling no one would challenge him now.

"Petra knows better than most what it's like to be constantly on the run," he addressed the camp. His face glowed in triumph, but his voice had turned conciliatory. "Our scouts risk their lives every day so the rest of us can live in relative security. They're out there, always on the move, not knowing half the time where they'll find us next. Petra puts her life on the line to protect us. Danis gave his life to do the same."

I glanced at Petra, who showed no sign that she appreciated either the compliment or the reminder. Her gaze was locked on a space directly in front of her, her bloodshot eyes unblinking.

"What would happen," my dad continued, "if instead of expending our resources on running and hiding, we devoted them to standing and fighting? What would happen if, instead of thinking of this compound as a temporary bivouac, we thought of it as a base of operations to begin the work of rebuilding?"

He waited for a reaction. I'm not sure people heard him right, or maybe they were too stunned by his final word to say anything.

Finally Aleka repeated the word. "Rebuilding?"

My dad nodded vigorously. For a second I thought his craggy face was about to split in a smile. He seemed like a kid who'd kept a secret for days and now couldn't wait to spill it. He didn't budge from his stance, but to my eyes he looked like he was practically dancing.

Aleka pursued, "And when did you arrive at this decision?"

"It's a decision we had to make," he said. "Sooner or later. Losing the truck forced us to make the decision sooner. But I'm not going to say I'm not thankful for that."

Across the circle, Araz swore softly.

"Laman," Aleka tried again. "The survival colonies abandoned reclamation projects decades ago. Mobility has been our ally."

"And our curse," he said. "Our goad and our torment."

He raised his voice, addressing us all, silencing the objection I saw forming on Aleka's lips. "We've been running too long," he said. "Never knowing where we'd find shelter, never knowing when we'd run out of places to run. For fifty years or more, we've had nothing like a place we could call home."

A few heads nodded around the circle. Far to my left, away from Wali and the other teens, Korah took a step forward. I hadn't seen her since the day of the rain, but whatever had been wrong with her yesterday hadn't done a thing to dampen her glow. Her blue eyes homed in on my dad, laser-sharp.

"I've never had a place I could call my own," he repeated, his voice oddly nostalgic. "None of us has. We've gotten so used to just passing through, we've never really looked at a site like this and seen its potential. But," and his voice rose until the skeleton buildings echoed it back, "I see the potential here. The potential to make a stand. To win back some of what we've lost."

Yov jumped to his feet. "Then what was the point of forcing us to trash all our stuff?" He sounded genuinely angry. "What was the point of that little exercise if you were planning to park our butts here?"

"Take your seat," my dad growled.

Yov reddened, his hands forming fists. But then, mouthing silent curses, he folded his lanky body back to the ground.

"I've thought long and hard about this," my dad said, his eyes raking the crowd. No one else stood, no one else spoke. "I've done nothing for the past twenty-five years but think about what's best for this colony. And I think now the only reason I didn't see it before was that I'd fallen into bad habits. Rituals. Maybe I was more vulnerable to that because I've spent so much time trying to sharpen our routines to perfection. But the worst habit of all is believing we have to follow the same habits forever. To the end, whatever that might be."

"Are you suggesting," Aleka said slowly, "a permanent settlement?"

This time, miraculously, he did smile. It wasn't much, a crinkling at one corner of his lips, but it was definitely there. On that face that never smiled, though, it looked less like a smile than a leer.

"I'm suggesting we've hidden in the shadows too long," he said. "Hidden like insects afraid to venture into the light for fear of getting stomped on. This is our chance, people. It might be the best chance we get. Aren't you sick of running? Sick of hiding? Sick of letting *them* call the shots?"

More heads nodded, though I couldn't tell if they were agreeing with his plan or only with his picture of how miserable their life was.

"That's right," he said, his hideous smile broadening.

"We've been living as if *we're* the ones responsible for what happened to our world. As if we have to atone for what someone else did fifty years ago. But life isn't a penance for the past, people. Life isn't about looking back. It's about looking ahead."

"Laman," Aleka interrupted once more, a note of desperation in her voice, "is this wise?"

"It's necessary," he said bluntly. "Yesterday's wisdom isn't always good enough for today. In fact, the received wisdom of the past can prevent us from facing the challenges of the present. I've got Querry to thank for reminding me of that."

Aleka's mouth opened, but she didn't say a word. Neither did anyone else.

Neither did I. Hearing my name, so unexpectedly, in the middle of this wild speech made my ears and face burn. I dropped my eyes as everyone turned to look at me.

"Querry?" Aleka found her voice and spoke into the wind-whipped silence.

"That's right," he said.

His footsteps approached, his gnarled hand hovered in front of my face. His fingernails showed against his sun-browned skin, long and filthy.

"Come here, son," he said.

I looked into his eyes. With the sun behind him they glistened as black as coals.

"What are you doing?" I whispered.

"Preparing for a war," he hissed back. "Choose a side."

Then he gripped my hand and drew me to my feet.

"Bravo, Space Boy," Yov seethed in a voice filled with loathing.

With his arm around my shoulders, my dad walked me to the center of the circle. People murmured all around me like the wind. His arm felt like a weight. I couldn't look anyone in the eye.

"Just yesterday," he said, "Querry helped me see we can't run forever. He helped me see there are some things too precious to risk losing. And one of those things, maybe the most important of those things, is our faith in each other and our hope for the future."

I tried to remember how I'd helped him see those things, but my memory of the last couple days had become as full of holes as my memory of the past fourteen years. All I could remember was his arm lashing out at me, connecting, the rattle of teeth in my jaw.

"We lost Danis," my dad said. "He was a good man, and a good soldier. We lost a vehicle. That's not the same as losing a man, but when you have as little as we do, every loss hurts. Some of you might not know this, but I've given names to all the trucks. The one we lost was Aggie."

That drew some quiet laughs. I tried to pull away from his arm, but he held on tight.

"We can survive those losses," he continued. "We can survive the loss of any one person, any one thing. We all die, right? Yet we survive. Why?" Without waiting for an answer, he went on. "Because of the colony. The colony is the key. If we lose that . . ."

He looked at me strangely, then addressed the crowd again.

"Well, let's just say I don't intend to. And I'd like to thank Querry for showing me that we were on the verge of losing it. That if we didn't make a change, we might just lose it for good."

Aleka shook her head slowly, her eyes closed, but she still seemed unable to say a word.

That's when my dad stepped away from me and did something I'd never seen him, or anyone, do. Holding his hands out toward me, he brought them together, slowly at first, then faster, until the palms of his hands made a smacking sound when they hit. Faster and faster, he did this strange thing, as odd and senseless, I thought, as any of the rituals he'd said we could do without. But then, to my amazement, others in camp began to do the same thing, haltingly, as if they'd just remembered it was something you could do, something you were supposed to do, even if they couldn't remember why. The officers started it, Aleka a bit behind the others but ultimately, as if she'd decided she had no choice, bringing her pale hands listlessly together. Then the rest of the grown-ups added to the chorus, Petra and Araz and Kin and a few others excepted, and the little kids skipping across the walls were drawn by the commotion and started doing it too, giggling delightedly as they did, and the teenagers

135

eventually, grudgingly, joined in, all except Wali and Kelmen and Yov, and Korah put her hand to her mouth and whistled, and the echoes reverberated across the ruined compound like the marching feet of an army ten times our size. It was the most noise by far I'd heard the camp make. The shelled buildings hummed with the sound.

I stood in the center of it with my dad facing me, his dark eyes lit by a triumphant glow. I tried to peer through those eyes, to see the man or not-man underneath, but there was nothing to see. All I could see was that somehow, in a way I couldn't begin to understand, he'd taken people's minds off the truck, and the footprints, and the collection jars, and Danis, and quarantine, and everything else in their lives. It wasn't about any of those things anymore. Whether they liked him or hated him, supported or suspected him for the direction he'd decided to take us, it was all about him.

When he finally signaled for silence and the hand-smacking noise died down, people rose from their seats, looking flushed and feverish. He led us around the place, pointing out features we hadn't paid attention to before, details only he had discerned: the sightlines from certain second-story windows, the sub-basements that could be used for storage or defense or surprise attack, the supply of untouched brick and stone and wood in an outbuilding that could be used to repair broken structures or build new ones. He told us we could tear down the weakest of the houses, the ones closest to the crater, and salvage their materials to reinforce the strongest. He spoke of how we could redesign the compound for maximum strength, resurrect the gate that at one time had circled the whole, repair the buried pipes that had carried water and waste to and from the desert. He painted pictures of a day to come when we'd be able to use those pipes to channel water from the river and sky, maybe figure out a way to use sand or clay to filter it for drinking, even recover some of the dead garden plots that littered the place like sandboxes. He said we might be able to generate fibers for essentials like rope and cloth and canvas, or develop methods to clean and repair the supply we already had. Given time, we might expand, grow our city, discover ways to make our own brick and metal and glass, build cool and comfortable houses we could rely on to block the heat of day. It was not an easy project he envisioned, he knew that, not something that would be accomplished in a day or a week or a year. It had taken the civilization before us centuries to achieve what he had in mind, a few short years to tear it down. But the advantage we had over them, he said, was that we had learned from their mistakes. We knew our limitations. We would begin anew tomorrow.

During the whole tour, I'd been getting sidelong looks from grown-ups and teens, mostly curious, some admiring, some doubtful. I tried to avoid the stares. My dad had apparently forgotten about me by then, or was too busy with the others to pay me any mind. I kept my eyes on him the whole time, only glancing back once or twice at Aleka, who stayed at the rear of the group without saying a word, her brow knitted. Occasionally I'd hear a snort or a laugh from Petra, who seemed to find the whole thing simply hilarious. For once, Yov and Wali were nowhere to be seen. Korah, though, absolutely glowed. She looked at me a couple times, her eyes both radiant and defiant, but I dropped my gaze in a hurry.

When he was done, my dad let us knock off for the rest of the day. Save our strength for the main event tomorrow. With the camp a bundle of nervous energy, he must have realized nothing more would be accomplished today, anyway.

I went up to Aleka after my dad returned to head-quarters. Her face looked even paler than usual, and her eyes were haunted.

"Well," I said. "You told me he'd have a plan."

She flinched as if I'd bitten her. "This," she stammered. "This I never anticipated."

"Do you still believe in him now?" I pursued. "You still want me to help him?"

She didn't answer, only passed a hand over her forehead and wandered off like a sleepwalker.

The Skaldi, my dad hadn't named them once. Apparently, they weren't part of the plan.

QUEST

If I was expecting my dad to tone it down the next day, he quickly dispelled that illusion.

So I guess it was a good thing I wasn't expecting it.

He started up again as soon as we got to work on what he'd decided would be our first project, breaking ground for a more permanent defensive perimeter than the tents and tilting fence posts we'd managed to string together so far. The wall he had in mind, he announced, would circle the entire compound, ten feet high and with guard towers at each of its cardinal points. It would have a locking gate no intruder could breach, barred portholes so our sharpshooters could track and take down an advancing enemy. It would be built, incredibly enough, out of the scrap wood and metal and brick from collapsed houses, along with the bags of sand and cement we'd found in the sub-basement of one of the outbuildings. It didn't matter that we lacked bolts and screws and saws, that we barely had enough tools or water or knowhow to mix cement. It didn't seem to matter that eventually we'd run out of ammo for the guns and fuel for the flamethrowers, and at that point any human or non-human enemy could walk right up to our wall and crawl over it without breaking a sweat. Somehow, my dad insisted, this imaginary barricade would be strong enough to repel an army of hungry Skaldi.

We were standing at the site of the dig on the eastern ridge of the hill, gripping our handful of shovels and rakes and trowels, half the camp itching to get started and the other half shaking their heads in disbelief, when my dad turned to me.

"Querry," he said, holding out his shovel. "How'd you like to break first ground?"

All eyes instantly fell on me. There was no way I could avoid doing what he'd asked without making a fool of myself, so I pulled myself erect and tried my best to stare down the crowd as I grabbed the crooked handle of the shovel.

For a second we held the shovel together, his hand right above mine. Then he let go and took a step back.

"Go ahead," he nodded. "Show us what you've got."

I pressed the tip of the shovel against the ground, wiggling it until it bit through the crust. When I felt the blade catch, I planted my foot on its heel and stamped. The shovel sliced easily through the parched soil. I put my weight into it, thrust with my arms and shoulders, and hefted a pile of red-brown dirt. Then I straightened, turned with the anthill-size mound balanced on the blade, and dumped it on the ground a few feet away. A wedge-shaped hole, about a foot across and a half-foot deep, marked my labors.

"Good work," my dad said, giving me another of his grisly smiles. His face looked like it might rip in two. "All right, people," he said. "Querry's gotten us started. Let's keep the momentum going."

Everyone moved toward the hole I'd begun.

"You're a real hero, Space Boy," Yov hissed in my ear before getting to work.

I ignored him and joined in, plunging the shovel again and again into the hole. Korah took her place beside me, while Yov grabbed Wali and Kelmen and set up shop farther down the line. Korah had tied her hair back in a ponytail and shucked her uniform jacket, revealing a white tank top sweat-stained to a shade of mustard yellow. The muscles of her shoulders glistened as she stabbed her blade into the ground. I stood close enough to smell her musky scent, close enough to see the wet strands of hair that came free from her ponytail and trailed along her cheek. At one point our swinging shovels clanged, and she shot me a smile before lowering her head again to her work.

Down the line Yov sang in a deep, raspy voice: "Nobody knows the trouble I've seen. . . ." Wali laughed so hard I thought he'd pee his pants.

We worked for a couple hours, the sun climbing to its peak, punishing and inescapable. We took shifts so no one would totally exhaust themselves: some people dug, others smoothed and leveled the ditch, and others carted the dirt away and dumped it over the side of the hill, where it vanished into a fine spray before settling to the plain below. When my dad finally called a break, we rested in the hot shade and looked at our handiwork.

The trench we'd begun digging was about two feet wide and five deep, and so far, with the lack of tools and the strength-sapping sun, we'd created a jagged line maybe thirty feet long, with a rough patchwork of sticks propping up the sides. It looked more like an open wound in the ground than the foundation of anything that would stand above the surface. If I'd had to estimate the perimeter of the compound, I'd have guessed about a half-mile. Which meant somewhere around a hundred similar shifts to dig the trench, not to mention all the work that would go into preparing it and erecting the barrier itself. Maybe we could run two shifts a day.

At the end of which, if we ever got to the end, we'd have a wall protecting basically nothing.

I thought of a story I'd heard once, I couldn't remember where. Maybe from the old woman. About a guy whose job, or I guess his sentence, was to roll a rock uphill, only to watch it tumble back down every time he reached the top. Till now, I'd thought the story had to do with the tragedy of never seeing your dreams fulfilled. But at the moment, I felt like it carried a warning to be careful what you dreamed in the first place.

After a while we got back to work. The gash in the ground grew incrementally longer. Mika, the person in camp next to Araz who knew the most about building things, inspected our progress and told my dad it looked okay except for the places where the ground had proven sandier than we'd thought and the walls of the trench had collapsed. She suggested diverting the trench around those spots, or reinforcing the walls with stronger pieces of lumber. What she thought about the project itself she didn't say.

While we worked, my dad hobbled around the site, passing on Mika's instructions, shouting encouragement. One time he picked up a shovel and lowered himself into the ditch, then went to work flinging dirt onto the ground, the blade of his shovel blurring and glinting in the afternoon sun. I saw Korah watching him, her cheeks flushed beneath smudges, her eyes gleaming.

After about fifteen minutes, though, he was beat, his uniform sweat-soaked, his lank hair glued to his forehead. He handed the shovel up to one of the workers and accepted their hand to haul him out of the ditch. His foot slipped on the crumbling edge a couple times before he managed to make solid ground.

"Thought I'd show you kids how it's done," he panted. He flashed us a look, then ducked his eyes and limped off to check in with his officers.

"That was truly inspirational," Yov growled. Korah glared at him, but I thought her own face registered disappointment that my dad hadn't succeeded in digging the ditch and building the wall all by himself.

In another hour Aleka came over. By this time the flying dust had stuck to wet skin and coated all of us in red, making us look like the clay figures the little kids sculpted sometimes and played made-up stories with. The only dolls they had, which always ended up ground to dust after a day's playing. You could still see the whites of people's eyes and patches of skin here and there, but grit caked everything, including our lips, and our hair hung heavy with beads of muddy brown.

"This seems like it's going well," Aleka said. But this time I definitely heard the strain in her voice.

"If you think this is going well," Yov grumbled, "I've got a dead truck I'd love to sell you."

"Not funny," Korah sang out.

"Not meant to be," he shot back.

"Not helpful either," she fumed.

Yov rested an elbow on the stick he was using in place of a shovel and smirked at her. "Not meant to be that, either."

"All right," Aleka said. "Let's call it a day and get cleaned up. Yov, you can collect the tools. Korah, come with me."

"Uh-oh," Yov grinned as Korah climbed out of the ditch. "Looks like someone's going to get a spanking."

The teens close enough to hear him cracked up, Wali hardest of all. Yov's smile widened.

"Well, all right, people," he hollered, doing a bad imitation of my dad's voice. He limped down the line, his back hunched and his hips jerking spastically. "Hand 'em over. No time like the present. Let's get a move on!"

The teenagers laughed even harder. Some of the grown-ups laughed too.

I ignored Yov's routine and handed him my own digging stick, which I'd been using ever since one of the adults swiped my shovel. I saw that Aleka and Korah had stopped a short distance away. Korah, her arms and hair a solid shade of red, was gesturing energetically and saying something I couldn't make out. All I heard was the rich sound of her voice. Aleka was listening, it seemed, but shaking her head the whole time. Finally Korah stopped gesticulating and walked off, her arms crossed tightly over her stomach. She did look, oddly enough, like a little girl who'd just been bawled out by her mother.

A clattering noise made me jump. Yov had thrown the tools to the ground right at my feet. I looked around and realized the other workers had sought the shade, leaving me alone with him. His smile had faded, and his long, gaunt face looked pained, as if his teeth hurt. His eyes blazed as hot as the late-day sun.

"Look, Space . . . Querry." He swallowed as if to get the taste of my name out of his mouth. "When are you going to tell the old man to give it a rest?"

"What do you mean?"

He let a long string of brown liquid drip to the ground.

"Our fearless leader," he said. "Can't you talk some sense into him?"

"If the work's a problem . . ."

"It's not the work," he snarled. "And you know it. It's this place. The place he's apparently decided to turn into his own little personal nirvana. It's crazy."

"How so?"

"God damn it!" With his cheeks coated in dust and his hair sticking out every which way, his face looked wild and desperate. "You know exactly what I'm talking about. This place is dangerous. It's been dangerous since the day we arrived. And yet here we are, in plain sight of anything that happens to be snooping around, and what are we doing? Prancing around like a bunch of Boy Scouts, building a fence that won't ever get built! What are we going to do next, sing campfire songs? Roast marshmallows?"

I had no idea what Boy Scouts or marshmallows were. They might be things I'd forgotten, or they might be things everyone had forgotten but still talked about. There were a lot of those things.

"What do you want me to do?" I said.

"Talk to the man!" His arms shot out and caught my shoulders. The stench of his breath bathed my face, hot and fetid. "Talk some sense into him!"

I shook free, more easily than I expected. In the second his hands had gripped me, I'd felt their strength, far greater than my own. "Back off, Yov."

He fell away from me, looking appalled. His breath came in husky bursts, and for the first time I could remember, he seemed unable to look me in the eye.

"Tell him," he said heavily. "Just tell him, for God's sake."

"He won't listen to me," I said. "He never has."

"Well, isn't that convenient." His red-veined eyes seemed to bulge beneath his brow. "Must be nice to always have that excuse. Crazy old man won't listen to poor little Querry. And so the rest of us have to pay the price."

I looked into his furious, miserable eyes, and for an odd moment I was moved to tell him what festered in my own mind. To tell him I knew what had happened to his father, knew why he was so angry at my dad, why he wanted others to suffer and rage too. More than that, I almost told him I agreed with him, that my dad had gone off the deep end and put all of us in jeopardy. I almost told him what I'd overheard during the interrogation of Petra, almost told him of Aleka's doubts, as well as my own. For that single moment, it seemed possible to tell him we had something in common: a common fear, a common enemy, maybe even a common purpose.

But I didn't tell him. I couldn't. Tell him I understood, sympathized, felt sorry? Tell him we were more alike than he realized? More alike than I had realized until this moment?

Yeah. And what would we do next? Sing campfire songs? Roast marshmallows?

"I'll talk to him," I said. "But don't expect any miracles."

His lips drew back as if to bite me, but he didn't try to stop me as I turned and walked away.

"You'll be sorry if you fail, little man," he spat at my back. "You'll all be sorry."

I left him standing there, coated in dust as red as blood. I was already more sorry than he could possibly know.

The sun stood too tall to continue our work, so we spent the rest of the day puttering around camp and planning for tomorrow.

Muddy as we were, we couldn't really clean ourselves. The best we could do was chafe our bodies with crusty rags that removed as much skin as dirt. The camp crazies collected the dust, scooping it into their palms and looking around for their jars, only to remember they'd been stowed away and the officers had failed to return them despite my dad's change of plans. So they stuffed the dirt in their pockets for a later time. Then there were those who withdrew from the group, took off their uniforms, and beat their clothes against walls and fence posts until the air grew cloudy with miniature dust storms. Wali and Kelmen whacked their uniforms the hardest. Watching them, it wasn't too difficult to figure out who they'd rather be beating.

But lots of people, probably the majority, seemed too exhausted to wipe down at all, and they went through the remainder of the day coated in a second skin of dust. As evening fell they sat by the bomb-scarred wall of the building we'd designated as the commissary and waited with clenched hands and drawn faces for Tyris to dole out another paltry serving of canned rations. There'd been a time, recent enough for me to remember, when people had stood in an orderly line to receive their food. But that time now seemed as distant as my own forgotten past.

Yov didn't make an appearance at dinner. In fact, he vanished right after our conversation, leaving the tools behind for me to pick up and deposit in their basement storage space. While people sat in silence and wolfed down their meager meal, while they prepared for bed, some of them unsure what to do now that their rituals had been interrupted and their pockets hung with their own dirty skin, Yov kept to himself, hidden away somewhere. For the rest of the day I kept an eye out for him, but he never showed. His absence brought a knot to my stomach that grew larger and tighter as the day dragged into night.

It wasn't just his threat that made me anxious. It was my pledge.

By the time we finished dinner, I knew I couldn't delay any longer. All meal long, my dad had pulled me around as he congratulated people for their hard work and bucked them up for tomorrow's repeat performance. He shook hands, patted backs, told everyone from the oldest and weariest to the youngest and most oblivious that we'd made a great start and we really needed to pour it on now. He exchanged quiet words with his supporters, reminding them of the sacrifices people like Danis had made, telling them they were honoring his memory by fulfilling the dreams heroes like him had died for. To those who remained unconvinced, disgruntled, or openly hostile he changed his tune, challenging them in a soft but unyielding voice to have faith, to work for the benefit of the colony, to put aside differences in the name of the common good. No one said a word back to him. Those not too angry to speak seemed too tired to think and too busy licking their fingers for the last greasy traces of food. All he got were grateful smiles from disciples like Korah, ominous glares from holdouts like Araz. Petra was harder to pin down, what with all the blinking and her natural ability to evade. Aleka he didn't bother trying to convince, which was just as well, since she kept her thoughts, and her person, to herself.

The whole time, while I stood by his side, unable to say a word and not invited to anyway, the speech I knew I would have to deliver gathered in the back of my mind, in the part of my memory not too damaged to call back. Every so often in the middle of a conversation he'd turn to me, nod, brace an arm behind my back, and I'd look at him evenly, the effort to control what I couldn't show making my lip tremble. Then he'd grab my elbow and steer me to the next person crouched over their meal, and the whole thing would start all over again. The worst was when he launched into his speech in front of Korah. I saw the light beaming from a face she'd somehow restored to its flawless beauty, and I couldn't do anything but squirm.

"This is what it means to be a leader," she whispered to me, her breath warm on my ear, her hand squeezing my arm. When our eyes met, I thought I saw the soft promise I'd never seen her show anyone but Wali. Whether my dad heard her, whether he saw that look too before he dragged me away, I couldn't tell.

When it was finally over, when we'd visited every last clump of exhausted, famished workers, he walked me to the crest of the hill and we stood looking out over a land drained of light and life. "You'll have to learn to do this," he said. "Someday."

"What do you mean?"

"When I'm gone," he said, speaking so low the wind tossed his words almost beyond my hearing. "They'll need you then. To carry on."

To carry on *what*? I almost screamed. "Dad . . ."

"Come on," he said. "It's getting late."

We strolled over to the group of officers who sat apart from the workers, their faces growing shadows in the twilight. Aleka stood to the side, so still and silent she might have been one of the pillars left over from the time before.

"Tomorrow it's Querry's turn," he said. His voice took in the group, but his eyes rested on her. "He can supervise the fence construction. Take charge."

"Dad," I protested.

"Aleka will help you," he said. "It'll be all right."

"No," I said. "It won't."

Aleka turned her gaze to me. The other officers stiffened as if I'd burst open and let loose a stream of Skaldi. Only my dad seemed unfazed.

"It'll be all right, son," he said quietly.

"Dad," I said. "I'm sorry I—I'm sorry about what happened. I should have listened. But this isn't the way. The way to win the war."

He faced me squarely, his eyes showing not triumph but something else—weariness, sadness, maybe respect. It was too dark to tell.

"You'll learn, Querry," he said. "All of us remember that time. The time when you have to make a choice. No matter how dark it looks. When the alternative is much, much worse."

"I don't know how . . ." I began. *I don't know how to tell you*, I recited in my head. *All the things I have to tell you, all the things I never have. . . .* But my riddled memory failed me, and I couldn't complete the thought.

He stepped closer, his eyes boring into mine. I couldn't mistake the sorrow in their coal-black depths. "Then it's time you learned," was all he said. He signaled to the other officers and strode away.

I turned to Aleka, but her gaze held neither promise nor encouragement. Her face and eyes blended with the gray of her uniform.

"I did try," I said.

"I know you did."

"He's gone crazy, hasn't he?"

She opened her hands in bewilderment. "I don't know what to tell you, Querry. All I can say is that the Laman Genn I know wouldn't do this."

"Maybe you don't know him anymore, then."

"Maybe neither of us does."

"Maybe," I said, "this isn't him."

She opened her mouth as if to respond, then turned away and wouldn't say another word.

I went to bed sure I'd wake to a night terror. Almost looking forward to it. Wishing for a nightmare I couldn't remember to cancel out the one I could.

10
LOST

Screams woke me.

At first I thought they lived in my head. Then I realized they were coming from all around me. Screams, magnified by the stillness of the night, rebounding off the ghost-town buildings. Screams of people I knew. Maybe. It was impossible to tell. Screams are just screams.

I sprang to my feet and searched the moonless dark for the source. I could barely make out shadowy figures in the distance and hear the slap of running feet. A gunshot sounded, an unidentifiable voice responded with shouts and curses.

Then a jet of fire bloomed in the night. In its glare I saw Araz standing on the edge of the crater holding a flame-thrower, others in camouflage uniforms racing in every direction. Some darted between the pillars and walls of crumbled buildings, others plunged deeper into the night. Some I thought I saw stumble and fall into the crater. I couldn't tell whether they were escaping from the stream of fire or from something else. I couldn't tell if they were the people I'd known for the past six months or something else.

But I did know one thing.

This was no night terror.

It was real.

Without a thought as to what I was doing, I leaped over the wall and ran toward Araz. My feet, bootless, suffered the piercing sting of rocks at every stride. In the swirling dark I nearly collided with a group of little kids who appeared out of the night, running in the opposite direction. Their screams of terror chilled my blood. But I kept moving toward Araz, dodging piles of brick and stone I could sense more than see. My lungs drew air laced with the smell of gasoline and burning wood, though nothing seemed to be on fire. The only things clearly visible in the whole camp were the driver and the outlines of the buildings into which he shot flickering tongues of flame.

"What is it?" I screamed at him over the rush of the flamethrower. Sweat covered his face and his eyes shone wildly in the orange glow.

"Skaldi!" he screamed back. He shot another gout of flame at something only he could see, or at nothing at all.

"Where's my dad?"

He didn't answer. He sent a long, sweeping arc of fire toward the buildings closest to him, and I had to jump back to avoid the flames. My skin prickled and felt as if it was blistering.

Half-blinded by the firelight, I spun and headed for the building where my dad had set up his quarters. I could just make out its shadow, separate from the other dim shapes that rose around it. I slammed against rock, pitched blindly forward. For a horrifying second I thought I had tumbled into the crater, but then my hands hit solid ground. Ignoring the pinpricks of pain from my scraped palms, I scrambled to my feet and ran toward the command building. Blurry figures brushed past me, too filmy to see clearly but firm enough to bruise my shoulder and spin me from my feet. I had no idea if they were people fleeing the Skaldi or Skaldi fleeing the man who flourished the flame gun.

"Dad!" I yelled into the night. "Dad!"

I thought I heard a weak voice answer, "Querry!" But before I had a chance to listen for a repetition, the flames erupted again and swallowed all sound in their exultant roar.

I reached the door of headquarters, pawed for the empty frame, swung myself into the front hall. For a moment I stopped short in total darkness. Then, moving as cautiously as my rising panic would let me, I picked my way past broken pieces of furniture to the room where I'd witnessed Petra's interrogation. My gut twisted as I remembered that day. Nothing stirred in the dark, no sound of voices or anything else. I passed through the archway that led to the back room where my dad slept, but it was as dark and silent as the rest of the house.

"Dad?" I breathed. "Dad?"

Nothing.

I slid one foot forward, then the next, groped for the place where I knew he'd laid his mat. I fell to my knees and felt around on the ground in front of me. My fingers found the mat, a coarse and scratchy piece of canvas, but no one lying on it. I thought I felt some lingering warmth from a body, but my feverish hands might have been playing tricks on me.

I stood and peered into darkness my eyes refused to penetrate. I wondered if he'd started sleeping in his third-story armory, if he was up there right now watching the chaos on the ground.

Or worse, if he was the cause of it.

The flamethrower sprang to life once more, and the outline of the room's sole window came into focus. The throaty noise emerged in bursts, the sound of screams resuming every time the weapon fell silent. The window flickered black and orange as the flames rose and fell.

Then I heard a voice, in the gaps of flame, faint but unmistakable. "Where's Querry?" he shouted over the other noises. "Where's Querry?"

"Dad!" I ran for the archway, knocking my shoulder against the wall, and sprinted blindly through the interrogation room. The flamethrower gave me just enough light to detect the front door and fling myself through it.

Araz remained visible in the distance, flames seeming to spout from his arms. Small fires had sprung up in the ruins of the buildings around him, so he looked like a gardener tending bushes of flame. What had caught fire, whether fuel or bodies or our meager supplies, I couldn't tell. No other figures were in sight, though the sound of their voices, calling for help or for each other, could still be heard when the flames fell silent. I couldn't determine what direction my dad's voice had come from, and I didn't know whether to risk another race across the compound's courtyard, another close encounter with the gaping crater. So I stood still and lifted my voice as loud as I could make it.

"Dad!"

No answer.

"Dad!"

"Querry!" The voice came from the direction of my own sleeping place. We must have run past each other in the dark.

"I'm coming!" I yelled, but then I felt a hand grip my arm and I spun, a scream about to form on my lips.

"Shh!" a voice said. "It's me."

The voice was Korah's.

She stood so close I could feel her warm breath on my ear and see the sweep of her dark hair blurring the night. Then Araz's flamethrower exploded again, and in the brief burst of brilliance I saw her face, soft and comforting yet full of concern.

"We've got to get you out of here," she whispered. "Before that thing finds us."

"How did it . . . ?"

"It's been here all along," she said. "We just didn't know it." She tugged my arm. "Come on. This way."

I resisted. "My dad . . ."

She stopped pulling. Even in the dark her eyes seemed to melt with sorrow and pity.

"It *is* your dad," she said. "I'm so sorry."

I staggered, caught myself against her shoulder. I thought I'd prepared myself for this, but hearing the words from her lips, it felt like the world had ended.

Aleka's instinct had been right. The Skaldi had taken my dad. When it had infected him, why it had waited till now to strike, I might never know. But he was gone. The madness I'd thought was his was the creature's madness, thwarting our will, forcing us to stay until it was ready to spring its trap. If I'd only been able to stop it, maybe this night would never have come. I couldn't have saved him, but maybe I could have saved his camp.

But I hadn't stopped it. I had helped.

I hadn't wanted to, but I had. Aleka and I had been the only two who might have been able to expose the monster in our midst. But we'd failed, and so whatever happened tonight would be on my conscience as well as hers.

And if she died, it would be on mine alone.

"We have to go back," I said haltingly. "To tell Araz. So he knows what to kill."

"We'd never make it." The pressure on my arm became

more insistent. "We have to hide someplace it won't find us."

"But Wali and the others . . ."

"Will have to fend for themselves." In the firelight her face grew grave and tender. "I'm sorry, Querry. I loved your father too. But you know he would have wanted you to be safe."

I did know. I knew it to my shame.

"Come on," Korah urged, her fingers massaging my arm. "We can't waste time."

I looked into her eyes. They seemed to create a light all their own. She had been one of my dad's staunchest supporters, I thought bitterly. She had seen his actions as those of a leader, not a madman, not a monster. She had even forgiven him for what happened to her own father. If we survived this night, she would grieve with me.

I threw one last look in the direction I'd heard the Skaldi speaking with my lost father's voice, then I turned and followed her.

She led the way past rubble, flattened herself against buildings, peered around corners before gesturing for me to follow. Bit by bit we made our way from the central area of the compound to the perimeter, where we'd started building the doomed wall. I could tell by the increase in wind that we'd neared the edge of the hill, but I couldn't see the hole we'd made. The screams of the others grew fainter, and the sound of Araz's flamethrower became little more than a pop or a hiccup, innocent as one of the blow-darts the little kids made out of hollowed branches.

We skirted the cliff. For a minute I thought she'd found some way down and was leading me out of camp altogether, but then I realized our steps pointed toward the bomb shelter. The only building where we could lock the creature out. I couldn't help admiring Korah for picking the shelter as the safest spot in camp.

"This way," she whispered.

She eased the front door open, slipped inside, and pulled me in after her. For a moment I had a dim view of the empty room, then the door closed and plunged us into total darkness. I heard a click as she turned the deadbolt, then another click and a beam of light sprang from her hand. I recognized her flashlight as the one Mika had used when she'd tried to fix the truck.

"Where's your mom?" I asked.

"She's safe," Korah said. "She's the one who sent me to look for you."

The beam danced across the floor, showing me a room as bare as a pit. The light reflected off metal: the handle to the trapdoor that led to the basement. Korah lifted the door and shone the light down the stairs.

"You first," she said.

Guided by the beam of her flashlight, I climbed down the stairs, which creaked beneath me as if they were about to break. The dirt floor felt shockingly cold against my bare feet. Korah lowered herself onto the stairs and started down. At the halfway point she stopped to pull the door closed and snapped the bolt. The sound echoed dully in the airtight room.

The room itself was as blank as I remembered it, gray walls and brown floor and nothing else now that the crates of food had been removed. The sounds from outside had died the moment the front door slammed shut, and in the silence I heard the faint hum of Korah's flashlight. She shone the light on all the corners of the room, ceiling and floor, checking in case anyone or anything had beaten us here. Then, satisfied, she sat cross-legged in the middle of the room and stood the flashlight beside her. I sat too, the light between us painting a yellow circle on the low ceiling.

Now that I had a moment to think, I realized my heart beat wildly and my breath came in staccato bursts. The image of my father hollowed out by the monsters he'd spent a lifetime fighting wouldn't let me go. Korah seemed surprisingly calm, resting back on her arms with her legs stretched in front of her, crossed at the ankles. She tossed her long black hair, which looked glossy and soft in the flashlight's glow. I tried to inhale her scent, but the air seemed too stale to carry it. How she kept her hair in perfect condition when everyone else in camp had a nest like twigs and straw I had no idea.

"How long do we have to stay here?" I asked.

"Until it's gone," she said simply. "Why?"

"You could go crazy in this place." Then, realizing what a stupid thing it was to say, I felt my face turn warm.

She laughed, the same unforced laugh I remembered from our conversation at the swimming pool. The sound echoed loudly. "Oh, Querry." She reached over to squeeze my arm. "I'll try to make the time go faster."

I thought she'd let go of my arm, but instead she used it to pull herself closer. The flashlight between us wobbled. Our hips touched.

"Do we need this light?" she asked, reaching between her leg and mine.

"I—" The thought of sitting there with her in the complete dark made my stomach lurch. "Maybe we should leave it on. In case anyone else comes."

"No one's coming," she said softly. "I've got you all to myself."

She turned to face me. Her lips parted slightly, but her amazing blue eyes stayed wide open.

"Let me get this off," she said, reaching for the flashlight without taking her eyes from mine. Her fingers brushed the cylinder and it clattered to the floor, but instead of picking it up she let her hand drop onto my thigh. The beam shining off the far wall gave me just enough light to see her flushed cheeks and soft eyes.

"I've been waiting for this moment," she whispered. "Ever since that night at the pool. I think you have too. Haven't you?"

Her hand stroked my leg. Her breath quickened.

"Korah," I said. "I thought you . . ."

She put a finger to my lips. "Whatever you thought, it's over now."

"But what about," I gulped, "what about Wali?"

"What about him?" she whispered back.

Her mouth loomed closer. I felt her breath, strangely cold on my cheek. Her eyes didn't even blink.

I closed my eyes just as her lips met mine. They moved against me, far drier and rougher than I'd imagined. There was no warmth to her touch. I opened my eyes and found her staring straight back.

That's when I realized I really could see through those luminous blue eyes.

And I realized at the same time there was nothing to see.

I jerked away as her lips drew back in a snarl that revealed pale, bloodless gums. Her head lunged forward in a convulsive motion, her teeth barely missing my throat. I scrambled away from her, backpedaling on my hands and heels. The bare ground scratched my already scraped skin. She rose to a crouch and launched herself toward me, and her body seemed to thin and lengthen in midair like an elastic band pulled tight.

She landed and slithered after me on her belly. Her arms and legs coiled against the dirt as if they'd been emptied of bones.

I heard a booming noise overhead and ran for the steps, but her hand clutched my ankle with an icy strength and pulled me to the ground. The red-handled pocketknife leaped to my fist, blade extended, slashing wildly. I felt contact, saw the ends of two fingers fly, but there was no blood. What remained of her hand gripped my ankle so tightly I felt the fingernails sink into my skin, and though I grappled for the stairs she pulled me down toward her waiting mouth.

It had opened so wide there was no face left, only teeth like strips of peeling flesh.

Then I heard another boom, louder than the first, and saw a blurry shape come crashing down the stairs, narrowly missing me and the Skaldi as it landed with a metallic clang on the basement floor.

I heard a puff of compressed air and another blur flew past me, and the thing that had been Korah fell back, its faceless mouth splitting in an inhuman scream. Sharp nails raked my ankle as it let go. Its arms and legs flailed wildly, its head twisted nearly backward, but something pinned its writhing body to the ground. Through the dust and frantic motion I couldn't make out what held it, but when its head turned toward me I could see its eyes again, all trace of blue gone, burning white-hot in its withered face with torment and loathing.

A hand touched my shoulder. I flinched, looked up into the face of Aleka. A harpoon gun lay across her arm, a flamethrower was strapped to her back. Her fist closed on my shoulder and pulled me painfully to my feet.

"Go," she said hoarsely. Her face was streaked with dirt and tears.

Trembling, I set my foot on the stairs. My knees wobbled but held. I looked back for a second at the creature that lay there, teeth bared in its once beautiful face. Then Aleka's body blocked my view, and as she advanced on the Skaldi I turned and climbed. At the top of the stairs I heard the roar of the flames behind me, the screams of the thing they consumed. How Aleka could stand it I didn't want to think. The heat burned through the uniform on my back, the screams seemed to penetrate my skull.

I stumbled to the front door, which hung from a single hinge. Throwing myself through the open frame, I collapsed onto the ground, and my stomach emptied of what little was in it. But the screams followed me.

The thing screamed and screamed. The echoes multiplied its scream into a thousand screams.

For the first time since my accident, I knew those screams were something I'd never be able to forget, no matter how hard I tried.

COST

I stayed on my knees until Aleka exited the building where the Skaldi had burned.

At first I shrank from the fire in her hands, the singed fabric of her clothes. But she wouldn't let me stay down. With her help, I struggled to my feet, too shaky and sick with the loss of Korah to care about my soiled shirt front. I felt a trembling in my chest that I knew would turn to tears if I gave in to it.

"Let's go find Laman," she said.

My reunion with him was brief. We met midway between the bomb shelter and headquarters, along with a few others, including Araz. The flamethrower, still smoking, hung from the driver's broad back. My dad approached me, looked me up and down, his face haggard in the first feeble light of dawn. His uniform was buttoned to the top just like the night before, his bearing in it as erect and unyielding as it had been then. The Skaldi had convinced me he was the infected one, but now I realized that had been another of its lies. He was battered and bruised, but he was himself. Why I'd doubted him so easily, why he'd made it so easy for me to doubt, were questions I couldn't answer.

But we had no time to ask questions, no opportunity for more than a bare acknowledgment that we were both alive. Before he had a chance to say a word, Araz stepped to his side and grabbed his elbow.

"Game's up, Laman," the driver said. Next to him my dad looked like a child, or a very old man. "Come with me."

My dad didn't respond at first. He simply looked at the man who'd been his chauffeur, his brow wrinkling as if he couldn't imagine what the problem was. Then he nodded once, curtly, and let Araz lead him away. The rest of the camp straggled after them.

Araz put him in the house that had been his head-quarters. He took his gun away and posted Kelmen at the side window, Kin at the front door. He even stripped the cloth curtains away so the guards could keep a better eye on him. He also removed the canvas bedsheet to prevent the prisoner, so he said, from doing anything rash. The one officer who'd survived the night's attack he sent to guard the weapons. Then Araz went to check on Keely and the rest of the little kids, to survey the damage to camp, to recover the bodies of the dead. To take charge of the colony my dad had once commanded.

I went with him. He wouldn't let me near my dad's cell, anyway.

As dawn marbled the sky we looked out over the wreckage of our camp. Long black streaks from Araz's flamethrower scarred the ground, and the tents we'd strung up dangled from their lines, charred and smoldering. In some spots the floors of gutted houses still glowed like hot coals. Many of the fence posts had been knocked down in people's haste to find or escape the intruder, while other sections had tipped over just enough to present lethal spikes. Wisps of black smoke twined around the building where the creature had met its end. The air hung heavy with the smell of oil and burned things.

The ditch we'd started the day before had survived, parts of it collapsed from running feet. In the harsh light of dawn, it looked like a mocking smile.

Six people had died in the attack: Korah, her mother Mika, three officers, and the man with the picture of the light tower, who'd fallen into the crater in his panic to get away. Had the creature gone after human victims immediately, the death toll would almost certainly have been much higher. But for some reason, it had attacked our equipment before seeking out its prey. The tires of the trucks were slashed, their fuel lines bleeding into the dirt. The water drums had been tipped over, spilling their contents into soil eager to lap up any moisture it could find. Shovels had been snapped in two, canteens punctured and torn. The weapons, stored high in the tower room and guarded by a single officer, had been spared, as had the flamethrowers, too risky for the creature to touch. But much of what we relied on to survive had been trampled into the dust. My dad had posted sentries, Petra included, in all the best locations: high in the naked windows of houses, out on the precipice of the hill. But his choices, I realized, were based on past practice. We'd never had to worry about our supplies before, because it was always our bodies we'd had to protect. And so, once the creature managed to slip past the sentries, it found itself free to go on its rampage. Considering how easily it had torn the camp apart, it might have finished us all off if Mika's scream hadn't sounded an alarm.

The scream hadn't helped her, though. We found her lying among the ruins, her head twisted crazily to the side, her mouth frozen open and her eyes wide and empty. When two workers tried to lift her they found there was no weight to her body at all, and her skin sloughed off like dust in their fingers. They wrapped her in canvas and set her aside.

In the case of the officers, there wasn't enough left to wrap. So far as we could reconstruct, the creature had started with them, moving from one to the next and depositing their tattered uniforms in the dust before jumping to Mika. She must have woken as it attacked her, giving her a split-second to scream. That had been enough to wake those lying nearby, whose own screams woke others, and the creature had fled to a new victim before it had time to consume Mika as thoroughly as the officers. It had made the jump to Korah probably for no better reason than that she had come first to her mother's aid. Unarmed and unprepared, she'd been defenseless against its attack. It had taken her body as it had taken her mother's, then grabbed the flashlight and set out to hunt for me.

I wished Korah hadn't been roused by her mother's dying scream. I wished she hadn't been awake when the creature scoured her soul.

Aside from the man guarding the weapons hoard, the only member of the officer corps to survive was Aleka. She told us she'd been restless and unable to sleep, so she'd been roaming the outskirts of camp when the others met their fate. What she'd been looking for, and whether she'd found it, she wouldn't say. While Araz shot blindly into the night and everyone else ran away, Aleka returned to the sleeping quarters and found Mika, and when she spotted boot prints leading from the body, she set out in search of whoever had made them. She had no idea, she said, that Korah housed the creature until by pure luck Araz's flamethrower revealed the two of us heading for the bomb shelter, somewhere the real Korah had far too much train-ing to go. "She knew we never lock ourselves in," Aleka said, and though she said it without any accusation in her voice, I cringed to think how stupid I'd been. Arriving at the

171

shelter, she'd been lucky once again to find the hinges so old and rusty she was able to force the door with the butt of her harpoon gun, lucky a third time that the creature had toyed with me before striking. Otherwise, I'd have been its final victim.

It sickened me when I thought of that, when I remembered the monster's burned-out eyes and corpse-gray teeth. Twice now, counting the night at the swimming pool, I had been careless, letting my feelings for Korah override the caution my dad had tried to instill in me. My stomach twisted with shame and dread when I imagined what would have happened if Aleka hadn't been there.

But I couldn't feel thankful for the way I'd been saved. The sounds of Korah burning, even if it wasn't really Korah, haunted me and wouldn't let go.

And another thought made me tremble in the pit of my being: How had the creature known so much about us? How had it known the best way to cripple the colony would be to damage our supplies, kill our officers and mechanic? How had it even known who our officers and mechanic were? No one wore a uniform that distinguished them from anyone else, and even if they did, how could Skaldi know about chain of command or rank? Petra's words resounded in my mind, forcing me to ask: How did the Skaldi *know*?

Even more terrifying, how did it know so much about *me*?

My attraction to Korah. Our talk at the pool. Even my suspicions about my dad. It had known all those things, had spoken just the right words to get me to go along with it. And it had used its knowledge to hunt specifically for me. I couldn't believe it had sought me out simply because I was the single person in camp most likely to follow Korah wherever she led. Almost everyone trusted her. Almost anyone would have gone with her to their death.

It made no sense, but what if the thing the Skaldi *knew* had to do with me?

We spent the first part of the day restoring what order we could to camp. Supplies the creature had failed to destroy we consolidated in a single corner of the commissary. Supplies it had damaged beyond repair we left lying in the dust. Mika's body we moved to a secluded spot for later disposal. I felt her remains shifting like sand inside the wrapping and knew we'd never open it again. A brief debate took place about how to recover the body of the man at the bottom of the crater, but in the end we left him where he was. The empty uniforms of the fallen officers we folded and set beside Mika's shroud. What we would use in place of Korah's body when it came time for the burials was a mystery.

"We could search the shelter," Wali proposed. "Once it cools down. We might find something. . . ."

His voice broke and he turned away. Nessa wrapped him in her arms, holding him while he shook with sobs. Though I kept to myself what I had witnessed in the shelter, I doubted there'd be anything left to find.

With all our attention focused on our fellow colonists, it didn't occur to anyone right away to search for the body the Skaldi had arrived in. Personally, I'd have preferred not to know. Araz, though, insisted on it. So we spent another couple hours hunting through camp, starting at the site of the attacks and fanning outward from there. We found hundreds of footprints, most of them so blurred and confused they could have been anyone's. Even Petra, who had followed wordlessly as my dad was incarcerated and as Araz led the clean-up operation, shook her head and shrugged over signs she normally proved so confident at reading. But nothing else turned up, no skin, no hair, no teeth, and eventually Araz called the search off. Maybe, like Danis and the three officers, there'd been next to nothing left of the body that had carried the creature to camp, and the chaos of the night had trampled that little bit into the dust.

The sun beat down on us by the time we'd cleaned up as best we could. Exhaustion and grief rimmed everyone's eyes. But today, there'd be no relief from the brutal afternoon, no break to spend seeking out shreds of shade. No time, either, to mourn. Our new leader and his handpicked accomplices had decided not to waste a moment before revealing their own master plan.

The first step of which involved erasing the memory of the past.

They marched my dad under armed guard to the central clearing, the same place he'd made his speech a couple days before. His guard, Wali, prodded him with a rifle to the back. My dad's uniform had been blackened by fire and his limp seemed more pronounced than usual, but he held himself erect and struggled not to stumble as Wali roughly positioned him before us. Araz took the stage his commander had formerly occupied. A couple paces to the big man's side, their arms crossed behind their backs, stood Kin and, to my disgust but not surprise, Yov. This was the first I'd seen of him since the day before, and looking into his smug face and gloating eyes made my blood boil.

Araz motioned for quiet, needlessly, since everyone watched the proceedings in a silence bordering on trance. The driver's squat face and brawny arms stood in sharp contrast to my dad's lean, whittled frame. Araz was in his mid-thirties, so he would have been younger than I was now when my dad first took charge of camp. I'd always thought he admired and respected the man whose truck he'd driven for the past five years.

"Laman Genn," he said, "your failed leadership has placed the colony at dire risk. Your own officers, along with an innocent child and her mother, were the first to suffer from your indiscretion. We have come here to exact justice."

"On whose authority?" my dad said in a calm voice. Across the distance, his eyes sought mine. I looked away, unable to bear his scrutiny, unable to stand his humiliation.

"On the authority of the dead," Araz replied gruffly. Though deeper than my dad's, his voice lacked the razor sharpness of his former commander's. "On the authority of the survivors."

"A popular uprising," my dad said, "normally relies on the will of the people."

For a moment Araz didn't seem to know what to say to that. Then he spread his hands and smiled at the forty-some remaining colonists.

"Anyone who supports the leadership of Laman Genn," he said, "is welcome to join him now."

Nobody budged. Nobody even met his glare. The little kids danced over the felled buildings, focused only on their game. I wondered if they knew about Korah. I felt my foot lift hesitantly, but then, seeing my dad make a sharp movement with his hand, I stopped short.

"Satisfied?" Araz said.

"Only that people are scared, and grieving," my dad said. "We suffered a terrible blow last night. But we can't let our grief destroy who we are. We must—"

"Enough speeches, Laman," Araz cut him off. "If we'd had less talk and more action before, we might not be where we are now."

I saw a few heads nod around the circle, a few expressions of agreement or anger or contempt. Mostly, though, I saw people with strained faces and terrified eyes, people who didn't know what to believe or what to do. Not like Wali, whose grief over Korah's death had driven him to Araz's side. Or Yov, who'd hated my dad for years. The others might side with the camp's new commander, but only out of fear, not conviction.

It occurred to me just then to wonder if my dad had ever had any friends in the colony. Any real friends. Or only followers.

"Do you deny," Araz directed his words at my dad, "that despite incontrovertible evidence pointing to a Skaldi presence in this compound, you failed to order quarantine procedures as is mandated in such cases?"

"Quarantine lies at the discretion of the commander," my dad said.

"And do you deny," Araz continued as if my dad hadn't spoken, "that it was on your orders that our weapons were sequestered in a location accessible only to you?"

"Guns," my dad said, "would not have saved us last night."

"And do you deny further," Araz rumbled on, "that it was on your authority that the colony was forced to remain, defenseless, in its current encampment?"

"I deny your construction of events," my dad said, but his voice had grown weary.

"And so"—Araz ignored my dad's answer once again and cast his voice at the audience—"while you armed yourself for an illusory conflict against your own people, you neglected your primary charge as commander of Survival Colony Nine, which is the protection of its members from a very real enemy, an enemy only constant vigilance can hope to defeat."

My dad said nothing, just shook his head slowly.

Araz smiled as if the case was closed. "Enough talk," he said again. "Justice will be done."

He turned briefly to Wali, who edged closer to my dad, his normally cool face murderous. Yov and Kin took a step forward to emphasize the threat.

Araz turned back to face the crowd. He used my dad's name, but he addressed the camp as a whole. "Laman Genn, for treasonous behavior, for dereliction of your duty as commander of Survival Colony Nine to protect and serve its people, for reckless endangerment of the colony leading to the brutal slaughter of six of our comrades, we, the leadership of Survival Colony Nine, sentence you to death by public hanging on the morning of the day following this."

A sharp intake of breath circled the camp. Even the people who had seemed to approve of Araz's lecture fell into a shocked silence. I was too stunned to breathe at all.

"That sounds like the way justice was served in the time before," my dad said quietly. He looked up at the taller man with no fear in his eyes, only sadness. "Are you sure you want to do that, son?"

"He's not your son!" Yov nearly screamed. "You're not our father!"

The shrillness in his voice sent a cold wave down my back.

My dad directed his mournful eyes at Yov. "You're right," he said. "I'm not." I expected him to continue, to transform

Yov's outburst into another teachable moment, but he simply looked across camp at me, his craggy face tired and resigned.

That was when Aleka stepped into the circle. I'd been so focused on my dad, I'd forgotten about her entirely.

"This has gone on long enough," she said. "Araz, you may have elected yourself leader of this camp, but you have no authority to order the execution of any of its members."

"The execution of traitors lies at the *discretion* of the commander," Araz smirked. "Lieutenant."

Aleka had reached my dad's side, but she didn't look at him. She kept her eyes leveled at the colony's new leader, who stood a head taller than her and easily twice as broad. The tips of her fingers rested on the silver pistol hanging at her belt.

"We will not become killers of our own," she said.

"No one would have died if not for this man," Kin spoke up, gesturing scornfully at my dad.

Aleka threw her frosty gaze on him. "We would all have died if not for this man. You owe your life to his protection. Many times over."

Kin scoffed and turned away.

"Don't think we've forgotten about you, Aleka," Araz growled. "Where were you when the Skaldi was feeding on our comrades?"

"Where were you when a child was crying out for release from living death?" she retorted. "I looked into the eyes of a girl I loved, and I watched my own flames burn her suffering away. Don't talk to me about loyalty to the colony, *comrade*."

For a minute they stood face to face, hands on holsters, eyes locked on each other. No one in camp seemed able to move. Yov and Kin's sneers lingered on their lips. My dad shook his head again, ever so slowly, as if he'd been through this all too many times before.

At last I found the will to step forward. Seeing me move, my dad turned an angry, cautioning look my way. But I didn't let it stop me this time.

"She's right, Araz," I said. "You can't do this."

"So speaks the traitor's protégé," Araz muttered, not taking his eyes off Aleka. "Better be thankful you're not up here with him, boy."

"I *am* up here with him," I said. "And I'm not going anywhere."

I stood shoulder to shoulder with Aleka. My heart pounded so hard I was sure everyone could hear it.

"Always by your captain's side, huh?" Araz said. "Even when he's consorting with the enemy."

Aleka lifted her chin in a gesture that reminded me of Korah. I could almost feel her strength flowing into me.

"The only enemy," she said, "is the one who wields power without compassion."

Araz's hand tightened on the handle of his pistol. His face seemed red enough to burst. But finally his shoulders relaxed and his arms fell to his sides. He looked around the circle at the eyes riveted on him.

"This isn't over," he said in a low rumble. He gestured to Wali, who jammed his rifle into my dad's back. "For his own safety and the safety of the colony, Laman Genn will be kept under house arrest until we've had a fair opportunity to discover his part in this. But I'm warning you," he said to Aleka and me, or to the camp as a whole. "Anyone who interferes with the investigation or who offers assistance to the prisoner will suffer the same punishment. I don't care who he is."

"That much is obvious," Aleka said, just short of open sarcasm. It surprised me to hear even that small concession to annoyance in her steady voice.

Araz pretended not to notice. "All personnel will report immediately to headquarters for the trials," he announced. "This camp is now under quarantine, by order of its commanding officer." A murmur passed through the crowd, but no one raised an objection. "Take him away." Araz signaled to Wali, and Wali thrust his gun in my dad's back until he started moving. The look of resignation and pity lingered in my dad's eyes as he turned his head to go. This time, he made no attempt to hide his limp.

While most of the camp made their way to headquarters, Aleka and I followed my dad to his jail cell. No one tried to stop us. Yov and Kin tagged along too, as did a few others—Petra, Tyris, the driver named Soon. They kept their eyes lowered and their mouths shut, and my dad gave no sign he knew they were there.

At the door to his prison he turned to face the small

crowd that trailed him. I still saw neither shame nor defiance in those dark eyes of his, only a profound sorrow and regret. The scar that seemed like it would never fade rested dark and grimy across his brow.

Aleka placed a hand on her lips as if to blow him a kiss, but she didn't.

"You brought this on yourself, Laman," she said.

"We both know what I brought on myself, Aleka," he said quietly. "But I am sorry I brought it on all of you."

Then he disappeared into the building and Wali's back blocked him from view.

Aleka stood silently, facing the empty doorway. Tyris and the others drifted toward headquarters. But Petra lingered, her cheeks puffed out, her eyes blinking a mile a minute. Then, out of nowhere, she laid a hand on Aleka's arm. She gave it a gentle squeeze before stomping off after the others, arms and legs pumping like a demon.

When we were alone, Aleka turned to me. Her eyes sharpened, but not with anger. "That was a brave thing you did."

"He doesn't deserve to die," I said. "Does he?"

"We've had enough death," she said. "The colony needs to come together, not tear itself apart. But I'm afraid that might not be enough to save him."

"What are we going to do?"

"First we're going to submit to the trials." She held out a hand to silence me. "Compliance is our best cover for now.

Beyond that, we wait. And hope. I'll do what I can, Querry. But I'll need you on my side. He'll need you too."

I made her a promise, right then and there. A promise to support her, the colony, my dad. A promise to fight if I needed to, to stop the fighting if I could. I didn't know if my promise would amount to anything, but I knew I had to make it. Even if everything my dad had done these past few days had been wrong, I knew that what he'd said to me last night had been right. The time had come to make a choice, and there was only one choice to make. More death couldn't bring back the ones we'd lost. More death couldn't restore Korah's eyes, her dreams, her smile.

I made the vow to Aleka, to my dad, maybe to myself. But in my mind's eye I saw Korah. Korah still alive and beautiful. Korah still Korah.

12
CAST

We broke camp at dawn.

Everyone saw it coming. Nothing remained for us here but bad memories and a jagged hole in the ground. The burials we held were brief, perfunctory, as if it really was just dust and sand we were burying. Even the people who'd been most enthusiastic about my dad's plan couldn't wait to clear out now that his plan had so tragically failed.

Other than the burials, we'd spent most of the previous day fulfilling Araz's quarantine order. Everyone lined up outside headquarters and, one by one, submitted to the trials, which Araz and his cronies conducted in the same room where I'd seen Petra's interrogation. I watched people come out shaking from the ordeal, mouths and hands bloody. The old woman had to be carried out by two colonists. When it was my turn, Yov took obvious delight in tightening the clamp on my fingers, jerking the pliers back and forth inside my mouth. But I didn't say a word, kept the pain to myself. Whether he and Araz really cared about ferreting out Skaldi or just relished the chance to inflict torment on the camp was anyone's guess. What they did to my dad when it came his turn I could only imagine.

Everyone passed the trials. The only person Araz exempted was Keely, supposedly on account of his age. You couldn't prove it by me, but apparently there were some perks to being the commander's son.

Once the trials ended and Araz pronounced the camp clean, he and Yov spent the dusk hours strolling the compound, deciding what to keep and what to leave behind. Without functional trucks, the second category far outweighed the first. The empty water barrels were the hardest thing to part with, but there was no way to imagine ourselves rolling them through the desert. We kept most of the stoves and propane tanks, blankets, bandages, pots, binoculars, tools, rope, both sets of walkie-talkies, some flints, and of course as much of the canned food as we could carry. We left behind all the tents, cots, and chairs, the fuel barrels, the most battered stoves, the emptiest propane tanks. Mika's flashlight Araz wanted to keep, but it had turned into a twisted hunk of metal within the charred circle that used to be the body of Korah. Personal items, dolls' heads and ballet slippers, even the craziest of colonists didn't dream of dragging along. The camp's new leaders allowed us to preserve collection jars to hold water, but the contents of the jars they scattered to the dust and wind.

And they kept our weapons. Accompanied by Yov, Wali, and the last officer from the old regime, Araz tramped up the stairs to the arsenal, came back down with arms full. The boxes of ammunition turned out to be emptier than anyone had suspected, and the fuel for the flamethrowers had run perilously low thanks to our new leader's own reckless shooting. He went around camp and demanded we turn over any stray weapon, then distributed a pistol to each of his lieutenants, depositing the rest with Kin for safekeeping. He seemed to take special pleasure in forcing Aleka to hand over her silver pistol. My knife remained safely in my jacket pocket, though what good it would do me at this point I couldn't imagine. But I kept it there. For luck.

The day of our departure, I rose with the rest of the camp and did my part to pack our remaining supplies. Out of habit I checked my sleeping area, but nothing showed except the mark of my body on the dusty ground. I hadn't seen Aleka since the evening before, when she'd walked off by herself toward the bomb shelter. My dad remained under guard, Wali standing at the door of headquarters with his rifle held stiffly across his chest. Araz had stationed himself in the front room of the same building, neither he nor Kin showing themselves the entire morning. They left the inspection to the fourth member of their cabal.

With a grin on his face and a swagger to his step, Yov strode out of the command building to supervise the exodus. He strutted among us, poking into rucksacks, throwing out items at random. The little kids almost never cried, but whatever he did to them this morning left them in tears. When he snatched the old woman's jar and flung it onto the pile of trash, I snapped.

"Give it back to her," I yelled at his retreating figure.

He barely turned. "Or what?"

"Or you'll have to deal with me."

Smiling, he returned to where I stood. A pistol, Aleka's silver pistol, hung at his belt.

"Getting pretty tough now that daddy's gone, aren't we?" he said. "Maybe you'd like to go along with him."

I tried to stare him down, but he wouldn't blink. The old woman crouched beside us, mumbling words or nonsense more softly than I could hear. I'm not sure how it would have ended if Aleka hadn't appeared and taken my arm.

"I know what you're trying to do," she murmured as she pulled me away. "But now is not the time."

"Good choice, Aleka," Yov called after us. "Little boys shouldn't try to play a man's game."

His mocking laughter surrounded me as I forced myself to focus on arranging my pack.

They led my dad out of his jail cell after all the preparations were completed, so the whole colony could line up to see him. He blinked in the bright light after most of a day indoors. They'd tied his hands in front of him, and a guide rope circled his waist. Maybe in deference to his bad hip, or maybe out of sheer sloppiness, the man at the other end of the rope, Kin, gave him some slack. Not enough to let him fall behind, much less to formulate a plan of yanking free and running. Araz emerged after him, arms crossed in triumph. The only thing that spared my dad from total humiliation was the fact that they hadn't tied the rope around his neck. That, and the fact that it was Kin, and not Yov, pulling it.

He didn't look humiliated, though. He held his head high and met people's eyes with an expression so composed they ended up dropping theirs. The worst you could say was that he tripped a little as he tried to keep up with the pace the younger man set.

Aleka was another story. As soon as she saw what they'd done to him, she charged at Araz, her pale eyes ablaze.

"This is how you treat the man who led this colony for half a lifetime?" she said venomously. "You're a child, Araz. You're not fit to wear the same uniform as him, much less to bind him like a . . ." She paused, trying to remember the right expression. "Dog on a leash."

"We've been over this," Araz said in a gratingly patient voice, like he was explaining a complicated procedure to a six-year-old. "The prisoner needs to be restrained for his own safety as well as the colony's. While the investigation proceeds."

"You're conducting an investigation?" Aleka said.

Araz nodded.

"By departing the site of the alleged crime?"

Another nod and, this time, a smile.

"And how do you plan to collect your evidence?"

"The nature of the offense," Araz said, still smiling, "is such that the evidence travels with the suspect."

"Which is another way of saying you *have* no evidence," she seethed. "This is shameful. Utterly shameful. If you were half the man you claim to be—"

"Aleka, let it go," my dad broke in. His voice sounded as calm as his jailer's, though cracked from lack of water. I noticed that, as with the day before, his words carried over the compound far more crisply than those of the camp's new leader. "Much as I appreciate your help—"

"I didn't ask for your opinion, Laman," she cut him off. She seemed as angry at him as at Araz, or maybe she was just angry, period.

But now that he'd interrupted, she didn't seem to remember what she'd been planning to say. "It's shameful," she repeated, spitting the words at no one or everyone. Then she stalked off, her face its usual mask, though her eyes could have bored through steel.

Yov appeared at his boss's side, grinning a lopsided grin.

"That is one tough lady," he drawled. "She send anybody to bed without supper?"

The usual suspects laughed. I wished Korah could have been there to shut their stupid mouths.

Kin handed the rope to Wali. He was joined by a second guard, Daren, another teenager who'd known nothing but my dad's leadership all his life. Both of them seemed only too happy to drag my dad away like the thing Aleka had said, a dog on a leash. They didn't give the rope any slack.

Araz shouted orders at the rest of us, his voice thin and husky as it floated over the compound. Yov and Kin roamed through camp double-checking our preparations. I ended up being picked to take care of the little kids. Hand-picked, in fact. By Yov.

"Querry-Werry can pway wiff da widdle babies," he gibed.

I didn't mind, though. It wasn't so bad being with them, the only people in camp who knew no more about the past than me. I liked to hear their silly questions, liked trying to answer them, knowing neither the questions nor the answers mattered. How big was the moon? Where did it go during the daytime? When I was with them, not remembering what had happened six months ago didn't seem that important, and remembering what had happened just yesterday didn't seem so awful.

I leaned over them as they wiggled into their oversize packs. I pulled the bags up on their shoulders, tightened or loosened straps, moved an item or two from a smaller kid's pack to a bigger kid's. Keely wrapped his warm hand around mine. Araz appeared too preoccupied with his own importance to notice that his son was consorting with the enemy.

"You ready to go?" I asked.

He nodded. The pack on his back looked like it should be carrying him.

"Where's Korah?" he said.

We marched all day in the path of the sun, but we didn't get far. We'd always known how important the trucks were, and we'd protected them and their fuel supply like living members of the colony. Even named them, if my dad was telling the truth. Turns out he'd been right to do so. We'd never experienced a march entirely without them, and it was grueling.

People collapsed or threw up from the heat, and we had to stop to revive them with what little water we had, what little shade we could find, a lone tree or a ripple in the land the sun didn't quite crest. I tried to keep the little kids preoccupied with stories or language games, but they fussed, threw tantrums I guess is the word for it, flinging themselves on the ground and refusing to budge, flailing at the dust as if they could pound it into submission. Nessa had to come help me pick them up and carry them, and even then, when they'd forced us to do what they were presumably trying to force us to do, they'd gotten so caught up in their grievances they would fight us off. Some would go boneless in their rescuer's arms. It's amazing how heavy a little kid can make himself. A couple times Yov came over and threatened them with what he'd do if they didn't stop whining, which obviously didn't help. And Araz was no use at all. He kept to the front of the column, his thick red neck visible between his cap and uniform collar, not turning his head once the whole time to keep tabs on the people he professed to lead.

My dad stayed at the rear of the column under Wali's watchful eye. They'd wanted to put him at the head where all could see, but his hip hadn't allowed it. How he was doing under the forced march I couldn't tell.

By the time night fell we'd traveled maybe ten miles northwest of the compound. We looked back in the dwindling light, but the hill where the gated community perched had fallen below our line of vision. Some people had looked back earlier, in fact they hadn't stopped looking back the whole day, stumbling and falling out of line. What they'd seen, if they'd seen anything, they didn't say. I'd stolen a quick glance when we'd covered about a half-mile, and I'd seen a place that appeared as if we'd never been there: skeleton buildings standing squat against a dirt-brown sky, everything that used to be ours, trucks and tents and useless fence posts, hidden from view by the walls and the hill and the distance. Yov, seeing me look back, jerked his head and spat in the dust behind us.

"Good riddance," he said to the spoiled sanctuary he himself had led us to. His voice bore so much spite you'd have thought the buildings would topple at the mere sound.

Our new leaders' plan, at least as much of it as they would let the rest of us in on, was to follow the path of the river, which curved gradually northwest a dozen miles past the compound. Rumor had it that mountains rose beyond our sight in that direction, with caves and precipices to conceal us from our pursuers, cooler water and air to shield us from the butchery of the sun. No one in camp had seen this haven, not even the old woman, and the question of whether to prepare ourselves for a fifty-mile hike or five-hundred was totally up in the air. We'd always carried around a couple maps from the old time, maps so torn and patched and faded you could barely make them out, but whether they corresponded to the actual landscape no one could say. For all we knew, the mountains might not be there at all, or they might be so far from the track of the river we'd die of thirst before we reached them. Or—Petra's warning sounded in my mind—they might be the exact place the Skaldi wanted us to reach. I didn't know whether Araz had consulted with her, and I doubted he'd take her advice in any event.

But compared to the alternatives, I guess the new plan wasn't all bad. At worst, it kept us moving. And maybe that was better than standing still.

It was certainly better than looking back.

As darkness gripped the land, we shed our packs and sprawled on a patch of dead ground near enough to the river to reach it in a couple hours' hike, but not so near we'd be sitting ducks for the Skaldi. The creatures didn't seem to need water themselves. Whatever kept the bodies they stole going wasn't fluid. But in the early days of the survival colonies, my dad had told me, they'd wiped out whole units that had been desperate enough or unwary enough to camp on the riverbanks. People who'd forgotten the world had changed. Or who had just liked the sound of the water at night, a flow and gurgle that seemed to wash everything away.

Petra volunteered to scout out the land between our camp and the river, and our new leader gave her the go-ahead. Not that he had much choice. Everyone else was exhausted from the day's hike, himself included. Araz had been driving a truck for the past five years, and though no better fed than the rest of us, he'd gotten pretty soft around the middle. He didn't even bother giving orders before he staggered off to the spot he'd chosen as his command post, a bare crest overlooking the encampment's western periphery.

Once we'd set up what was left of camp and I'd made sure the little kids were tucked in for the night—lacking only their one storybook and the girl who used to read it to them—I followed Araz to the command post. I found him standing with Yov at his side, the two of them poring over one of our maps. It was almost comical to see them squinting and pointing at it like it held the answers to all our questions. But I swallowed the words that came to mind and approached them with what I hoped was a neutral, even a friendly expression on my face.

"I'd like to see my dad," I said before either of them had a chance to stop me.

Araz lowered the map and frowned. "He's not in a spa,

you know. Or a retirement village. You do get that, don't you?"

I had no idea what either of those things was, and I doubted he knew any better than I did.

"Space Boy only understands what he wants to," Yov said. "Nothing penetrates that thick skull of his except his daddy's sermons."

"I want to see my dad," I repeated. I tried to keep my voice calm, but it wasn't easy. Yov's taunting words made me feel as if a hot bubble was trying to burst through my chest.

Araz glared at me in the descending darkness. I noticed how close-set his eyes were, how square his head and jowls. His thick neck resembled the cactuses we sometimes found, his head the lumpy knob growing out of the base. We left those alone. They weren't edible.

"I'll give you five minutes," he said. "And don't get any ideas. Kin and Wali will be there."

"Thank you," I said. I couldn't bring myself to add "sir," but he didn't seem to expect it. As I left, I saw him take out his walkie-talkie. Yov had already turned his back to me and was fingering the remains of the map like a talisman.

I walked down the hill to the area where my dad sat. Without buildings or tents, they couldn't put him in solitary confinement, but they'd moved him as far away from the others as they could. A dead tree, its bare branches densely tangled, stood on the eastern outskirts of camp, and Araz had set up the prison there. In the couple minutes it took me to walk to the site, I rehearsed what I might say to him. But I gave up as soon as I saw the guards clustered around him, weapons drawn. It turned out Araz hadn't trusted Kin and Wali to guard one restrained, famished, exhausted prisoner, because Kelmen and Daren had joined the party, too.

My dad did seem happy to see me, though. His eyes didn't exactly light up and his face spared me the ghastly smile, but he sat straighter against the tree trunk when he saw me coming. He lifted his hands in greeting, the rope still binding his wrists.

"Querry," he said. "It's good of you to come. Aleka was just by. They wouldn't let me visit with her, though."

My eyes flickered over the circle of guards who ringed the tree. All looked smugly satisfied. Kin smiled an ugly, nearly toothless grin. I saw that, not satisfied with binding the prisoner's hands, they'd tied his torso to the trunk as well.

"How are you doing, Dad?"

"Oh, not bad," he said in an unconvincingly jovial voice. "A bit stiff. But they're keeping me comfortable."

I stared at his bound hands and body, his ragged uniform, his right leg held ramrod straight. The lines of his face could have been carved with a knife. Wali hovered over him, gripping the butt of his rifle, and I could tell he was just waiting for the order to use it. But my dad met my eyes with a calm and even contented look, and I tried to compose my face to match the man I saw before me.

I thought of all the things I wanted to ask him, all the

things I no longer could. Why he'd made the choices he'd made, whether he regretted them now. How he thought this would all turn out, with him alive and back on top or with him gone and the rest of us no better off than before. Whether he blamed himself for what had happened. Whether he blamed me.

If so, whether he'd ever be able to forgive me.

"Dad . . ."

He held up his bound hands, the right palm facing me in the familiar signal. "Focus," he said. "Stay alert. You're going to need that." He forked his fingers and pointed them straight at me.

Then he did something I'd never seen. With his fingers still forked, he raised them perpendicular to the ground, so they formed a *V*. He looked meaningfully at me for a moment, his dark eyes piercing the shadows that veiled his face. Then he dropped his hands and settled back against the tree.

"It was good to see you, son," he said. I watched his eyelids close before Kin interposed his body between us.

"Time to go," the scout said.

I wandered back to my spot in camp, feeling flushed and dazed. He'd clearly been trying to give me a signal, something he couldn't say in front of the guards. The "focus" gesture was a brilliant way to do it: familiar to everyone, but not so familiar they would notice the slight variation. My dad might be beaten down and worn out, but he'd still found a way to send me a message.

The only problem was, I couldn't make out what it meant.

Victory? Vigilance? I racked my brain for *V* words, but none seemed to have anything to do with the two of us, the situation we were in, the survival of the colony. Maybe, I thought, it hadn't been a *V* after all, but a way of pointing out something I should have seen, something in his captors' hands or in the branches of the tree, something I had now missed my chance to see. Maybe it hadn't been a *V* but a *two*. Or maybe it had been half a *W*, a sign for Wali.

Not wanting to attract attention, I collapsed onto the ground and turned on my side. Mechanically, I rubbed the spot in my jacket where the knife rested. Then, making sure no one was looking, I took it out, unfolding two blades to form a *V*. I stared at it for a long time before snapping it shut and returning it to its hiding place.

Leave it to my dad, I thought as I prepared for another sleepless night, to make my life more complicated even after he'd been stripped of his power to command. Leave it to him to make even his best and most urgent attempt to communicate with me impossible to read.

13

BURST

Aleka stooped by my side.

Her eyes shone like silver moons in her pale face. I opened my mouth to ask what was going on, but she silenced me with a finger to her lips.

"It's time," she whispered.

"Time for what?" Darkness still draped the land, but it had the grainy quality of approaching dawn.

"You remember your promise," she said. "Now it's time."

"To do what?"

She probed my eyes. "To do what needs to be done." She stood and held out a hand. "Are you with us?"

It was then I saw the others standing in the splotchy darkness behind her. Petra. Soon. Nekane, a young woman with long, prematurely gray hair. The two teens who hadn't joined Araz's goon squad, Nessa and the big quiet guy named Adem. All of them eyeing me expectantly, as if they couldn't do whatever they intended to do without me. Or at least, without knowing whether I would stand with them or stand in their way.

"It's my dad," I said.

Aleka nodded. "We have reason to believe Araz and Yov intend to carry out the execution first thing in the morning. Apparently, they're concerned about information he may be spreading."

I thought about my dad's sign to me last evening, a sign I'd been struggling to understand when I'd fallen into a restless sleep. Could it be that the camp's new leaders knew more about it than I did? Or was it that they didn't know, and that was what they were afraid of?

I took Aleka's hand and stood. "We're going to free him," I said.

"We're going to try." She pressed something into my hand. My fingers closed around its handle, still clammy from her touch. I'd held guns before, my dad had insisted I learn how to take them apart, keep them clean, load and aim. I'd never fired one, though. He was adamant about not wasting ammunition, and they were no good against Skaldi anyway. Even when he'd showed me his secret arsenal, I'd never thought a day might come when I'd have to use one against a member of my own colony.

"How did you . . . ?"

"There'll be time for that later," she said. "Now it's time to listen."

She signaled for us to huddle close. I looked around the circle at their eyes, shining and intense in their shadowed faces. I could hear everyone breathing, though they tried to suppress the sound.

"Remember," Aleka said, "we don't shoot unless we have to. Our plan is to free Laman quickly and quietly, then head for the river. If anyone gets separated from the group, we rendezvous at the following coordinates." She held up a series of fingers in rapid succession, and I strained to remember what they meant. "Querry will stay with me. The rest of you know what to do."

The others nodded and, led by Petra, melted into the gray darkness.

We waited a minute before Aleka gave my arm a gentle tug. I tucked the gun into my belt, and we headed east, the same direction the others had taken. Though they couldn't be far in front, it seemed Petra's knack for invisibility had cloaked them all. "They'll deal with the guards," Aleka whispered to me. "It'll be up to you and me to free him."

"Why us?"

"Because he won't trust anyone else."

"And you trust them? Petra, the others? Nessa is one of Yov's—"

"I trust them," she said. "There's a lot you don't know, Querry. A lot I haven't been able to tell you." She didn't look at me, but I saw the strain and sadness in the twin curved lines around her mouth. "I'm sorry I wasn't able to prepare you for this. But you've been watched closely. Until tonight. Wali was assigned to keep track of you. What they don't know is that Wali is one of ours."

I remembered Wali's rifle jabbing into my dad's back, looming over his head. I remembered his fury the night at the swimming pool, his anguish the night Korah died. One of ours?

But then I remembered him hanging around my resting place after last night's interview. I'd wondered if he planned to question me about my conversation with my dad, threaten me with his muscles or his gun, but he'd wandered off before I settled down to sleep. At the time, I'd been too preoccupied with my dad's cryptic signal to think anything of it.

"But how—?"

"There's no time to explain," she said. "Just remember, Querry, things aren't always what they seem. You have more friends than you know."

I nodded, trying to believe her. "What's the plan?"

"Kin is on guard duty with three others," Aleka said. "Araz and Yov are, to the best of our knowledge, stationed at the command post, there," and she signaled across camp to the hill where I'd met them the evening before. I could see nothing from that distance, no lights or movement to indicate their location. "They're in communication with Kin via walkie-talkie, so we don't think they'll put in an appearance at the prison site until the time they've chosen for the execution. If they do show up, that may complicate things."

I couldn't be sure, but it seemed a grimace flickered across her face as she said that.

"The others will flank the camp," she continued, "and Soon's contingent will seek to draw off as many guards as possible. If the guards follow the protocol they learned under Laman, they'll leave at least two of them behind. It's possible Kin will contact Araz at this point. If he does, the plan is off and we'll have to try something else."

Her frown deepened, but she went on.

"If all goes well, we'll have a few minutes' opening to make our move. Petra's team will have the tougher job. They'll need to overpower the remaining guards with a minimum of noise and fuss. Then you and I will release Laman and make for the river, where other members of our colony will be waiting for us." She sniffed, an almost laugh. "At least, that's the plan."

I was no tactician, but I'd spent enough time around my dad to recognize that their plan was as full of holes as my memory. What if the guards didn't bite at the decoy, what if Kin did contact the camp's leaders or one of them made an unscheduled visit to check on their prisoner, what if shots were fired, what if my dad insisted on peppering us with questions, what if his hip, stiffer than usual from cramped sitting, wouldn't allow him to keep up? "Why are you doing this?" I asked.

"Because we still believe in him," she said. "And in the colony. We don't know for certain what Araz and Yov are up to, but we know it can't be for the good of our people."

A sudden fear gripped me. "The kids—"

"Are meeting us by the river," she said in a soothing voice. "Everything's been taken care of. All you need to do, and this might be the toughest part of all, is convince Laman Genn to go along with a plan he didn't personally develop."

I caught her eye, caught that hint of a smile I'd seen on her lips once before. It seemed like months ago, though I knew it had been only days. I realized she knew as well as I did how risky the plan was. Probably better than I did. She'd served as Laman Genn's second-in-command, and the man wrote the book on risk. But she was willing to risk her life, they all were, to rescue a man who'd given them every reason to doubt.

"Thank you," I said.

She stopped for the first time since we'd left the others, her eyes searching my face. Then, unexpectedly, she reached out and laid a hand on my cheek. Her touch lingered for a second, warm and surprisingly gentle, before her fingers slid off.

"Save that for an hour from now," she said. "If we pull this off, we'll all have reason to be thankful."

We resumed our silent journey to the prison site. The sky remained a peppery dark, but the first hints of amber rimmed the horizon. We'd left the main body of camp behind, which meant less chance of discovery, though we needed to take care not to call attention to ourselves by tripping on the rough ground. Having arrived at this place only a few hours before, I hadn't had time to learn its layout, and it would have been easy to lose my way. Everything looked different in the dark. But Aleka glided forward with confidence, never slowing or glancing to either side, and I felt sure that if I stuck with her I'd be all right.

Before long I saw the solitary tree where they'd set up their prison, its twisted outline stark against the dim glow on the horizon. I couldn't make out human figures, but it occurred to me that if we got much closer we'd be totally exposed to their eyes.

The thought must have occurred to Aleka, too. "This way," she whispered, and led me to a low hill that broke the ground to our left. We crouched behind the natural barricade and peered over the edge, but the distance and the tree's silhouette made it impossible to see the people we knew must be there.

"We'll wait here," Aleka said. Her eyes scanned the sky, looking, maybe, for some sign or signal, or measuring the time till daylight.

"How will we know?"

"We'll know. Be still and listen."

I noticed the walkie-talkie hanging at her belt. Apparently, Petra had been busy tonight. "Couldn't we call them?"

"Araz might pick up the frequency," she said. "Hush now."

I held my breath and closed my eyes, trying to reach

out with my ears into the undisturbed night. All I heard was Aleka's steady breathing beside me. That comforted me somewhat, though I still felt a knot of tension in my stomach. The pressure built as the moments passed by. Not knowing what to listen for, I thought nothing of it when a sound like a rising wind sighed in the distance.

"That's it," Aleka said softly, her voice startling me after the long silence. "Soon's group has been successful. Let's go."

"Are you sure?"

"That was Soon's whistle. He carved it himself. Very ingenious, very useful. Let's go."

We rose to a crouch and started off in a long arc, staying always to the left of our target, where rocks and the occasional tree stump broke the open ground. We kept low and used what cover we could find. I still saw nothing except the prison tree, but Aleka always seemed to know when to pause and when it was safe to move again. Within a minute of stop-and-go running we had drawn near enough to the tree for me to make out two figures standing in its larger shadow, a third seated at its base. Soon's group, as well as the two other guards, were nowhere to be seen.

"Get down!" Aleka hissed, and I dropped to the ground beside her. We'd fallen in open ground with no cover to speak of, but I hoped that with the distance and speckled darkness we might be mistaken for a part of the landscape. She placed a cautioning hand behind my head as we rose on our elbows to survey the scene. Her fingers prickled along the spot where I'd had my accident six months ago.

The guards' backs were to us. They'd taken a couple steps away from the tree, so my dad's shape could be seen as well, resting against the trunk. He seemed to be asleep. One of the guards was obviously Kin: short and stumpy, with bow-legs and arms that barely hung to his waist. His head jutted forward as he sighted into the predawn gloom. The other, tall and broad, was Kelmen. I hoped he'd prove as slow-witted about the rescue as he did about everything else.

"We wait for Petra," Aleka breathed in a whisper hardly more audible than Soon's wind whistle.

We waited. Each second seemed like an hour. I didn't dare move, didn't dare ask any questions. But my mind raced like my dad's on overdrive. I ran down a long list of worries: why we'd put this off till dawn, when Petra would show up, how we'd know if Kin had called for backup, whether Soon's group had managed to detain the other two guards, what would happen if they hadn't. Still nothing moved in the dim light. I saw Kin confer with Kelmen, their voices too low to make out words. Then I heard a distinct rustling, and the guards spun, weapons drawn, aiming at the branches of the tree.

Not fast enough.

A dark shape fell from the knot of branches, swept their legs from under them, chopped at their arms. I heard the guards cry out in pain. Aleka leaped up and ran, and I followed a step behind her, sprinting low over the rough ground, keeping my eyes on the confused jumble of bodies at the tree's base.

We pulled up in front of the tree as Petra disentangled herself from the guards and stood, pointing their pistols at them, one in each of her hands. The pale darkness disgorged another figure: Nekane, whose look of surprise showed that Petra had decided to wing it as usual. How the scout had gotten into the branches without us seeing her or the guards hearing her was beyond me.

"Well done, Petra," Aleka said. She sounded as impressed as I was.

"Piece of cake," Petra said blithely. She tucked one of the guns in her belt and, keeping the other trained on Kin and Kelmen, dangled their walkie-talkie in front of their eyes. "Or should I say, like taking candy from a baby."

Kin's eyes bugged with rage, but he kept his mouth shut. Kelmen, as usual, looked like he'd just heard something in a completely different language.

"Bind and gag them," Aleka said. She leveled her own gun at the prostrate guards while Nekane produced the rope and rags. Within seconds the two were lashed together, the scout looking like an underfed twin that had grown out of its giant brother's back.

"You're on, Querry," Aleka said.

I took out the red-handled pocketknife and squatted by my dad. A single glance told me how exhausted he was: though the ruckus of Petra's one-woman show had started to rouse him, his eyes had yet to open. His face appeared pale and drawn, his hair seemed to have grayed even further in the hours since I last saw him. No visible cuts or bruises marred his face and hands, but I suspected Kin and Kelmen had spent the first part of the night working him over, the former for malicious fun, the latter out of some dim sense of duty.

His eyes finally struggled open as I sawed at the ropes around his wrists. At first he looked confused, even frightened. I thought about the many times he'd stood over me, silently watching before shaking me from sleep, and I wondered what he'd seen those times.

"Querry," he said now. The confusion in his eyes registered in his voice as well.

"It's okay, Dad," I said. "We're getting you out of here."

"Out," he said dreamily. Then his eyes snapped into bright focus and his voice sharpened. "No!" he said. "It's not safe. You'll be—"

"Laman," Aleka said, stepping beside me. "Querry's with us. We're all here."

By now I'd freed him from the ropes. He tried to push himself upright by bracing his back against the tree, but his bad leg gave out under him. Aleka and I each caught one of his arms and helped him to his feet.

"What is this?" he asked, looking around at the small group of rescuers. His eyes had lost all signs of sleep and regained their dark intensity. "Aleka, you know the plan, you know the need to save—"

"The plan has changed," she said. "There's simply no time. If we'd waited any longer, you might not be here."

"Then so be it," he said. "No man is worth taking that chance."

I looked from him to Aleka. Their eyes locked, their jaws set. Ragged as he was, pale as she was, neither seemed ready to back down.

"What do you mean?" I asked.

He remained silent. Aleka hesitated, her eyes dropping for a moment, then volunteered, "The plan, Querry, was to save you first. Then, and only then, to free Laman. We discussed this days ago, when the first real signs of trouble cropped up in camp. If ever the camp's leadership were to change . . ."

"You'd have Querry on the first train out of here," my dad finished. "And if it wasn't feasible to bring me along, you'd leave me behind."

"And return for you later," Aleka added. "Which we may no longer have the opportunity to do. You know what they're planning for you, Laman."

"That doesn't change anything," he said.

"But why me?" I said. "What do you mean you have to save me? Save me from what? From the Skaldi?"

Both of them looked at me, then back at each other. I could sense a contest going on between them, entirely unspoken. But I still had no idea what they couldn't or wouldn't say.

"There isn't time for this, Laman," Aleka said at last, and I heard an uncharacteristic tremor in her voice. "I take full responsibility for what we've done. But we're here now. What can you possibly accomplish by sacrificing yourself?"

"I can secure the future of this colony," he said defiantly.

"By saving me?" I said.

Neither of them answered. Neither of them would even look at me. All the unexplained events of the past week came rushing back to my mind: how my dad had assigned Aleka to guard me that night in the hollow, how Petra had insisted the Skaldi were searching for something or someone, how the creature that had killed Korah had come looking for one specific victim. They'd driven us here, Petra had said, so they could take back what they'd lost. But the time was coming, Aleka had warned, when my dad might not be able to protect me anymore.

Not protect his camp. Protect *me*.

The question Yov had raised that night in the hollow bubbled out in words I knew as my own but in a shrill tone I hardly recognized: *"What's so special about me?"*

"Funny," a familiar, mocking voice spoke from behind us. "I was just about to ask that myself."

Everyone whirled. In the split-second before she turned I saw the frantic look in Aleka's eyes. Then I saw the owner of the voice, just as he spoke again.

"She's a smart lady, Laman," he said. "You should have beat it while you had the chance."

The voice belonged to Yov.

He stepped forward. The silver pistol that had been Aleka's flashed as it caught the traces of coming dawn. His usual crooked smile spread across his face, and a cruel light kindled in his eyes.

Petra instantly dropped the walkie-talkie and pointed the guards' weapons at him. My hand reached for the gun at my belt.

"Put those down," Aleka ordered in a voice I'd never heard from her before.

My hand froze. Petra wavered, her eyes flicking from Aleka to Yov. Aleka drew her gun, pointing it not at Yov but at the stunned scout.

"I said drop them," Aleka commanded.

Petra did, the weapons clattering to the ground.

"Aleka," my dad said, reaching toward her.

She held him back too. "I can't allow this," she said. Her gun swung in a circle around the small crowd, and we all backed away. Then she turned toward Yov, her gun still raised, her eyes pleading.

"We don't want to hurt you, Yov," she said.

His smile widened. "But we do want to hurt you," he said. "So I guess that gives us the advantage."

The dawn split with a sharp crack and a flash of light, but not from either of their guns. Yov's face twisted, his features etched by the gunfire's brief glare. Then he grabbed his leg above the knee and crumpled to the ground, his weapon flying loose. Aleka spun, shrieking, "I told you not to shoot!" I followed her frenzied eyes and saw Soon with his command group of Nessa and Adem, his gun raised, his face frozen in shock.

Yov rolled on the ground, gripping his leg and cursing. I heard footsteps in the distance, the faint sound of voices. Petra had recovered all three of the dropped weapons and stood facing Aleka, whose eyes gaped wide and whose gun hung limply from her hand.

"We have to go, Aleka," Petra said. Her voice shook. "Now."

"We can't leave him," Aleka said dully.

"We have no choice," Petra said. She placed a hand on Aleka's arm and gently pried the gun from her fingers. Aleka didn't resist at all.

Petra turned to my dad. Two guns rested in her grip, two more at her belt. "It's now or never, Laman."

He stood rooted to the spot, his hands hanging in front of him as if he was the one who'd fired on Yov. His face looked as drained as Aleka's, his eyes as empty as hers of will or decision.

"Come on, Dad," I said, taking his arm. "Petra's right. This is our chance."

He didn't budge.

"Dad?"

"He's not your father!" Yov screamed from the ground, where he lay doubled over in pain. "You're not his son!"

His words sliced through me like a blade.

"Yov," Aleka groaned. She didn't sound angry. She sounded like she was begging him.

"Ask him yourself!" Yov's voice rose hysterically. "Ask him!"

"Dad?" I said.

He didn't answer. He didn't even acknowledge me. Five minutes ago he'd looked like a man waking from a dream. Now he looked like a man unable to wake from a nightmare.

The sound of voices and running feet grew louder. Any second I was sure we'd be able to see them coming for us.

It was Aleka who finally got him to move. Shaking herself from her own paralysis, she grabbed his arm forcefully, tugged until his feet followed. "Come on, Querry," she said. She cast a final look at Yov, whose body was contorted in pain, his face twisted with fury. The others trooped after her. We started running, the man who called himself my father hopping on one leg while grabbing hold of Aleka's shoulder and mine to keep himself upright. We didn't stop until the guards, the tree, the curses of the downed man, and the commotion of the roused camp vanished in distance and silence.

PAST

We traveled through the brightening dawn until we reached the river.

A brief skirmish with a couple members of our former colony who caught us at the camp's western edge turned into nothing when they abruptly retreated. Which was a good thing, because we had to stop many times to let Laman Genn rest. By the time we arrived at the rendezvous point he could barely walk, requiring the assistance of two or more of his rescuers to stay on his feet.

I kept my distance. He looked so weary, so frail, I had to fight the urge to dash to his side. The members of our colony who had joined us at the river came up to shake his hand, speak his name, pat him on the shoulder. Tyris helped him arrange his limbs on the ground, then knelt by his side to check his pulse and breathing, to massage his crippled hip with her skilled fingers. When she rose, I saw tears creeping down her cheeks. Nessa fluttered around him, bringing him water in a squashed and dirty canteen, holding her hand behind his head to help him drink. The whole time he was being fussed over, he met people's eyes gratefully but with fatigue written in every line of his face. Beneath his knotted beard, his lips moved in what might have been words of thanks or merely mute acknowledgment of the company of the faithful.

As Aleka had promised, we found the little kids clustered by the riverbank, along with their parents or caregivers. It was Wali who'd rounded them up and led them away from camp when he was supposed to be guarding me, Wali who'd given Petra the information she needed to steal the weapons. Laman gripped his shoulder and looked long into his eyes before collapsing in exhaustion. The only child Wali hadn't been able to rescue was Keely, who'd been sleeping at the command post with his father. It dismayed me to think of the youngest member of our colony left all alone in the rebel camp, but there was nothing we could do about it now.

Totaling everyone up, it seemed a little more than half the colony, or about twenty-five people, had decided to stick with their former commander, the rest choosing to take their chances with Araz and Yov. Whether the new leaders would consider our splinter colony enough of a threat or an embarrassment to track us down was up for debate. Aleka speculated they would, but she predicted they wouldn't come after us until they could do so in force. Petra kept watch just in case. As soon as Laman got settled she slipped out of camp, dodging both the praise and the apologies Aleka tried to lavish on her. But even with our best scout on watch, we didn't dare remain by the river long, not with both human and inhuman enemies who might easily track us there. We'd have to chart a course through territory Petra had already determined to be Skaldi-controlled, and hope we could elude not only the creatures we feared but the colony we'd deserted.

Walking through the new camp, avoiding and being avoided by everyone else, it quickly became apparent to me why the rescue operation had waited till near dawn. An enormous amount of preparation had gone on during the night, with much of the colony's remaining food and tools spirited away along with the little kids. Petra, as usual, had gone well beyond her assignment, nabbing a couple flamethrowers and a second walkie-talkie to complement the one she'd taken from Kin. If nothing else, the depletion of their supplies might lead our former colony to hunt us down.

It occurred to me, too, that we couldn't be sure everyone in our new camp was truly on our side. Maybe we harbored a rebel spy right now, someone waiting for their chance to report back to Araz. Wali sure had looked like he'd wanted to smash the prisoner's head. And who had tipped off Yov about the escape plan? Aleka could say what she wanted about how many friends I had, but just hours before, she'd been ready to turn on her own people to protect Yov, while Laman Genn had spent a whole half-year deceiving me about who he was. Who *I* was. And it wasn't just him: everyone in camp, *everyone*, had apparently agreed to play his little game. The only people who might be innocent were kids like Keely, and them only because they were too clueless to know whose father was who.

I still had no idea who I was. And now it turned out I had no idea who anyone else was, either.

We hung around by the river until late morning, when Laman's eyes finally blinked open and his piercing gaze came to rest on the packs neatly lined up and ready for evacuation. All we waited for, I guess, was his go-ahead. So he and Aleka huddled like old times, their heads close together, his bushy and brown, hers close-cropped and silver-blond. Finally, they told us we were moving out. Figuring that the leaders of the rebel camp, once Yov could walk, would abandon their original plan and come after us, Aleka announced that we would chart a course to the east, with Petra scouting ahead, in hopes of doubling back on our former colony and getting behind them. We had to be careful, though. As always, we had to keep the river in mind if not in actual sight, and since the rebels had the same need, they might easily intercept us. Petra argued briefly with her commanding officers, reminding them that she'd found strong signs of Skaldi farther east after the attack in the hollow, but Aleka countered that the rebels posed a more immediate threat. The best we could do, she told our half-colony while her commander made a final, limping check of our preparations, was load up on water while we could, stay alert on the road, and hope to replenish our bottles by night without getting caught by either of our enemies. It wasn't much of a plan, but then, what was?

Through the afternoon, as we backtracked under a murderous sun with only a couple hours' break during the worst of the day, I kept wondering if the man at the head of the column was going to make the first move or if I should. That we would have to talk sometime soon I had no doubt. If only to justify himself, he wouldn't let the opportunity pass. Yet as the day wore on and he kept silent, limping along beside Aleka with a stick to support him and without so much as a backward glance at me, I began to wonder if he was actually going to leave me in the dark about this. That would be just like him: expect me to follow his every word when his every word was a lie, then abandon me to my own devices when he finally had a chance to tell me the truth. By late afternoon, when Petra met up with us to report that the rebels were falling behind and he responded with his usual curt nod, my mind reeled with that familiar feeling of dislocation, as if the world refused to come into focus.

"Any sign of Skaldi?" he asked.

"What do you want to hear?" she said. "The real answer, or the censored-for-Laman's-ears answer?"

He gritted his teeth. "Surprise me."

"It's a heavily infested area," she said. "I haven't seen

anything on the move yet, but I've picked up way more signs than usual. They could be anywhere. Or everywhere."

Aleka joined their conversation. "Did you see Yov?"

"They were carrying him," Petra admitted. "But that must mean he's okay," she added.

"And is there any reason to believe they'll be able to pick up our trail?" her commander said.

Petra smiled witheringly. "Kin's their lead scout. There's no reason to believe they'd be able to pick up the trail of a herd of buffalo if one bit them on the rear."

And he nodded again, went back to his hobbling march, and left my world to tip a little more into a blur of unreality.

But it turned out my first hunch was right. Nearly eight hours after we'd begun our march, when we finally stopped several miles from the river to bed down in the last light of the vanishing day, he came over to where I was spreading out a towel-size scrap of canvas and prepared to sit across from me. His hip had taken such a beating in the past seventy-two hours that he had to reach out a hand to lower himself, his right leg held stiff and straight as his crutch. I didn't look at him while he struggled to find a pain-free position, just kept to my chore far past the point when it was done. I smoothed the blanket, plucked rocks from beneath it, flattened it again. He watched me for minutes before he spoke.

"It's about time for a water run," he said. "You interested?"

I continued making my miniscule bed. That had to be the smoothest piece of canvas of all time.

"Or guard duty," he said. "Petra says we've shaken Araz, but she's extra-jumpy about Skaldi, and she can't do it all by herself."

My hands kept smoothing, smoothing, moving stones, flattening scratchy wrinkles into the blankness of the cloth.

"All right," he said. "You've made your point. But we do have to talk."

I still wouldn't look at him. "More fatherly advice?" I said.

"Not this time, Laman." The name sounded ridiculous on my tongue, though I'd been practicing it in my head all day.

"I don't expect you to forgive," he said. His voice had the gruff sound it always carried when he gave me orders or grilled me on protocol. No concessions, no apologies. "But maybe you can understand."

He shifted position, tried to sit cross-legged, but gave up, wincing as the hip snapped into place. He drew a deep breath and began.

"You came to this colony just over six months ago," he said. "You and Aleka and Yov. You were the last survivors of a colony that had been decimated by Skaldi. Survival Colony Twenty-Seven, for what that's worth. When we came across you in the desert you were just about dead. All three of you. Heat stroke, dehydration. And you . . . you were unconscious. Had been for three days, according to Aleka."

My hands paused in their routine. I didn't want to say anything, but the words spilled out on their own. "Aleka and Yov . . ."

"Yov is her son," he said. "Her sole surviving child. She lost another during the attack."

"She told me his dad—her husband I guess—was dead."

"Consumed by Skaldi years ago," he nodded. "I've tried to do what I can in his place, but . . ."

"You've tried to do that a lot."

He let it pass. "I welcomed the three of you into the colony, as I would any survivors. But the adjustment hasn't been easy. Aleka was the commander of Survival Colony Twenty-Seven. The last commander it ever had. And serving together has been . . . well, challenging."

"So is lying to your minions a part of the job description?" I said. "Or is that just an added bonus?"

Once again he ignored me. "The first few weeks were the roughest. We both fought to protect our own, and we didn't always see eye to eye. Still don't, as you may have noticed. Her relationship with Yov has only complicated matters. I've had to walk a fine line with those two. And earlier today, when his life was threatened . . . Well, you have no idea what she's suffered, watching him become what he's become."

I resumed my mechanical task, palming stones, only half listening to his words. Still, I couldn't help trying to put Aleka's face together with Yov's, to think of him as her little boy, her baby, someone she'd held in her arms and rocked and sang to. I tried, but I couldn't do it. All I could see were the hard lines of her face, the stony judgment of her eyes. All

I could remember was how he'd pointed a gun at all of us, how she'd done the same.

"But her ultimate allegiance remains with the colony," he continued. "Even after what happened today. As a former commander, she knows we can fight most effectively as a unit. I have no doubt she'd defend the colony, under . . . similar circumstances, if she was forced to make the choice."

"You have a lot of faith in the colony," I said.

"I have to."

"More than you have in people?"

He kept silent for a moment, then said, "The colony is its people."

"Enough faith that you'd lie to save it?"

"Querry . . ."

"That's not my name!" I raised my head and found myself looking directly into his eyes. The stone I held seemed to pulse in my hand. "The least you can do is call me by my real name." I swallowed. "Whatever it is."

"That is your real name," he said. "When we took you in, when we made the decision to treat you as my son, we kept your name."

"Thanks a lot."

"It wasn't entirely for you," he said. "We felt, Aleka and I, Tyris as well, that some continuity with your past might aid your recovery. Spark your memory." He cleared his throat. "So far, it hasn't seemed to help."

He fell silent, but kept his dark eyes fixed on mine. I

looked away, angry at myself that even now, I couldn't return his gaze. But I knew the tension in my chest wasn't all anger. My past hovered between us, perceptible if invisible. I sensed he knew what it was. I sensed, too, that he knew more than he planned to tell me. But less was more than nothing, and so I waited.

"This is going to be hard for you to hear," he said. "Frankly, it's hard for us to believe. But we've withheld it from you all this time, and it hasn't done any good. Maybe the truth will."

He drew another deep breath before continuing.

"The blow to your head isn't what erased your memory," he said. "At least, we don't think it is. According to Aleka, you were showing signs of confusion before it happened. It was sudden, as it always is with Skaldi. But we're reasonably confident you were deprived of your memory by a mechanism we've never known, one we didn't think possible prior to this point."

I expected him to finish, but he paused, forcing me to look at him once more. Shadow hooded his eyes, but their fire burned deep under his ragged brows.

"What?" I said. "What was it?"

"We believe," he said, "that you were infected by Skaldi. That one had taken possession of you, however briefly. We believe that's what stripped your memory away."

I stared at him. "But that's—"

"Impossible," he completed. "We know. Or so we thought.

No one's ever survived a Skaldi attack, to our knowledge. No one, that is," and a terrible smile briefly lifted the corners of his mouth, "until you."

My stomach swooped in horror as a rush of images flooded my mind. Korah's gray-white gums. Her tattered face, her otherworldly screams. The burned-out eyes of her ravaged mother. The monster in the hollow loping toward us, teeth flashing like knives in its blank, fixed face. No one had ever seen Skaldi outside a host, seen it and lived to tell what they saw. All we saw were the bodies they stole, and when they finished feeding, all we saw were the scraps they left behind. Danis. The officers. Korah's father. Bodies without souls, bodies with barely enough left to count as bodies.

Impossible.

But if Laman's story was true, one of those things had taken control of me. And, for some reason, had spared my body, leaving its mark only on my shredded mind.

"You can see now why you're so important to the colony," Laman Genn said, and even with all that had happened he could barely restrain the eagerness in his voice. "Somehow, in a way we don't pretend to understand, you withstood a Skaldi attack. The creature took hold of you, tried to consume you, but failed. We think, Aleka thinks, the effort to master you destroyed it, because after it fled she could find no sign of it. In fact," he added grimly, "by the time it abandoned your body it had left itself practically nowhere else to go."

My mouth had gone so dry I had trouble forming words. "Aleka saw it happen?"

"She saw you convulse as it happened," he said. "She had attempted to track the Skaldi through your camp, had seen one victim after another fall before it. All the usual factors—darkness, the confusion of the attack—made it impossible for her to follow its movements with certainty. All she saw was a fellow colonist collapse beside you, then your body go into what appeared to be a seizure. A violent one. When you relaxed and opened your eyes she assumed you were infected and was about to feed you to the fire, but something stopped her."

I thought again of Korah, of Aleka's words: *I looked into the eyes of a girl I loved.* I couldn't bear to say the rest, even to myself. "What stopped her?"

A weird light shone in his face. "She says, and these are her exact words, that there was no hatred in your eyes. No cruelty or malice. Just confusion. You seemed disoriented, couldn't recall your name or anything about yourself. You said you felt dizzy and sick to your stomach, and then you stumbled and fell. She saw your head strike the ground. When you arrived at our camp you'd been unconscious since that moment. We performed all the tests on you, as we did on Aleka and Yov and the rest of the camp as a precaution, but we saw no further sign of the Skaldi's presence."

He licked his lips, leaning forward as if itching to peer into my mind, my past. The stones I'd arranged without thought or plan lay spread between us in a crooked line like a stitch in the dead ground. I had the strange feeling that so long as the barrier remained in place, he'd be unable to touch me.

"So you believe . . ." I began guardedly.

"That there's something about you the Skaldi can't reach," he said. "Yes. Something neither we nor they knew existed. Some power, some . . . we don't know what to call it. Not strong enough to protect you entirely from damage. But strong enough, it may be, if you could remember what it is and help us harness it, to protect us all."

His eyes flicked over my face, searching, eager. For a second I thought I saw the veil drop, and I knew he was hiding something.

"You know what it is," I said. "The thing that protected me."

"I swear to you I don't."

I almost laughed. "You're a lousy liar, Laman," I said. "If you didn't at least suspect something, we wouldn't be having this conversation."

He rocked back, seemed to wrestle with himself. Finally he spoke again.

"I've heard rumors," he said. "From the early days of the survival colonies. I didn't believe them at the time. People talked of—experiments. Attempts to find a cure. Even though we didn't know what the disease was. And even though there wasn't enough left of the bodies that caught it to take a decent sample."

"So now you've got a body," I said.

He drew a deep breath, let it out. "Now we've got a body."

"So what's stopping you from taking your sample?"

For the first time since the conversation began, his eyes flared with anger. "We no longer have the means," he said. "If we ever did. All we have is you."

His voice fell silent. I dropped my eyes from his penetrating gaze and turned them inward, trying to feel the thing he told me I held within, the power he couldn't or wouldn't name. The experiment, if that's what it was, that had been performed on my body. I felt nothing, though. Nothing but the absence I'd carried in my gut as long as I could remember. Maybe, I thought, I'd possessed this power all my life. Or maybe it had come to me only when I needed it. Either way, I could no more *remember* it than I could remember my heart doing its work or my brain sending its signals. "So you took me in to save yourselves," I said.

The anger never left his eyes. "We took you in because you would have died if we hadn't," he said bluntly. "We've taken in others under similar circumstances. But there's no point denying that our interest in you changed once we learned your history. Enough so that we decided, all of us, Aleka and Yov included, to treat you as if you'd always been with us. For the two of them, that meant withholding their own history from you as well. We agreed to create a past that would serve in place of your actual past, until it returned. If it returned. Until such time as you could tell us yourself what happened that night." He looked levelly at me. "As commander, I assumed the primary responsibility to sustain that fiction."

"But why?" I said. "If Aleka and Yov knew who I really was, why not just tell me?"

"That's complicated," he said, so matter-of-factly he might have been talking about a troop maneuver and not the lie that had controlled my life. "Aleka was in favor of disclosing the circumstances of your coming to us, but it was Tyris's opinion that you'd feel safer if you thought you were among friends and family. That the truth of what the Skaldi had done to you and your colony might overwhelm you, even further the damage. You have to realize, we were shooting in the dark. Nothing like this had ever happened to us. But we felt, I felt, that to help you regain your memory we'd have to establish a relationship of trust."

"By lying to me."

"If that's the way you choose to see it."

"What other way is there?"

"We were on the brink," he said. "We'd been on the brink as long as I could remember. And suddenly, unexpectedly, beyond all possibility of life as we knew it, an opportunity presented itself to fight back. To recover some of what we'd lost. I wasn't about to let that opportunity pass us by. If the price of saving our species was keeping the truth from one of its members, that was a price I was willing to pay."

"What a fatherly thing to do," I said.

He glared at me, brows lowered. "You're in no position to judge," he said. "A father cares enough about his children to—"

"Sacrifice one of them?" I said. "The one who just happens not to be his own?"

"I'm not going to apologize to you, Querry," he said. "If that's what you're looking for, you've got the wrong man. I took on the role of your father because I strongly believed you would respond to me as you would not to a stranger. That you would listen to me, learn what you needed from me. And then, when the time came, if the time came, it would no longer matter how it had come. When the time came, you'd tell me what you yourself had learned, and help me use that knowledge for the salvation of our kind."

I mulled that over. It seemed incredible that he'd think I'd help him after finding out what he'd done. But then, it seemed incredible that he'd done it at all.

"The memory exercises," I said. "Were those your idea too?"

"Tyris's," he said. "They were all she could think of. And we have reason to believe they have made a difference. Prevented you from losing more. And possibly"—here he paused for a long time—"helped you begin the process of recovery."

At first I had no idea what he meant. Then it hit me, and I felt my stomach drop like one of the stones that lay before me. "The dreams," I said. "The night terrors. You think that means my memory's coming back?"

He nodded slowly, warily. "Tyris believes the dreams might represent your mind's unconscious attempts to access your past. Attempts that, as we both know, have been unsuccessful so far. She believes the terror associated with those dreams might be a result of the event you're trying to remember, the event you can't remember. If it's true you were subjected to some sort of—procedure, it might be that the terror has as much to do with that as with the attack. But Tyris believes the intensifying of the panic attacks means you may be close to calling those memories back into consciousness."

"Intensifying?" I said. "You really have been keeping an eye on me, haven't you?"

He said nothing.

"And what makes you so sure I'll ever remember?" I said. "Maybe there's nothing *to* remember. Or maybe it's gone for good."

"Nothing is sure," he said. "All we know is that if *you* can't remember, no one can. Aleka and Yov don't know what it was that protected you. And there's no one else left."

"That's a pretty slim hope," I said.

He smiled humorlessly. "A slim hope is all we have."

His eyes locked on mine, but this time I didn't look away. I simply sat and stared at the man in front of me, the man who could confess so calmly to deceiving the person he called his son. But there was one thing more I needed from him, one more piece of my past I wanted to hear from his lips. So I said, "What about my real family? My father and mother? What happened to them?"

"Lost," he said. "To the Skaldi."

"So you're all I have left."

He nodded almost imperceptibly.

"Well, guess what, Laman," I said. "I didn't have a choice before. I do now."

I stood and walked away from him.

"Where are you going?" he said.

I didn't stop, didn't turn, didn't acknowledge him in any way.

"It was no accident," he called out. "The one that took Korah. It was no accident it sought you first. I didn't want to admit they could outflank us, outsmart us. But it's the only possible explanation. Petra was right, Querry. They're hunting you. They know."

I felt a shiver run down my back, but I kept going.

"I'm not your father," I heard him say. "But I'm still the commander of your colony. Let me help you."

This time I did turn to face him. Crouching on the ground in his grubby coat and beard, with his head jutting forward and his eyes lit by a fierce light, he looked about as much like the commander of a survival colony as the lunatics who hoarded their own spit and eyelashes. The arc of stones I'd placed between us enclosed him like a crazy cage. Within their circle he seemed, at long last, like the man he'd always been. The only difference was, now I could see him for what he truly was.

I took the red-handled knife from my pocket, flung it toward him. It skidded to a stop at his feet, inscription facing up. He looked at it, at me, but made no effort to touch it.

"You're nothing to me, Laman," I said, and walked away.

15

BEAST

A voice spoke to me, telling me that the people and places we know will always be there.

"But that's not really true, is it?" I asked.

No answer came. Instead, a figure approached me, wrapped in darkness like a cloak of shadows. From its depths a bleached hand emerged, groping. I stood paralyzed, my mouth wide but the sound refusing to leave my throat. The darkness surrounding the figure seemed to grow, obliterating the world, turning all to night. As if through a storm of black dust I saw swirling forms in violent motion, heard the terrified cries of loved ones. Wind and distance muffled their voices, but I thought I heard them begging me for help.

Then all sound ceased and the veil of darkness lifted just

enough for me to see that the ground at my feet was strewn with bodies.

Anguish contorted their limbs and faces. Spirals of smoke curled from their vacant eyes. As I watched, their bodies disintegrated, sinking into the dust as if they'd never been. I sensed two hazy figures standing on the periphery of my vision, but the creature's arm brushed them aside before I could reach out to them or call their names.

It turned its full attention to me. Its maw stretched wide, enveloping me in a smell as sickly as curdled blood, and a wordless howl rushed over me like a gale. I felt ensnared, suffocated, consumed. My gut heaved as though my insides had been wrenched from my body. The world wavered and grew black, a candle's flame sputtering in the wind.

Something whispered to me, as if the creature's wail had turned to words. I couldn't make the words out, but the whisper tugged at my body, my mind, urging me to follow it into the dark.

Then I experienced a sudden outpouring of warmth, as if a fire had bloomed deep inside my blood and bones. The whisper slid into a panicked shriek, and a feeling of relief washed over me. The heat no longer seemed to come from my veins but from outside, as if the fire had been transferred to the thing that had attacked me. I couldn't see it, but I could hear it thrashing at my feet. I took a step forward but found myself falling, falling toward the unseen ground, falling into darkness.

The voice sounded again from the void, pronouncing a single word: "Querry!"

Querry.

I clung to that word like a lifeline.

But I didn't know what it meant.

The next thing I knew, the darkness surrounded me, and I saw it was the natural darkness of night, silvered by a tiny slice of moon.

My skin felt cold and wet. My pulse hammered in my temples. But nothing shared the night with me, no sound except my own breath broke the stillness. The ground held only the common dust of this dead world. I was alone.

I'd been asleep. I'd been dreaming. The significance of that fact didn't strike me for a second.

I'd been dreaming.

And I remembered the dream. It chilled me to remember it, but I did. I could play back the details just as I'd experienced them in my sleep, and each time I replayed them they grew stronger, sharper. The voice, the whitened hand, the bodies, the whisper, the fire, the fall. The details became solid shapes in my mind, and the feelings of horror and relief they produced became as firm as my own flesh. And I knew what that meant.

This wasn't just a dream.

It was a memory.

It was a memory of the night memory had failed. A glimpse of the attack that had stripped my identity away.

After six months of nothing, a fragment of my past had finally returned.

I rose to a sitting position, hugged my knees. From the corner of camp where I'd moved my blanket, the moon's slanted smile showed me the shapes of sleeping bodies, the half a colony that had followed Laman Genn deeper into the Skaldi stronghold. I couldn't tell which of the huddled forms belonged to him, which to Aleka. Last night he'd let me walk off undisturbed, and neither of them had approached me as I lay down and fell into a feverish half-sleep. I'd listened to the sound of my own blood rushing in my ears, felt the presence of my own thoughts crowding my mind like ghosts. I'd struggled to locate the power I supposedly possessed, the power that had driven the creature away. I tried to detect any last trace of that creature lurking in my cells or bloodstream, eating at the roots of my being. I remembered what Korah had said that night at the pool. What did Skaldi feel like? Did Skaldi know they were Skaldi?

But I felt nothing. No power, no parasite. All I felt was me.

And now this dream, this memory. I didn't understand it completely, couldn't grasp what had happened to the creature that had threatened my life. But I got the gist. Laman had lied about many things, but not about the attack that had brought me to Survival Colony 9. I *had* been infected. One of the Skaldi had tried to hollow me out, to drain me like Korah, like Danis, like Mika. It had succeeded in gaining access. But it had failed to complete its work. Somehow I had driven it away. Something in my body, born there or put there, had stopped it. The creature had killed my memory, but it hadn't killed me.

And that meant there was yet another part of me I knew nothing about, a part that no one, not even the Skaldi, knew. The creature that attacked me hadn't known. It had seen me as just another body, one more tidbit on its way to devouring Survival Colony 27. But when it tried to feast on my body, it was the one that experienced pain. It was the one that got consumed. Triumph had turned to torment, and its body had crumbled to cinders and ash.

I guess that should have made me happy.

I was alive. The invader had fled. Whatever had fought off the infection had succeeded. I was me.

But that thought didn't make me happy. It didn't make me want to forgive, much less forget.

For the past six months, Laman Genn had been hounding me for a single reason: he wanted to pick my brain for the secret he thought I possessed. If he found out a shred of my memory had returned, the hounding would never stop. Not from him, not from any of them. They'd poke at my mind—and if they figured out a way to do it, my body—in an effort to tap the power they wanted for themselves. As more memories surfaced, as I recovered more of the life I'd lost, I'd lose it once again to their dreams, their demands. If I finally got to the bottom of it, learned who I was and how I'd fought the Skaldi off, I'd become an experiment for good. A pawn, not a person. Other colonies might even get into the Querry business.

I'd never be free of them.

The moon cut a bright scar in the sky. I squeezed my sides, tried to clear my head. There had to be another way. A way to discover who I was without the members of Survival Colony 9 finding out, tricking me, trapping me, using me for their own ends.

Then it hit me.

I could never be me as long as I stayed with them. Which meant the only chance I had of being me was to leave them behind.

I rose to a crouch, training my eyes on the sleeping bodies. I waited a couple breathless seconds in case anyone stirred. I knew Petra roamed somewhere out in the night, keeping watch on camp, but I trusted her not to show up except in an emergency. When I felt sure everyone was sound asleep, I crossed to the area where we'd piled our supplies. There wasn't much left, but I didn't need much. In fact, the less the better. Speed and secrecy were what I needed most. I reached out for the battered rucksack I'd been carrying the past six months.

I had just laid my hand on its scratchy surface when a scraping sound from behind me made my heart freeze. I spun, my hands held guiltily in front of me, my lips poised to formulate a lie.

But no one had moved. My heart thudded in my ears as

I stood there a long minute, trying to detect a change in the sleeping forms, but there was nothing to see.

The scraping sound caught my ears again, louder this time, closer. I held my breath, stared into the wan moonlight.

Nothing.

Then I saw it.

Something had entered our camp.

Where it had come from I couldn't tell. One second I saw only dust and darkness, and the next a pale shape appeared, not thirty feet from me. For the briefest moment I thought it might be Petra, returning from her surveillance to check on our safety or report something to Laman. Or maybe, I thought, Petra had been overconfident and we'd been tracked by someone from the rebel camp, a scout, a spy.

But it didn't take much more than a moment to realize the thing before me wasn't Petra. It wasn't one of Araz's people.

It wasn't even human.

It had been, though. Before its body fell prey to the Skaldi.

My heart rose to my throat as I got my first good look at it: a being no larger than Keely, creeping on all fours into our camp. But its face, I realized with relief, had never belonged to Araz's son. Its features looked not childlike but terribly old, wasted and worn. Its oversize head drooped at the end of a scrawny neck, its hands and feet scraped the ground as it dragged itself across the dusty terrain. The moonlight showed skin the same red-brown color as the dirt, arms and legs so bony it might have had no flesh at all. It looked like it had crawled through the desert for weeks, its stolen body deteriorating moment by moment, until practically all that was left of it was dust.

My mind flashed back to the day we'd found the gated compound. Wali had sworn he'd seen something in the distance, something the color of the land crawling on all fours. This thing matched his description to the letter.

I braced for its approach. There was just me between it and the rest of the colony, all of them fast asleep and defenseless a hundred feet away. Maybe I'd have a chance to test Laman's theory for real. A chance to save the people who had lied to me.

But it didn't come near me, or anyone else. It veered away from the cluster of bodies and crawled along the edge of camp, moving with painful slowness. I thought I heard a sound coming from it, a feeble cry, nothing like the wail I remembered from my dream. I watched as it crept inch by inch around our campsite, its head wobbling on its emaciated neck. Its body seemed to diminish even further as I watched, as if it was crumbling to dust before my eyes. Then the darkness closed over it and it was gone.

I let out the breath I hadn't realized I was holding. I told myself it must have been a dream, that my mind must still be reeling from its first solid memory in six months.

But when I went to investigate the path the crawling

creature had taken, I found a definite trail. Twin furrows in the dust, exactly what you'd expect from a body dragging itself on hands and knees. I traced the trail back the way it had entered camp, saw that the grooves continued far into the night. Then I reversed course and followed to the point where the creature had disappeared, and once again the trail stretched as far as I could see. The thing that had made the trail, though, had passed beyond my sight.

I returned to camp, skirting the sleepers, back to the supply cache. My legs trembled, but not from the danger that had just passed. I had no idea what would have happened if this Skaldi had attacked, whether the power that had protected me once would have protected me again. But I felt no fear. What I felt was so new I barely recognized it.

I felt excitement.

It couldn't be a coincidence. Of that I felt certain. The very night my first memory returned, a Skaldi unlike any I'd heard of had entered our camp. A Skaldi that had worn its host body down to near nothing yet failed to attack when a fresh supply fell within its reach. There had to be a connection.

My heart beat faster as I realized what the connection was.

This was the one. The one that had erased my memory. It had to be.

The creature that had attacked me had suffered, been damaged in some way. My dream, my memory told me that.

Though everything had been dark and cloudy, I remembered its scream, remembered it falling away from me, its body burning as if my skin had turned into a living flame. I thought the creature had burned away completely. So did Laman and Aleka.

But what if it hadn't?

What if it had merely been wounded, weakened? What if it had fled to one of the half-consumed bodies that lay at my feet, hidden there while Aleka tended to me? There'd been no reason, and no time, for her to scorch all the bodies after the attack ended. As soon as she could, she'd hit the road with Yov and me, desperate for help. And now, after six months of whatever it took for a Skaldi to recover from injuries its kind had never known, it had come back to find me. To finish the job it had started.

Or, I thought with another burst of excitement, maybe it had spent the past six months trying to get *away* from me. Only now, after all that time, it had failed.

My mind jumped at the thought. It all made sense. The Skaldi that had stolen Korah's body had known things—about the colony, about her, about me—that it couldn't have known unless it had also stolen her memory. Skaldi were mimics—how could they pretend to be us if they didn't share our thoughts? If they didn't assimilate the host's mind along with the body? It came as a surprise that no one had ever suggested this to me before. Maybe it was because people like Laman Genn preferred to think of Skaldi as dumb brutes that they refused to believe the things that *copied* us also *became* us.

But in the case of the one that attacked me, my memory was all it got. For six months it had held my past inside its wasted body, somehow clinging to that emptied shell far longer than we'd believed Skaldi could. But now, after a half-year of hiding, it had stumbled across our camp. Too weak or frightened to attack, it had crept away as fast as it could. But it had left behind a fragment of the memory it had stolen: the memory of the attack, the memory that haunted it as much as it tortured me.

And that meant that if I could find the creature again, maybe I could force it to restore the rest of what it had taken.

My past. My life. Myself.

I felt something flame inside me at the thought of confronting it. Defeating it. Winning back what I had lost.

Not for Laman, not for Survival Colony 9, not for the human race.

For me.

I snuck back to where we'd unloaded our supplies. Trying to move fast but as stealthily as Petra, I stuffed all I could fit into my old rucksack. I took a canteen, three cans of food, a length of rope, a tattered bedroll. I looked around for guns and ammunition, but Laman and Aleka had kept them hidden. In the end I decided they'd be useless anyway. I did take a pocketknife for carving, a tinder and flint for making fire, a jar for rainwater. I considered a couple other things, a shovel, an extra pair of boots, but I didn't want to waste time or weigh myself down. I thought about trading my knife for the one Laman had left where I'd thrown it, but I let it lie. Its pale letters glowed like bone against its red flesh.

I hoisted the rucksack onto my shoulders and tiptoed to the spot where the colony lay sleeping. For a moment I stood over them, silently reciting their names, as I'd done time and again that first week following the attack. Wali. Nessa. Tyris. Soon. Nekane. Adem. The old woman whose name I'd never learned. All the others I'd believed were my own. I watched Aleka, who slept on her side, her long legs crossed at the ankles, her head cradled in her arms. I felt a pang when my eyes came to rest on the huddle of little kids, sleeping on their stomachs with their knees bunched up to their chests or on their backs with their arms flung every which way, the circle of adults forming an ineffectual barricade around them. I wondered what would happen to them. If they'd live to see another year. If they'd miss or even remember me.

My eyes lingered on the man who'd pretended to be my father. He slept on his back beside his followers, his bearded mouth open, his breath issuing in a rattling snore. I'd spent hours with him every day, learned his lessons and rules, thought I'd learned who he was. But it had all been a deception, and I couldn't forgive him for that. I couldn't forget the way he'd looked at me, dark fire burning in his eyes, when he told me a lie so basic I never thought to question its truth.

Your name is Querry Genn.

But in one way and one way only, I did thank him. He'd taught me everything I needed to know to survive on my own. I could guide myself by sunlight or rare stars, hunt for the few sources of food that survived in this dying world, tie a fast knot or strike a larger opponent where it'd hurt most. Why he'd taught me these things didn't matter anymore. He'd told me my time was coming, and he'd been right.

He just hadn't known he wouldn't be with me when it came.

I tightened the straps of my rucksack and followed the creature's trail toward a row of stunted trees that edged the camp. I turned back only once. I'm not sure if I said good-bye. The word poised in my mind and on my lips, but if I spoke it aloud it was too quiet for even me to hear.

TRUST

Morning, hot and red, found me miles from camp, miles from anywhere.

I'd avoided Petra somehow, hadn't seen her on the way out. She'd been my biggest worry. I'd been dreading the thought of facing her, trying to explain myself, hearing her scoff at my explanation. Lacking any weapon other than the pocketknife, I'd snapped a branch from one of the trees, tested its broken end against my palm. It felt sharp as a thorn, and might work as a spear. But after what I'd seen her do the morning we freed Laman, I doubted I would stand a chance against her. I doubted even more that I was prepared to skewer a fellow human being. So I was relieved I didn't have to test either theory.

With the camp behind me, I focused on following the

Skaldi's trail. It angled toward the river, roughly three miles to the west, then forked northwestward to follow the water's edge. It ran remarkably straight and true, and as the sun crept over my right shoulder, I had no doubt I'd catch up to the thing that had made it. But somehow the creature eluded me, stayed always out of sight. I puzzled over how something moving that slowly could outrun me, but I reminded myself that I knew next to nothing about its abilities. It had gotten past Petra, so it had to have something going for it. Maybe it had sensed me following and increased its pace, or maybe it had recovered its strength once it got out of my range. The thing Wali had seen the day we discovered the compound had disappeared too, moved out of reach of Aleka's binoculars. But we'd seen no trail that day, hadn't even looked for one, and as long as I could see a trail, I wasn't worried about losing the creature, or myself, in the desert.

And tracing the river had other advantages. Aside from water, it offered wet rocks where edible creatures liked to hide. None of them with less than six legs, but you had to take what you could get. Even more important, keeping to the riverbank gave me my best chance of staying ahead of Laman. I knew he would start looking for me the instant he found me gone, and he had Petra on his side. But I also knew he wouldn't expect me to travel toward danger, which meant toward the west and most of all toward water. Petra would look for footprints, not the creature's trail, so I walked on the pebbly shoreline, where I wouldn't leave as much of a mark.

If I moved fast, I figured I could stay ahead of any pursuit from my former colony. It occurred to me that Araz and Yov might be hunting for me as well, trying to get their hands on the power Laman had told them I possessed. In fact, maybe that's why they took over the colony: not so much to do away with him as to get at me. If so, they'd expect to find me with Laman's colony, not on my own. And if Petra was right that Kin couldn't track a whole colony, there was no way he could track a solitary hiker.

It gave me only a slim edge to know more about my own position and movements than anyone else, but it was all I had. And after six months of knowing less about myself than anyone, it was about time I had the advantage.

The Skaldi presented another story, impossible to figure out, impossible to predict. As soon as I left camp I wrapped the blunt end of my walking stick in a rag, hoping I could light it with my flint in case I needed a weapon against them, or in case I needed something to threaten the one I was pursuing. But I knew my makeshift weapon was nowhere near as effective as a flamethrower, and I wasn't about to walk through the desert lugging one of those. From what I understood of Petra's conversations with Laman, the Skaldi had set up a line to the east, squeezing us along the river's bend toward the northwest. But traveling solo, I might just slip through their net. Or if not, I would have to hope that Laman's story and my own memory really were true.

I stifled a quiet laugh at the thought that I was actually

chasing Skaldi instead of the other way around. I hoped that unexpected twist would work to my advantage.

Through the better part of the morning, my plan seemed to be paying off. The sun climbed, revealing the empty land around me. My shadow shortened and pooled at my feet. The creature's trail held steady, but nothing else met my eye. I took a swig of water and settled into a hard march, hoping to catch up to my prey or at least cover as much ground as possible before the sun reached its meridian.

But then, maybe an hour before noon, I hit a major roadblock.

Not a living one. A leftover from the wars that had given us this dead land. It was the remains of a mine field, no telling exactly how long or wide, the land pockmarked with craters where the charges had gone off, other unexploded mines showing as dark disks beneath the veil of dust. Laman had told me the combatants of a half-century ago often seeded the rivers with minefields. In fact, any body of water, even a dried-up lake half-filled with muddy sludge, had become as precious as gold in the waning days of the old world. Chances were whoever had planted this field had blown themselves to bits along with the ones they called their enemy. But I couldn't risk a walk through what was left. I searched for the creature's trail, but it became confused at the field's edge, maybe plowing straight through, maybe hooking to the east. I stood there a long, painful minute, my legs tightening with the desire to move forward. But my head knew better.

I wanted my past back. Just not enough to risk losing my future.

I backtracked a quarter-mile and took a wide detour to the east, probably wider than I needed, but Laman had warned me about outlying mines planted to trick the unwary. By the time I'd circumnavigated the field and returned to my route by the river's edge, a new problem rose, or hung, before me: the sun. Much as I hated to lose more time, I knew I'd have to take a break soon. The camp buzzed with stories of people who had plodded forward looking for shade and water, only to collapse in the dust. Once, we'd found the decomposing remains of someone who'd been too fatigued and dehydrated to realize he was dying. We could tell that was what had killed him because there were still bones, and unless they're in a huge hurry, Skaldi don't leave bones. I'd been drinking sparingly throughout the morning, small sips every fifteen minutes or so, not only to make it last but because that was about as much of the oily fluid as I could stand to hold in my stomach at a time. But I had started to feel headachy and woozy, and I knew I needed to find shade before confusion set in. Once I crossed that line, I couldn't count on myself to stay by the river's edge. I could just as easily end up walking myself to death in search of a mirage that stayed always a step or two beyond reach.

I'd just about convinced myself the creature itself was a mirage when I found its trail again, arrowing straight along the riverbank as if it had never deviated an inch from its course despite the minefield. The temptation to follow took all my waning strength to fight. But I reminded myself that I hadn't sidestepped the mines just so I could kill myself slowly an hour later. The trail still showed. The creature might tire. I could rest a couple hours through the full blaze of day and wake refreshed and ready to make up lost time.

The riverbank provided some shade, so that seemed an obvious place to take a break. But then I saw a white blur on the horizon, something I felt confident was more than heat distortion. I approached it cautiously, though it didn't have the look of anything I needed to fear. Within a quarter hour I confirmed what I'd hoped to find: a broken section of pipeline, the kind that used to pump fuel across the land. We'd found scattered pieces of these lines every so often, never with much of the original pipe left, because the fuel supply had been one of the first things to be targeted by air strikes. Occasionally we'd found sections sticking up from the ground, most times flat on their bellies, the metal struts that had supported them collapsed or buried in the sand. The first time we came across one, I made a fool of myself by asking Laman if there was still oil inside. Yov had had a field day with that one.

The length of pipe spanned about thirty feet, with jagged ends and a huge crack down the middle, empty of everything but dust. It had collapsed completely, so it was a cinch to climb inside. The pipe itself was made of plastic, luckily, because the metal ones got too hot to touch at midday. Not much room, and not exactly what I'd call cool, but it kept me out of the direct sunlight. The smell of oil or gas or tar that had probably been overpowering a half-century ago had been completely erased by the ever-present scent of dust and decay. And the creature's trail, I was gratified to see, held steady right past the pipe, so I could pick it up again the moment I finished my rest.

I stayed inside the pipe a couple hours, not really sleeping. My eyelids felt heavy enough to fall, but every time they started to close I'd jerk awake with the fear that I'd heard some noise, the stamp of a boot, the scraping sound of the Skaldi I was pursuing. Probably nothing more than wind in the pipe or the rustle of my own attempts to find a comfortable position, but I'd never been so completely alone, and the quiet of a land without people dwarfed the hushed movements of our life as a colony. Out here by myself, it was hard not to magnify every squeak and shuffle into the rumble of an approaching army. That, plus the nervous excitement in my stomach, kept me on high alert.

I replayed the memory from last night time and again, and though nothing new came to fill in the gaps in the sequence, the thought that I might be on the verge of recovering more of my past ran like an electric current through my body. I imagined myself waylaying the creature, intimidating it, forcing it, I had no idea how, to give back what it had stolen. I refused to let myself believe it was impossible, that the creature could snatch memory but not restore it. The hardest part was waiting. The curved plastic walls of the fuel pipe enclosed me like a cage, even though I knew they were the only thing protecting me from sunstroke and death.

Just a little while longer, I told myself as I peeked out of the pipe to see how far the sun had limped across the sky. Just another hour, another few minutes, another few seconds, and I'd be free again. The trail would be there. I would find the creature at the end of it.

And I would find myself, too.

When at long last the sun started its descent, I climbed out of the pipe, stretched my legs, and continued on my way. Within minutes my resting place vanished into the blankness of the land. My shadow grew long again, a dagger slicing the ground to the east. The creature's trail held amazingly steady, its endurance hard to believe. Tyris, the closest thing to an authority on the Skaldi we had, always maintained that the creatures needed new bodies on a regular basis, staying in each host only long enough to carry them to their next victim. She didn't know *why* they tore through bodies so fast, but their relentlessness and insatiable hunger, she said, suggested that they did. That, she speculated, explained why they went on killing rampages when they had the chance: they stored up energy by consuming as many bodies as they could, leaving themselves only one final body as a vehicle to their next meal. What happened to them if they failed to find a new host we had no idea, though we'd always assumed their last body simply disintegrated and became part of the dust we tramped on. What would happen to them if they ever succeeded in destroying all of us we didn't even bother to think about.

But if I was right, this thing had been creeping through the desert for six months in a hollowed-out corpse, and still it showed no signs of slowing or stopping. Either it had gained some unheard-of energy when it attacked me, or it wasn't what I thought it was after all. Its trail tempted and tormented me as I plunged deeper into uncharted territory. If I could only catch up with it, I told myself, the answers to all my questions would lie within my grasp.

But as the day waned, the bitter realization sank into me that I would have to stop once again and find a relatively safe place to spend the night. The river had begun to wash out into the dull hue of the land, the cloud murk threatened to block any light from moon or stars, and I knew I'd never be able to follow the trail in the dead dark. I'd been walking, break excepted, for nearly twelve hours, and I couldn't take the chance of growing groggy or careless without sleep. Not with the possibility of other minefields in the vicinity, not with the risk of crossing paths with Araz, Laman, or anything else that might be in the area. I delayed as long as I could, squinting into the dusk, trying to distinguish the creature's trail from all the other nameless ripples in the land. But when the sun finally tumbled in a smear below the horizon, I knew I couldn't delay any longer.

The land had dimmed to shadows and outlines by the time I quit the river to seek shelter away from its shore. What light remained from the fading sun made the few visible shapes look like they'd been dunked in blood or doused in fire. I trod carefully, listening for movement, spooked by my own footsteps. Night falls fast in the desert, and I realized my desire to catch up with the creature had left me stumbling blindly in the dark.

I hadn't gone far before I caught my foot and fell over something I couldn't see.

Visions of my body exploding into fragments flashed through my mind. But I landed in one piece, my hands hitting the ground hard and my pack flying forward with a clatter to smack the back of my head. When I rose to my knees, I saw that I'd tripped over an object nearly the color of the land. For a second my heart leaped with the thought that this might be the creature itself, but it sat formless and motionless, a duffel-size lump with the solidity of clay. I rose, wiped my hands on my pants, and resumed my march, only to stub my toe on another blob a few steps on.

This time I halted and looked around me, letting my eyes grow accustomed to the dark. When they did, I spotted a collection of darker shapes lying against the dark ground, one every few paces or so. All of them roughly the same size, the size of a . . .

I stooped and reached for the nearest shape. My fingers closed around thick, heavy material, and when I pulled, I felt something like dirt shift inside. Probing further, I traced the edges of the material, touched a series of hard knobs, confirmed what it was.

A uniform top.

But what remained inside was far less than its wearer. I lifted it free from the ground and the last traces sifted invisibly into the dust at my feet. To my utter surprise, the cloth itself fell apart next, leaving me with nothing but a fistful of prickly fibers.

Trembling, I crept to the next bundle and felt it lightly. This one contained more to feel, a complete uniform, but no more inside. I moved breathlessly to the next, and the next. Some of them, like the one I'd tripped over, felt relatively intact. I didn't investigate deeply enough to see how much was left inside those. Others had been emptied of everything but air, while still others had disintegrated partially like the first. They formed a line, each one spaced roughly twenty feet from the next, leading back toward the river. I followed this new trail, shape by shape. I counted sixteen in all, along with spilled packs and the empty tank of a flamethrower. The rest I probably missed in the dark.

On the last one before the river, a bundle far bulkier than most, I found a gun and a walkie-talkie. I didn't need to look closely to know that this had been Araz.

I lowered myself carefully down the rocky bank, my eyes scanning the water's black surface. When I reached the river's edge I cupped my hands, dipped them into the rank water, brought them to my face. I shivered, though the water was warm.

Araz and Yov's colony was gone. Totally gone. Its leaders, its followers, and those who hadn't been old enough to make a choice. Like Keely. I hadn't seen a uniform his size, but he was so small I could easily have overlooked it. Nearly twenty colonists, trained fighters like Kin, bruisers like Kelmen, had been wiped out so quickly they hadn't had time to do anything but scatter and run. I had hated the rebels, wished them out of my life, but never wished them dead.

But it hadn't mattered. The Skaldi had wished differently. I knew now why Petra had seen nothing of them since yesterday's late afternoon report: they'd been waylaid in their pursuit of Laman's colony, and when it ended, their tattered remains were all the Skaldi had left behind.

Which Skaldi, I couldn't say. I barely believed the pitiful thing crawling through Laman's camp could have destroyed the rebels so completely, especially when it hadn't touched anyone the night before. But I'd been there last night, and if my suspicion was right about it, its main objective at that point had been to get away. If this really was the same creature that had stolen my memory, it had wiped out Survival Colony Twenty-Seven all on its own. Who knew what it could do when there was no one to stop it?

I'd been so focused on tracking this wounded thing, I'd forgotten that wounded things can be the most dangerous.

A movement out of the corner of my eye made me

freeze. Something stood at the water's edge, a dark shape not ten feet from where I crouched. I had no time to light my tree-branch torch, and I doubted such a small fire would scare it off anyway. If Tyris was right, Skaldi feed until the last body is left. And now a new body had walked right into the middle of its feast.

I rose to face it. What else could I do?

But then I noticed that the thing I'd seen had backed away, as if it was as startled by me as I was by it. I debated what to do for a second before calling out.

"Who's there?"

"It's me," said a child's voice. "Keely."

Relief flooded me, followed by a new wave of fear. "Keely," I said. "Are you all right?"

"I hid under Daddy," he said. "It didn't see me."

I struck a spark from my flint, saw his terrified face in the brief glow. I knew it was wrong to feel this way, but I couldn't help giving thanks that Araz's remains were complete enough to shield his tiny son. "Is there . . ." I meant to finish, "anyone else?" But I couldn't ask him that.

"Keely," I said. "There's something I have to do. It won't hurt. Can I . . ." I felt sick asking. "Can you come over here?"

Obediently, he took a series of small steps until he stood right before me. I could barely make out his face in the gloom. His cheeks were drawn and his teeth chattered, but his eyes, I thought, gazed back at me in trust. I tried to will mine to look the same.

"I'm just going to check to see if you're okay," I said, and I took his two small hands in one of mine. With my other hand, I gripped the ends of his fingers, wiggling them hard at the very tips.

A look of confused delight crept over his face. "This little piggy went to market," he whispered.

I tried to smile back. "Now I'm going to check your teeth."

"My teeth?" But he opened his mouth without protest.

I unfastened my rucksack and took out a strip of cloth and my glass jar. Stuffing the rag inside, I struck the flint until I got a corner of the fabric to catch, then set the home-made lantern at our feet. In the yellow light I inspected each of Keely's tiny teeth, held each one between fingers that seemed clumsy and blunt, pulled as hard as I could without hurting him. On the top row, a tooth wiggled and came loose with a slight tearing of tissue.

I looked at him, horrified, then saw a dark spot of blood welling at the root. He smiled a brand-new smile.

"We'll have to save this one for the . . ." I tried to remember the name of the thing the little kids talked about, some kind of boat that took baby teeth away. "The tooth ferry," I finished, and slipped the treasure into his hand. Then I closed my own hand around his and led him up from the riverbed.

I walked him along the bank, away from the violated bodies. His hand felt cold, but his teeth no longer chattered. Once, he gave my hand an instinctive squeeze, and

I squeezed back. He'd always trusted me, at least for the six months I could remember. Chances are he couldn't remember much more than I could. All he had, really, was trust.

We couldn't stay here, I knew. The thing that had done this might be coming back. Whatever my chances against it, Keely's stood at exactly zero. But I had no idea where the creature had gone, whose body it had slain last, so leaving this spot in the middle of the night didn't seem like an option either. I considered pocketing Araz's gun, but the thought of touching it turned my stomach, and what good would it be against Skaldi, anyway? Retracing my steps to Laman's camp seemed equally foolish. Not only would I have to deal with at least one minefield I could no longer detect, but if the Skaldi that had killed the rebels wasn't the one I thought it was, I could be leading it straight back to Survival Colony 9.

I stood there far longer than I should, trying to focus, coming no closer to a decision. Keely shivered beside me.

"Querry," he said. "I'm cold."

That was what finally made up my mind. He was my responsibility now, at least until I found someone else to take care of him. Whatever lay ahead of us in the night, the one thing I knew for sure was that death lay behind. I might not be any good at making decisions, but I had to be better than a kid who'd just lost his first baby tooth.

"Come on," I said, and we started off into the night, leaving the carnage of the rebel camp by the riverside.

NEST

Keely and I marched deep into the night.

When he got too tired to walk I strapped my rucksack across my chest and carried him on my back. When he got too sleepy to cling to me I switched him to the front and held him in my arms. A half-starved five-year-old doesn't weigh much, and though my muscles grew numb, they also seemed strangely tireless, immune to fatigue or pain. His thin chest breathed against mine, his soft exhalations caressed my neck. I put my head down and forged ahead, one step at a time.

I abandoned the area right by the river in case of mines, but I tried to stay on course to the northwest. Even if there'd been enough light to spot yesterday's trail, I wouldn't have hunted for it, preferring not to think about it at all. My only thought was to put as much distance as possible between the child I held and the memory of the night. Let the thing catch us if it could. I didn't know where we were going, or what we might find. I didn't know if our next step would land us in a crater or lead us straight into the arms of the Skaldi. All I could do was walk on through the night, holding the one living thing that was mine to hold for as long as I could hold it.

Eventually, though, I had to set Keely down and get some sleep. The risen moon had shrunk to a fingernail-shaped sliver, and all across the darkened land there was nothing like shelter to be seen. So I lay down on my bedroll, draping an arm around Keely to keep him close. Not safe, just close. He murmured in his sleep, eyelids fluttering. Dreaming, I guess. I closed my eyes wondering if either of us would open them again.

But when a dreamless night passed and the sun rose on another day, I rose with it. Keely slept on, so I shook him gently, watched his brown eyes open. He seemed momentarily confused to see me, then he smiled. I wondered how much sorrow a single night could erase for a kid his age. If he asked about his dad, I didn't know what I would say.

He didn't, though. He watched me puncture the lid of a can with my pocketknife, accepted the couple mouthfuls of stringy yellow stuff I offered him, and waited for me to swallow some of the tasteless food myself. Then he took my hand and followed along, cupping the meal to his mouth and licking his palm as we went.

Now that the crisis of the night had fallen behind us and

I could look at the situation in the brutal light of day, I had to admit that taking care of Keely presented some real problems. To begin with, his presence changed my plan—such as it was—from fight to flight. I'd glanced around for the Skaldi's trail as soon as we woke up, but as I'd half-feared and half-hoped, it had vanished during our nighttime march. Whether the creature had stopped or changed course, I doubted we'd find it again. Maybe that was a good thing. But it meant I now had no particular destination in mind, and no particular goal except to get as far away from the ruins of Keely's camp as I could.

And with Keely in tow, that might not be so easy. Though he seemed satisfied with the bare-bones meal I'd given him, an extra mouth to feed meant my cans would run out twice as fast, forcing me to spend time hunting for what little food the barren land provided. So long as we stayed within hiking distance of the river our water would last, but Keely drank much more than I did, in tiny but frequent sips, and that meant more river runs to refill my canteen and jar. He also stopped for bathroom breaks all the time, and he could never predict when they were coming, so they never coincided with a time we were actually at the river. The best I could do to erase our scent was dig a ditch with my knife, cover it once he was done, and hope the camp crazies were wrong and the Skaldi's sense of smell wasn't as keen as they said.

The biggest problem of all, though, was how slowly my new companion forced us to move. He didn't drag his feet or waste time playing, but he got tired and needed to rest, he took baby steps, and I didn't think I could carry him forever. If a situation arose that called for speed, I could run, but where would that leave Keely?

I knew the answer to that. Nowhere.

And I knew I couldn't leave him. But watching his tangled brown hair bob along by my side, I couldn't help thinking how much easier it would be if I could.

By mid-morning we'd walked maybe two miles, less than half the distance I'd have covered on my own. A good two hours of that time had been devoted to naps and potty breaks. I'd become an expert at digging holes and finding shelter in the tiniest of divots, and for a short time I'd discovered that I could get Keely to pick up the pace if I turned our march into a kind of game, like tag minus the hard running. As high sun approached, though, a change settled over the land, from flat and sterile emptiness to a more varied terrain, low hills spotted with rocks and scrub brush, and that made it even harder for Keely to keep up. I tugged his hand, lifted him onto my shoulders, distracted him with nonsense jokes, anything I could think of to keep him moving. All I had left in my favor was that he hadn't asked me where we were going or when we would get there. Which was a very good thing, because I had yet to figure that out myself.

While Keely rested in the lee of a hill during the day's hottest hours, I debated what to do next. The only thing I knew for certain was that I had to stay near the river. I could keep trekking northwest, in hopes of finding . . . something. Araz's fabled mountains. The Skaldi I'd lost overnight. A new colony to take Keely off my hands. Or I could backtrack, hope against hope to avoid whatever had slain the rebels, maybe even find some way to reunite Keely with Laman without being nabbed myself. But when I thought of that, I knew I was fooling myself. Survival Colony 9 would never willingly let me go. My plan had blown up in my face, but it was still the best I had. I'd stay on course and hope for a revelation or a miracle.

"You ready?" I said to Keely, who lay yawning and stretching from his nap.

He nodded and took my hand. At the moment, that seemed like miracle enough for me.

Over the next hour, the hills became steeper and more widely spaced. I found myself panting as I trudged up each rise with him on my back, catching my breath at the top and recovering it fully only at the bottom of each downslope, just in time to lose it again. I wondered if we might be nearing the mountains after all. I'd never seen mountains, so I had no idea what led up to them. The trees here I couldn't place, low and spreading and blanketed in rusty needles, interspersed with bushes and boulders that could either hide us or conceal whatever might be lying in wait. I kept my eyes trained on the unsparing landscape, but nothing moved except our own shadows, linked by the thread of our twined hands.

Anxiety made me determined to keep Keely close. But

as the day wore on he got fidgety, and I found it harder and harder to distract him. We hadn't done much talking or anything I'd call playing since the game of marching tag fizzled, and by mid-afternoon it felt like our roles had switched: now he was the one who'd develop sudden spurts of energy, while I was the one who wasn't always up to joining him. Probably that came from giving him piggyback rides the first half of the day. I decided to give him a job scouting ahead, not far enough that I couldn't run him down if I needed to. That seemed to please him, and every time I caught up he'd give me a scouting report. "I'm Petra," he said. "And you're Laman." I smiled for his sake, though the reminder of Petra's superhuman skill and of the commander she served made me glance anxiously back the way we'd come.

About two hours past his midday nap, I let him climb to the top of the steepest hill we'd encountered so far while I took a break in the shade of a rusty tree. I was beat. I'd been trying to save on food and water since our last refill at the river, which basically meant none for me, all for him. Add to that the hills and the pounding of the afternoon sun, and I felt like a rag wrung dry. The ground beneath the tree blistered my back, but I lay out of the direct sun, and at least I could close my eyes for a second to escape the blinding day.

That's when I heard him call out, "Querry!"

I jumped to my feet, realizing I'd been on the verge of nodding off. Instantly I spotted his small figure standing stock still at the hill's crest, a slender brown body engulfed by the solid brown waste of land and sky. He turned to face me, his arm gesturing urgently, a "come quick!" motion. My exhaustion forgotten, I sprinted to where he stood.

When I reached his side, he pointed. But there was no need.

The ground sloped sharply away at our feet, forming a broad bowl where it met with other, lower hills far beneath us. Within the hollow of these hills, maybe a mile northeast of where we stood, a huge spire reared out of the desert. It looked to be made of rock or soil, the same color as the surrounding terrain, though it appeared less a part of the land than a slim finger balanced precariously on the plain. I had no guess as to its actual height, but it seemed simply enormous, towering all alone with only a few bare, lowly knolls in its vicinity. It might have been a mountain, I thought, except it didn't look at all like what I'd imagined when people talked about mountains. Those sounded like welcoming places, places of peace, even of beauty. This looked like an ugly growth, as if an explosion from long ago had burst the face of the land and left this monstrosity behind as a grave marker.

Keely peered up at me eagerly. "Can we go there, Querry?"

I glanced at him uncertainly, then back at the spire. To his eyes, it must have seemed like a play place, a place to explore, or at least to break up the monotony of the day. To me, it seemed like the kind of place we should stay away from. Yet at the same time, I had to admit I was curious to find out what it was, if only to know how wide a berth to give it. Plus it looked shadier in the valley between the hills, and at this point getting out of the sunlight seemed a good enough reason to take a detour.

"We have to be careful," I said. "You stay with me."

Without a word of agreement or disagreement, he set off down the slope, playing Petra's part except without an ounce of her stealth or caution.

I followed him. The hill dipped steeply and the soil lay rocky and loose, but we kept our feet. Clouds of dust billowed around us, especially him as he skidded downhill. During the entire descent, all I could think was how visible we'd be to anything scouting the hillside. I kept half an eye on Keely, the other half on the neighboring elevations, but nothing showed itself.

In less than half an hour we reached the saddle formed by adjacent slopes. Looking across the valley, it became apparent to me the spire was even more massive than it had seemed from above. It dominated the landscape, rising so high above the plain we might as well have been ants emerging from our anthill. It stood farther away than I had thought as well, two miles distant at least. I glanced at Keely, whose bright eyes focused on the single pinnacle rising from the empty land.

"You sure you're up for this?"

He didn't answer. He didn't have to. His face told me all I needed to know.

I turned to the hill we'd descended, traced our path in the dust, realized it would take double the time to climb back up. Two miles, if it was two miles, meant another hour minimum at Keely's pace. To reach the spire and return by nightfall would be pushing it, especially if he wanted to stay and play. But the arguments that had gotten me this far made me reluctant to turn back. We had half a canteen and a full jar of water, and as long as we could reach the river before we ran dry, did it really matter if we got back to where we started?

"Come on," I said to Keely, who was already tugging my sleeve. "And stay close."

For the next hour, in the stifling shade of the valley and the sporadic shelter of the strange trees, we marched toward the monolith. Or I marched, Keely skipped. As our goal advanced I got a better sense of its size and shape: about two hundred feet tall and maybe a third as wide, tapering slightly from base to rounded peak, and not as smooth or featureless as it had seemed from far away. On closer inspection it appeared more like mud than stone or soil, mud built up over the years and baked by the sun into lumps and swirls and dribbles. On size alone I'd have said it looked like one of the skyscrapers Laman had told me about, steel pylons that pierced the polluted sky. But the closest thing it resembled from my own experience was a termite mound, a hundred times bigger than the ones I'd seen.

At last the spire loomed directly above us, its shadow swollen to gigantic dimensions and flung far away to the east. I laid a hand cautiously on its warty surface, but it felt no different from any piece of rock or clay heated and dried by the sun. Its consistency exactly matched that of a termite mound, slightly porous but too hard to break with my bare hands. The only difference lay in the scale: where you could cup your palm around any of the bumps on the termite mounds I'd seen, both my arms weren't wide enough to girdle the monstrous bubbles that hung from the tower's side. A million termites couldn't have built this, not in a thousand years. I walked a circle around its base, craning my neck, squinting at the sunlight on its crown, but I saw nothing that might give me a clue to what this thing was, how it had come here. Maybe, I thought, it had been here forever, an ancient ruin left over from the death of the modern world.

When I completed my inspection, I found Keely standing beside the mound with his face angled up at the peak, a frown clouding his brow. Whatever he'd been hoping for, he must have realized he couldn't play with this thing. It wasn't even possible to climb. I could imagine how disappointed he must have felt after walking so far to get here. But now that we were here, he had to see that there was nothing to do but go back.

"Querry?" he said.

"Yeah?"

"I'm tired." His eyes looked teary, and his voice was a kid's pout.

I tried a smile. "Me too."

"I need a nap."

"I can carry you."

"No!" he said, more violently than I expected. "I want to nap here!"

"Keely . . ." I reached for his arm.

He swung and hit me with a balled fist. It didn't hurt, but I jerked back in shock.

"I want to nap here!" he said again.

"Let me carry you," I said. "You can sleep with me like you did last night."

Again I reached for him, and again he took a swing.

"You're not my daddy!" he said. "You can't tell me what to do."

Your daddy has been scattered to the wind, I thought. *He can't tell you what to do either.*

"Keely," I tried once more, but before I could continue he let out a scream that stunned me with its vehemence. I looked around as if someone might hear, but there were only the two of us, him red-faced with childish rage, me speechless with confusion and doubt.

I knew I could pick him up, fend off his fists for the few minutes it would take him to exhaust himself. But I was as tired as he was, and I didn't have the energy for a fight. I glanced back at the hill we'd started from, its slope smothered in shadow. At that moment, home base seemed as far away as the craters of the moon.

"All right," I said. "Come here."

I sat by the foot of the spire, patting the dust beside me. His mini-tantrum melted from his face, and he smiled.

I would let him fall asleep before taking him back, I decided. Give him a chance to dream off his disappointment and wake with what he'd left behind forgotten. I'd cover more ground with him asleep anyway.

He came over to me, but he didn't sit on the ground. Instead, he curled into my lap, his head tucked under my chin. Hesitantly, I lifted my hand and stroked his matted hair. He slipped a filthy thumb into his mouth, and instantly his breathing softened. I looked down to see his cheeks flexing and his eyelids flickering.

"Tell me a story," he said in a muffled whisper, just as his eyes slid closed.

I woke to catch the last rays of sun winking behind the hill where I'd hoped to deliver us by nightfall. Twilight blanketed the land, a muddy vagueness that turned brown to gray. Keely slept on in my lap, his thumb planted in his mouth, his sucking cheeks baby-smooth. The story he'd asked for remained untold.

We'd been asleep for hours.

"Keely!" I hissed. "Get up. We've got to go!"

He stirred, his eyelids struggling to open. Then his thirty pounds flopped back onto me and his eyes closed. The thumb never left his mouth.

"Keely." I shook him, lifted him from my chest, set him

273

on his feet. He refused to stand on his own. I propped him up and, not knowing what else to do, slapped him lightly on the cheeks. He winced and feebly waved his free hand, but still he wouldn't wake.

At last I gave up and lifted him into my arms.

"We're getting out of here," I whispered, and turned toward the hilltop's distant silhouette, a black knob against a crimson and purple sky.

In my arms he spoke at last. But his eyes stayed sealed, and his thumb-muted voice emerged as if from a dream.

"It's too late, Daddy," he said. "They're already here."

I spun in a wild circle to take in our surroundings, but I saw only what I'd seen before: dirt, rock, haunted trees, the lonely spire soaring above us. Detail had slid away with the dusk, making everything seem a shadow of itself. Then my ears caught a faint sound like moaning from above, and I stepped away from the pillar and stared into the darkening sky.

Things were crawling down the side of the spire.

Things pale yet dim as darkness, with livid skin and blunt, obscure faces. Their heads swung blindly from side to side as they descended. Their arms were long and veined as if they'd been flayed, but their trunks ended in a short, flat paddle like a larval tail. The walls of the tower glistened with a slick substance in their wake.

There were too many of them to count. More emerged each moment from the dimness at the peak of the spire and climbed steadily down.

I retreated, hugging Keely to my chest. His body remained limp, but I could feel his cheeks moving and hear their sucking sound.

When the first wave of the creatures reached a point ten feet from the base of the nest, they fell heavily onto their stomachs and lifted themselves to face me.

That's when I saw that they had no faces.

No eyes, no mouth, no features of any kind, only veined knobs like a fist stripped of flesh. Starting where their mouth would have been and stretching the length of their chest ran a gash, wide and ragged, as if they'd been ripped apart to expose the cavity of their bodies. But instead of revealing organs or muscle or bone, the gash opened on a smooth gray emptiness. The only signs of life were a waving motion at the torn edges of the gaping wound and a rotten smell that exhaled from within, accompanied by the chorus I'd heard, like the wailing of someone in pain.

I remembered Korah's story, the body of her father halfway corrupted by the thing that had taken him. I remembered Korah herself, her beauty changed to something reptilian, flesh and blood and bone dissolved to flailing skin. And I remembered my dream, my one link to the past, the excruciating feeling I'd experienced not of being invaded but of being consumed. No one had seen Skaldi before, Skaldi without the human hosts we'd always thought they nested inside. No one had seen them and lived.

Now I had seen them. And I knew what I was seeing.

Skaldi didn't enter you. Just the opposite. They drew you in, into the emptiness of their own bodies. They made you fill that emptiness, ingested you while they assumed your shape. When they moved on to their next victim, the scraps we found were the mimic coverings they had shed.

But I also knew that knowing this wouldn't save me.

The creatures circled us, dragging themselves blindly but surely on emaciated arms. Dozens more hung expectantly from the sides of the mound. Their swaying motion resembled a snake's.

The moaning grew louder as the creatures closed in. Still I could see nothing inside them, only a hollow space, dull and gray as dead tissue. I gathered myself to leap their squirming forms, but a feeling of horror made my legs tremble, and I dropped to my knees.

"Keely," I whispered to the inert bundle in my arms. He refused to wake from his dream. Then I realized it was better if his dream never ended, and I lowered my head and buried his sleeping eyes in my chest.

The creatures had drawn so close I could feel nothing but their icy breath, smell nothing but their suffocating stench. I tried to rise, but a crushing weight pinned me to the ground. Whatever power had protected me six months ago now seemed as remote as my stolen past. I closed my eyes and waited for the end.

But the Skaldi didn't strike. Their moans rose to a pitch of grief and pain.

Then I heard footsteps, a scuffing against dirt and stone. I raised my eyes to see that the creatures had flattened their bodies to the dust, arms outstretched. Their moans had died. The footsteps echoed in the stillness of the dusk as both the Skaldi and I waited for whoever or whatever was coming.

A moment later, a shadowy figure stepped from behind the nest. I couldn't distinguish a face, but the voice was unmistakable.

"Space Boy," the voice said. "Welcome to the family, little brother."

18
HOST

At first I thought the twilight had tricked my senses.

Then he stepped from the shadow of the pillar and I saw that it was him: tall, gangly, slouching, his face spread with the same smirk he'd been using to torment me for the past six months. He wore his usual filthy uniform, though his holster hung empty. Yet he approached the circle of Skaldi fearlessly, sliding with perfect confidence between their prostrate forms. Even more astonishing, a break appeared in their ranks to let him through. The circle closed once more as soon as he was past, and the creatures inched forward, groveling at his heels.

I tried to form words, but my mouth had gone dry. "Brother?"

His smile broadened. "Mom always said you were the smart one."

"But," I stammered. "Laman told me . . ."

"*Laman told me,*" he sneered. "Laman didn't know about Aleka and you. There's so much Laman didn't know. I told you not to follow his advice. But you wouldn't listen to your big brother, would you?"

"But," I tried again. "The camp. By the river. I thought you were . . ."

"Oh, that," he said, as if he was referring to a lost button or a skinned knee. He reached down, and one of the creatures lifted itself on skeletal arms to accept his caress. Watching his hand stroke its slimy back both mesmerized and repulsed me. "Rookie mistake," he said. "You can't kill us."

My mind whirred, stalled, sputtered to a halt. "Then you're . . ."

In answer, his smile yawned so wide it obliterated the rest of his face, as if his mouth formed the beginning of the gash I'd seen in the creatures at his feet. For a second there was nothing else, only a cavity like the empty skull of a thing long dead. Then the slit narrowed and the face became Yov's again, or what appeared to be Yov's, smugly grinning.

"We are," he said, "what we are."

"You're Skaldi." The fact that I was speaking to it seemed as incredible as the transformation.

It threw back Yov's head and hurled a long, mocking laugh into the twilit sky. The groveling creatures echoed its shout with ghostly moans.

There was only one way this could be, I thought

feverishly. The Skaldi that had destroyed the rebel camp had taken Yov's body. Somehow it had missed Keely, and then it had left in search of other victims. That was the only answer.

"Let Keely go," I said, knowing even as I said it that I couldn't bargain with Skaldi. "Do what you want with me, but let him go."

The thing with Yov's face smiled, malice glistening in its gray eyes. It lowered itself to sit among the squirming creatures, Yov's long legs stretched casually in front of it.

"We could have killed him six months ago if we'd wanted to," it said, speaking conversationally despite its ugly words. "But that was never our purpose."

"Six months?" I said dumbly. "How could you . . . ?"

The Skaldi tapped Yov's forehead with a long finger. At first I thought it was mimicking Laman's "focus" signal. But then I realized what it meant. This time I was so dumbfounded I could barely choke out the words.

"My memory," I said. "*You're* the one. *You* stole my memory."

"We *are* your memory," it gibed. "We take what we need, and throw the rest away."

My mind spun as its words sank in. I'd been right that my attacker hadn't been killed. But it hadn't been reduced to the creeping creature I'd seen. It had jumped from me to Yov. Against everything we thought we knew about them, it had kept his body intact for six long months, bleeding enough of Yov's stolen blood to pass the initial trials, remaining stable far beyond the point where anyone would suspect him. And the morning of Laman's rescue, when the one I'd thought was Yov had been shot in the leg and gone down screaming . . .

My eyes flickered over the wounded leg. The uniform showed no sign of a bullet entry. This shape-shifter had faked its own injury to fool Araz and his camp, and had restored itself when it no longer needed the disguise.

I met the creature's gaze. Its mimic face lit with a cruel smile. In its gaping mouth, Yov's yellow teeth seemed as tiny as a child's.

"How?" was all I could say.

The creature shrugged. "We don't ask *how*. We don't ask *why*. That's the thing that took the most getting used to. All the questions, the doubts. We had to learn to weed through that to get at what we wanted. To use your frailty for our own purposes."

Absently, it stroked the back of the nearest creature as it spoke.

"You and your brother taught us everything we needed to know. It was like waking up from a long, long sleep." Its voice sounded almost wistful. "So weak, so divided. You say one thing and do another. You call yourselves a colony, yet you let petty squabbles get in the way of your objectives. You wrangle over toys and trinkets. You follow a pair of pretty eyes into the dark, even if that means certain death."

I thought over my past six months in Survival Colony 9,

the past couple weeks. The creature's portrait of us—of me—sounded so true I felt compelled to argue. "We're not—"

It held up a hand as if asking for patience. "And your so-called leaders! Laman made it so easy for us. He must have suspected the compound was ours. Must have realized he couldn't hold it together once we trashed his truck. But he wouldn't face the truth. He wasted time sending that little bitch girlfriend of yours snooping around. We had to call one of the others to kill her off before he'd listen. Before he'd"—its teeth flashed like daggers—"focus."

It shook out Yov's legs and rose. The creatures cowered at its feet.

"And let's not forget the fabulous Space Boy," it jeered. "You couldn't have played it any better if we'd asked you to. Really, tracking our decoy right to our front door? Bravo."

Movement rippled among the Skaldi. A form emerged from their ranks: the crawling creature, its head bowed to the ground, its arms so emaciated it could barely drag its body forward. It lifted its head long enough to stare at me with vacant eyes, then it crumbled to dust at my feet.

"Mission accomplished," the thing that had been Yov purred. "It's been fun, Space Boy. But the game's over. Now it's time to go."

I met his eyes. They flamed red in a face that had wilted like dripping wax. I was surprised to find myself trembling, not with fear but with rage at the creature that had used my memory to attack the colony, and now was using the memory of people I'd known to mock their deaths. I wondered if Yov had always been as cruel as the one that had replaced him, if the monster that had consumed his body had inherited his soul. Was this twisted thing my real brother? Or had he ever been someone I looked up to, trusted, loved? Someone who loved me back?

Had he ever been someone like Korah, who loved her colony and her family enough to put herself in harm's way when the Skaldi struck?

"You haven't won," I said. My voice came out dry and cracked, but it grew stronger with each word. "You killed my brother, you had one of your little friends kill Korah, but you couldn't kill me. My memory is all you got."

A spasm passed over its stolen face, distorting it again, replacing Yov's smirk with the bulging knob of the Skaldi's blind forehead. Then Yov's features returned and the creature shook its head. When it spoke again its words sounded muffled and broken, as if it was losing the ability to work Yov's tongue and teeth.

"Your—memory is all we needed," it gasped. "Soon— there will be nothing left of you. Like there is nothing—left of them."

Again Yov's face buckled as if it was about to split open, and I sensed its deadly purpose coiling. I didn't know what it was that led me to continue taunting it.

"You call us weak," I said. "But you're the one that's weak. You steal people's bodies, people's memories. You use the strength of others to cover your weakness. You're afraid to fight on your own."

"No!" the voice burst from the monster's bottomless mouth, bringing with it the same stench of rot that breathed from the ring of lesser creatures. "Skaldi know no fear. No weakness. Skaldi know only death."

Once more the mask of Yov's face warped as the Skaldi-self strained to break free. Its lips twitched, its rabid eyes bugged. I knew there was no time left, no point in delaying what had to happen.

Gently, I laid Keely on the ground at my feet. He slept on, lost in whatever dream or nightmare had claimed him. Slowly, wearily, I stood and planted myself over his sleeping body. Then I raised my head to face the one I'd hated for so long, not knowing who or what I hated. My fists clenched as its frame melted away under the pressure of the monster Yov had become.

"Prove it," I said. My voice shook, and I hoped I sounded a lot braver than I felt. "Show yourself to me now."

With a shrug, the Skaldi threw off the last shreds of Yov's body and struck.

Its speed blinded me.

The instant it charged at me, it seemed as if a shroud settled over my eyes, and its form vanished into the darkness. The next instant, something powerful attached itself to my arms. It didn't feel like a body, a solid shape I could grasp or define, but a force that wrapped me in shadow and flooded my senses with the icy corpse-stink of its breath. A sickening sensation of being entombed in another's flesh washed over me, and my gut churned violently as I felt not only my body but something deep inside me being drained away. I tried to concentrate, to focus, but the more I tried, the muddier my thinking became. I seemed to be trapped at the bottom of a night-black pit, my body floundering amid the members of the two colonies the creature had consumed. I heard its mocking laugh in my head, urging me to kneel before it, to bow down as its latest sacrifice. It wanted me to give up, to surrender the parts of me it hadn't already claimed. For a long moment I forgot who I was, forgot that I was. There was no me, only it.

As in my dream, I heard a whisper. But this time I could make out what it said.

There was only one word.

Forget.

It would have been so easy to obey. I'd lost everything I'd ever called mine—my past, my hope, my people—and I almost felt as if it was my own voice telling me to give up. Did I really want to remember, if that meant remembering nothing but loss?

But another part of me fought back. A part of me that hadn't been drowned by the creature's venom bubbled up from the depths, and I clung to it as the waves buffeted me in the dark. It spoke to me not in words but in images: my game of catch with Laman, the trial where I stood beside

Aleka, my march through the night with Keely, my talk at the pool with Korah. I looked into her eyes as I had that night, and this time I saw the strength and love that shone within them. I focused on the light in her eyes, a frail blue flame in the surrounding darkness.

And then the darkness receded, and I returned. The flame spread outward from my chest to my arms, the tips of my fingers. My hands gripped something solid and sank in. The creature's taunting laugh turned to a shriek of pain, and the wall of darkness fell away, the suffocating stench retreating at the same time. A new smell wafted over me, the stink of burning flesh.

I opened my eyes.

The creature lay on the ground, convulsing, howling in pain. Wisps of smoke rose from its pale flesh, and in spots the sickly gray hue had turned an angry red. It thrashed so violently I couldn't tell for sure, but I thought the marks on its body matched the shape of my hands.

I staggered back, quaking with more than cold. But before I had time to think, to move, the Skaldi rose and lunged again.

Its force clutched me, its breath licked my face. Again I felt myself being turned inside out, exposed to its hunger, my skin raw and prickling as a newborn's. The world around me spun, the world inside me darkened. The name I called myself was snuffed out like a blown candle, and the only word that filled my mind was *Skaldi*.

But once again, when it seemed I could hold out no longer, a rush of memories flowed through my mind, and I felt a surge of air like a swimmer breaking the surface. The memories weren't all good, but they were mine, and I rode them back to the light. Laman giving me a tour of the weapons horde. Aleka guiding me the morning of the rescue. The old woman telling me about birds. Korah again, the first time she'd spoken to me, teaching me how to set up my tent, touching my hands as she showed me the way.

My own pulse became the pulse of a flamethrower. I shoved blindly and the Skaldi reeled, fell to its clawed hands on the ground. It tried to rise, but its arms gave out under it. Its tail thrashed feebly against the dust, threads of smoke curled from its blistered flesh. My own legs felt like rubber, but I faced it, waited for its next move.

Bracing itself with one hand, the Skaldi that had been Yov lifted its body shakily from the ground and pointed a single long, clawed finger at me. The scar that should have been its face split wide. The members of its colony reared from the dust in unison, and their skin peeled back like an opened wound.

With a speed I could hardly believe, they struck.

Some collided with my back, others my chest. All clutched at me, chewed my arms with their claws, clogged my nostrils with their breath. At their touch I gagged and nearly fell into the dead hollows of their bodies. A word echoed in my mind, a different word this time.

Querry.

Que . . .

Qu . . .

Then memory resurfaced, the sensation of fire flooded me once more, and the creatures broke contact, their writhing bodies dropping to the ground, their moans escalating to a high-pitched squeal. But they didn't stay down long. As if driven mad by their master, they flung themselves at me, strained to swallow me, to make me one of their own.

But they failed.

I did nothing. There was nothing I could do.

I stood, paralyzed by their speed, unable to resist when they clenched me in their arms. Too many came at me to catch them, grip them, fling them aside. I stood unsteadily, my head and heart pounding, dizzy and sick as if I'd gone a week without water. Memory was all that kept me on my feet, the fuel that fed an inner fire. At the creatures' touch, my flesh grew so hot it seemed as if my bones blazed. And the ground on all sides of me piled with pale bodies that twisted and clawed at the dust.

Finally it stopped. The creatures squirmed away, and I saw that though nothing ebbed from their bloodless flesh, their naked backs bubbled with red marks as if from an iron brand.

The leader hadn't moved from its spot. Its arm hung in the air, its body shuddered as if with heavy breaths. Its faceless face turned toward me once more, and I sensed a movement in its mind. A split second before it acted, I knew what it planned to do.

I scooped Keely's sleeping form into my arms and ran.

I heard the creatures in pursuit. When their stench told me I couldn't outrun them any longer, I dove to the ground, my body cocooned around Keely's to protect him from the assault.

Just in time.

They swarmed my back, grappled with me, slashed at my throat and wrists. I lay pinned to the ground by the iron strength of their claws, the dead weight of their bodies. Their breath hissed in my ears. The sickness inside them tore at me.

But they couldn't tear me from the child I shielded.

I knew I couldn't throw them off if I tried. So I made no effort to. I curled myself around Keely's frail form, and the creatures fell from me like dead skin. A force that came from somewhere other than my muscles, a force I felt as a hot coal glowing in the pit of my stomach and spreading outward like the path of a wildfire, defended me from their attack. I huddled around that flame and fought to hold on.

Time passed, but I had no way to mark its length. Sound and silence emitted the same dull roar. Memories slid and merged.

Finally, after what seemed an eternity, the creatures retreated. Their shrieks sliced the dark, pierced my heart. I lay shaking and weak, my stomach twisted and a foul taste in my mouth. Tears and darkness blurred my vision. I could barely see my attackers, barely keep from choking on the stench of their burned bodies. I didn't know what would happen if they came at me again.

They didn't, though.

Instead, a lot of things happened at once.

I heard shouts, voices. Footsteps hammered the ground so hard it shook. I lifted my head to see, but as I did, the soil collapsed beneath me. Instinctively, I clutched Keely's body. But the fall wasn't far, five feet at most, into the deeper darkness of underground. We landed softly not on dirt or stone but, incredibly, on human hands.

The hands lowered us carefully to the floor of the pit. Bodies brushed past me, nearly invisible in the dark but solid and alive with warmth. Fingers closed on my wrist. I tried to jerk away until I realized they were feeling for a pulse.

"Stay here," a gruff voice commanded. I didn't need to see her face to know it was Petra.

Her stocky body leaped over me, out of the hole. Heavy footsteps diminished as she ran. I felt another hand brush hair from my eyes, and a face I couldn't see leaned over to press dry lips to my forehead. Then it, too, vanished into the dark above.

The sky over my head blazed with twin ribbons of flame. The Skaldi wailed, a confused chorus of screams rising above the deep cough of the flamethrowers. I shivered as I remembered those screams from the night Korah died. But I took heart in the human voices that shouted in response, not

words I could distinguish but monosyllables of encouragement and resolve.

Then I heard Laman Genn's voice, sturdy and calm above
the chaos of battle.

"For the colony!" he called. "For our lost brothers and
sisters! Let none escape!"

The flamethrowers unfurled into the pitchy sky, and the
throats of the Skaldi howled in baffled rage and fear.

Carefully, making sure to keep track of Keely's body, I
lifted myself from the ground. Standing on tiptoes, I could
just peer over the edge of the pit.

In the orange glare of their two remaining flamethrowers, the last members of Survival Colony 9 marched in a
tight formation, driving the Skaldi away from the nest. Laman
and Petra I couldn't locate, and it was impossible to tell the
Skaldi leader from the rest of the blind, groping things. Some
lay dead, their bodies charred beyond recognition. Others
wriggled frantically away from the advancing line, but the
wide arc of the flamethrowers caught them and ignited them
with a crackling sound. Dozens, it seemed, would die, cut off
from the safety of their nest.

Still, I knew something was wrong.

I turned my eyes upward and saw in the flamethrowers' glow many more pale bodies scaling the spire.
Some had already vanished into the inky darkness at the
nest's peak. In a couple minutes of slow, painful climbing,
the others would reach the top, well beyond range of the

flamethrowers, and would be able to secrete themselves in their nest once more.

Laman's words rang in my ears.

Let none escape.

And I knew what he meant. He was determined to end it tonight.

I didn't want to leave Keely. I'd been watching him only a day, but already it seemed I'd had him with me a lifetime. And I didn't want to go back out there. I felt weak, dizzy, sick at heart and sick at soul. All I wanted was to curl up inside my hiding place and let the others finish the job.

But I knew if I didn't do something, the creatures would escape. And I knew I couldn't abandon my colony, not again, not now.

I knew the time had come.

I braced my hands on the crumbling lip of the pit and vaulted into the open. As soon as I did, I realized some of the bodies at my feet weren't Skaldi but my own people, burned by their fellow colonists to destroy the monsters that had tried to camouflage themselves with human forms. They'd been caught at all stages of the transformation, gray-white bodies with human faces, human bodies with gaping scars running their length. I didn't stop to identify the dead. I ran toward the row of attackers, waving my arms, trying to make myself heard above the din of battle.

"The nest!" I shouted. "Don't let them reach the nest!"

No one turned. They continued to march in a mechanical

line toward the retreating creatures, while the main body of Skaldi crawled nearer and nearer to safety.

More decoys, I realized. Sacrifices. Driven by the silent command of their leader, the Skaldi on the ground would forfeit their lives to allow the others to escape.

And if they did, their colony would win.

"The nest!" I shouted hoarsely. "They're getting away!"

No response came from the attackers. I stumbled with the effort to increase my speed, but I knew I was too late.

Then a hand gripped my arm and I turned to look into Laman Genn's eyes.

"Let's finish this now," he said.

He raised his walkie-talkie, spoke a few quiet words. I didn't hear the response, but he nodded as if satisfied.

"Petra's on it," he said. "Let's go."

"What is she—?"

"We'll wait for her to report back." Then he took my arm and, leaning heavily on a stick carved in the shape of a crutch, led me away from the noise and flames.

We stopped at the edge of the pit. To my relief, Keely's sleeping body lay where I'd left him. Laman said nothing for a long moment, just stood looking at me with keen but weary eyes. His face in the firelight was grimier than I'd ever seen, his hair and beard like that of a man who'd emerged from a lifetime in the desert. Which, I guess, he had.

Finally he broke the silence. "Their own tunnel," he said, indicating the pit. "Good to finally use one against them."

I saw then that the hole where Keely lay gave way to other holes, branches beneath the surface, snaking in every direction. "That's how they were getting around?"

He nodded. "Explains a lot. The surprise attacks, their ability to evade our sentries. How they made it appear as if they were everywhere, even to an experienced scout like Petra. They were right under our feet the whole time."

"You mean . . . ?"

"The crater," he confirmed. "That's how it got in that night." The lines around his eyes bunched with pain. "If only I'd figured it out sooner."

I felt my throat tighten. "You can't know everything."

"Huh." He averted his eyes, scratched the tangled mop of his hair. "You noticed."

"It was Yov," I said. "The Skaldi that led me here. The one that attacked me before. It was in our colony from the start. It summoned the one that killed Korah."

His face registered less surprise than I expected. "It's over now," he said.

"Is it?"

"Querry," he said, and I saw him reach toward me.

That's when the world shook with a muffled concussion, accompanied by a brilliant glare that threw our shadows into the far reaches of the night. We both spun, me a second before him. I saw the Skaldi nest blazing like a huge, grotesque candle. The fire shot high into the night, revealing for a moment the pale bodies of the creatures clinging to its sides.

Then another booming noise issued from deep within the nest, and I watched the black obelisk explode into fragments. Or I didn't watch. It happened too fast to watch. One second the spire stood there, the next chunks of fiery rock hailed around us and a pile of flaming rubble marked the spot where the nest had been. The forms of our companions still showed where they'd marched away from the nest, but the bodies that had clung to the nest were gone.

Laman frowned. He stared at his walkie-talkie. Then recognition lit his eyes.

"Petra!" he breathed, and began limping toward the remains of the nest.

He didn't make it. A black figure rose from the ground and launched itself at him. For a second my mind went blank. The thing struck Laman full in the chest and sent him sprawling, his crutch flying beyond his grasp.

I realized it was the Skaldi leader, charred and smoking but not dead. It rose above the helpless form of Laman Genn, its voracious mouth opening to consume him.

I had no time to think. As its jaws closed over Laman's body I threw myself at it, gripped its smoldering flesh and pulled with all my strength. My hands burned, waves of dizziness and nausea washed over me. But the creature, whether surprised by my assault or weakened by its own injuries, fell from its victim and rolled to the ground with me underneath. I could see nothing except its dark shape, but a hot liquid that had to be blood bathed my face and hands.

I rolled to the side, trying to throw it from me. My hand struck something on the ground, something small and smooth with marks like gashes along its surface. I gripped it, flicked it open, stabbed blindly upward. I felt my fist tear through the creature's chest, felt its body shudder. But still I remained trapped beneath it, unable to free myself.

Its breath hissed. Its body burned. Its maw was the darkness I could see, the darkness that covered the whole world. I struggled to keep from falling into that pit.

But I couldn't hold on, and the darkness closed around me.

GHOST

My eyes opened to a colorless dawn.

Daylight spilled in its queasy way over the world, illuminating an area of blighted ground and scrubby brush. I lay on my back with a rolled-up blanket beneath my head. Another wrap, equally threadbare, covered my legs. My hands, resting on the blanket, were swaddled in rags that did little to ease the burning pain in my palms. A hilltop rose in the distance, not the one I'd descended with Keely the day before. The air, though, hung thick with the smell of burning. Either the downed pillar was nearby or I'd carried the odor with me on my skin.

I lifted my head to look around, and instantly regretted it. A headache the size and shape of a fist connected with my temple, my eyes popping with pain. Nausea coiled through my stomach, my vision blurred. The morning I'd woken after the attack six months ago had been better than this. Then, I'd had no memory. Now, I felt like I had no strength, and no will either.

But I had to find out what had happened, what had become of Keely and Petra and Laman and the others. Had they lived or died? Had we won, truly won, or only gotten away, escaped with fewer and fewer of us left, like always?

Gritting my teeth, I kicked the blanket aside, lifted myself to one knee, and stood. My head and stomach protested, but my legs held. I took a couple hesitant steps, heard the blood pounding in my ears. That was the only sound I heard. I tilted my head delicately to listen for a human presence, but the world rested as still and dead as dust. If anyone had survived the battle, if they'd bound my wounds and carried me to this place, they'd left me to fend for myself.

But as soon as that thought crossed my mind, I knew it was wrong. They wouldn't leave me. I was the one who'd left them, but they had followed. Followed me right into the worst place I could imagine. They had fought for me there. Died for me there.

They weren't going to leave me. The question was, was I going to leave them?

I jumped at the sound of footsteps. Moving that fast made lights dance in front of my eyes. I staggered, almost fell, then felt a strong arm catch me and hold me up.

"Good morning, Querry," a voice said. It was Aleka's.

I searched her somber face. In the short time since I'd left camp, she seemed to have aged, becoming thinner, the lines of her face starker, her pale eyes larger in their dark sockets. The gray depths of those eyes held a well of pain. But as she looked at me, the whisper of a smile I'd seen on her lips surfaced again. She looked both worried and relieved, sorrowful and glad.

"What?" I said. "What is it?"

She didn't answer, just gripped my arm and guided me along with her. The look on her face never changed.

We passed more empty waste, the stub of a tree, the husks of vegetation past. My head and hands throbbed, the aroma of burning lingered in my nostrils. Then a familiar scent cut through the burning, the greasy smell of water. I realized we were near the river once more.

The camp had followed, what was left of it. Maybe fifteen people, adults and children, sprawled by the riverbank, faces and uniforms darkened by the night's fires. With relief, I saw that all the little kids had survived, Keely included. He looked at me as we walked by, and I tried to see in his dreamy eyes if any memory of the nest remained with him. Others, grown-ups and teens, roused themselves from their reclining positions and stared at me as we passed. I looked around for Petra, but her short, stocky frame was nowhere to be seen. Neither were the tangled hair and knotted beard of her commander. Fear clutched me, and I turned to Aleka.

"Petra," I began.

"Petra's gone," she said. "She was the one who destroyed the nest. From within."

"Then she . . ."

"Yes," she said. "She must have been hanging on to explosives all this time, waiting for her moment. No one but Laman knew, and he swears she said she'd get clear before the charges went off. But I think she never forgave herself for what happened to Danis. And I guess she decided to handle it her own way."

"Laman's alive?"

She nodded. "But he's lost a terrible amount of blood. The Skaldi that attacked him—"

"Was Yov," I said. "It was the same one that attacked me."

She nodded again, her lips and throat tightening with pain.

"Yov," I stammered, "I mean, the Skaldi—it told me you were . . ."

She said nothing, just met my questioning look with a solemn, steady gaze.

"Is it true?" I asked.

"The Skaldi lied about many things," she said gently. "But not about that."

A warmth spread through me as I regarded my forgotten mother. I stood awkwardly, not knowing whether to smile, shake her hand, throw my arms around her. But in a private place in my heart, the sting of betrayal kept my hands at my sides. "Why didn't you tell me?"

"It was the only way," she said. "The only way I knew to

ensure our safety. When we joined Laman's colony, I had no idea who I could trust. Out of desperation I'd told him about the attack, and it was obvious he was captivated. I sensed that if he knew you were my son, it could cause trouble." The somber smile touched her lips once more. "Call it a mother's intuition. So I agreed to participate in his deception as a condition of our joining the colony, and I kept to myself the truth about the boy he insisted on claiming as his own."

"You lied to him too," I said, not angrily. I was just amazed to hear that there were secrets Laman Genn hadn't known.

She reached out and touched my face as she'd done the morning we rescued him. Her fingers felt rough as if with years of accumulated scars, but their touch was warm. "The commander of a survival colony does what she must for the good of her people."

I smiled, even though what I had to ask her next filled me with fear. "And my—my dad," I said. "My real dad. Mine and Yov's. You said that he . . ."

"Is gone," she said softly. Her hand cupped to fit the curve of my chin. "There will be a chance to talk about him later. About him, and many other things. But there's only one place you need to be right now. And there's very little time."

At her words a chasm opened inside me, cold and empty. But I nodded, looked once more into her eyes. They were gray as clouded moons, deep as water, eyes that shone with a mixture of intensity and sorrow. I reached up and held her hand against my cheek.

"Yov had your eyes," I said.

She tried to smile. "Both my boys did."

She squeezed my hand, and the eyes we shared brightened with tears.

We walked on, through the shell-shocked camp, to the bank of the river. Everyone stared, but no one spoke, no one stood in our way. They all knew where we needed to go.

He lay by the water's edge, so pale and thin I thought he was already gone. His shirt and jacket were missing, and bloody stripes crisscrossed his chest and shoulders. For some reason his hair and beard had been shaved, showing even more clearly the hooked nose, gaunt cheeks, and wide, grim mouth of the man who had called himself my father. As I neared I saw that the crown of his head and his deeply corded neck were laced with gashes from the Skaldi's bite. Tyris knelt by his side, patting his wounds with a rag reddened by his own blood, while he stared placidly at the empty sky.

His eyes moved when our shadows fell on him, and his lips cracked in a soft smile, a natural smile that chased some of the deathly pallor from his face.

"I've brought you a visitor, Laman," Aleka said.

"No one I'd rather see," he said weakly. "How are you, Querry?"

"I'm okay," I said, catching myself before I added, "Dad."

"Have a seat," he said in the same thin voice, waving feebly at the ground beside him. The skin of his hand barely clothed the bones beneath. "You can go now," he said, his words meant either for Tyris or Aleka. Both left, Aleka squeezing my arm one last time before she climbed the bank and was gone.

I sat by his side. With Tyris no longer hovering over him, I could see that the slash marks were the least of his injuries. A thick bundle of cloth packed his stomach, soaked through with bright red. Tyris had no way to stop the bleeding, no way to repair the damage. The creature had torn a hole in him, and his life was ebbing away.

I didn't want to waste what little time we had left. I tried to focus on the most important things I needed to say. But exhaustion and grief clogged my thoughts, and the first thing that came to mind tumbled from my lips.

"Are they gone?" I asked. "The Skaldi?"

"I wish I knew." His voice, low and thready, carried a measured cadence. "Did Petra destroy *the* nest, or only *a* nest? But I have no way of answering that. I still know so little about them."

"What about—the one that attacked you?"

"Gone," he said. "Aleka had her flamethrower trained on it the whole time. You stabbed it with a blade, and that seems to have knocked the fight out of it. It struggled with you briefly then fell away, and she torched it."

I tried to imagine Aleka burning the body of the creature

303

that had murdered her firstborn son. "Did you know it was Yov?"

"I knew Yov lay behind the unrest in camp," he said. "But I didn't know the real reason until last night. And there was little I could do in any event, because of Aleka."

"You had him watched."

He winced at a sudden pain. "Korah," he said, his teeth gritted as if to trap what remained of his strength. "She kept an eye on him. And you. In case of trouble."

I thought again of bodies burning, this time not Yov's but Korah's. "You assigned her to watch us?"

"She volunteered," he said sorrowfully. "Insisted. When it became evident the strain was wearing on her, I relieved her of her duty. That didn't sit well with her, as you can imagine."

I remembered our conversation by the pool, her squabbles with Yov and Wali, her anger at me. Or at Laman. I remembered the kiss we'd almost shared, before the creature took her. I wished I'd known what she was going through. "So Wali took over . . ."

"But by then it was too late," he said. "The camp was lost, and any word I said against Yov would have imperiled us both. I did try to warn you, but . . ." His shoulders lifted incrementally.

"You tried to warn me?"

His head moved in a fraction of a nod.

"When?"

He said nothing for a long time, seeming to gather

himself inwardly. At last his chest settled into a calmer but shallower rhythm. "That night," he said. "After they took the camp."

My thoughts felt as thick as mud. All the days and nights flowed together in a single litany of sorrow. Then it came to me. "The sign you made. Not *V* but *Y*. *Y* for Yov. Focus on Yov."

"It was all I could think of," he sighed. "I knew by then that Yov was the ringleader, Araz only the figurehead. I suspected he'd been responsible for the truck, the tracks at the shelter. I even wondered if, somehow, he'd been consorting with the Skaldi. I thought if you watched him you might figure it out. As it happened, there was no time for that. The creature kept us all in the dark. It was more powerful than anything we've encountered."

I nodded, but impatience gnawed at me. His breath moved like a shadow, faint and uncertain. I felt it could flee at any moment. And there was still so much I needed to know.

"He—the creature spoke of the Skaldi as if they were a colony," I said. "A colony with him as its commander. It said they—he—learned about us from me and Yov. And then he passed that knowledge to the others."

Laman's chest rose in a long, slow, rattling sigh. I feared the strength had left him for good. But then his eyes sharpened on my face, and even without hair and beard he looked like the man I'd known, the man I'd thought I'd known.

"There's still a lot we don't understand, Querry," he said.

"A lot where all we're going on is speculation. Maybe this one was unique, something new. An evolved form. Its longevity suggests that. As does its unusual power of mimicry."

I nodded, wondering how much he'd seen last night. But I held my words as he continued.

"But the other way of looking at this is that its power came *from* you. From the attack that robbed you of your memory. If it's true the Skaldi acquire the attributes of their victims, it would stand to reason that it gained some of your power during that attack. Had it finished the job, there's no telling how potent it might have become. But thankfully, the same power prevented it from doing so. And if I were a gambling man," he said with a slight smile, "I'd bet that's because you're an evolved form too."

I ignored his final words. I just wasn't ready to go there. "And now it's gone."

His smile faded, and he nodded.

"Along with my memory?"

His eyes closed for a long minute. I noticed how thin his eyelids looked, like scraps of peeling bark. When he looked at me again the orbs seemed to have retreated deep into his skull. "I wish I had an answer for you, Querry," he said. "I truly do."

You must, I thought desperately. *If not you, then who?* "How will I know?" I blurted.

"Know?"

"*Know.*" I struggled to find the words. "Know if I'm the

one to blame for—everything. If it learned from me, got its power from me, then isn't it my fault? Aren't I the one who taught them how to think like us, trick us, trap us? You say it was an evolved form. But that means it evolved from *me*." I swallowed hard, feeling the bitterness of grief rising in my throat. "How will I know if it was me?"

His faraway eyes gave me a long, searching look, the kind I remembered from before I learned the truth. Before any of the things happened that had torn apart the world I thought I knew. "Querry," he said, "you can't live your life regretting what you can't change."

I hung my head so he wouldn't see the tears start in my eyes.

"It wasn't you who did this to us," he said. "You tried to warn me that night at the compound, but I wouldn't listen. I knew you were right, but—I fell in love with that ruined fortress. It reminded me of a place I barely remembered, a place I knew long ago. I couldn't bear to give it up. And so we lost Korah, and the colony was shattered, and now . . ." His voice broke with the remembrance. "It wasn't you, Querry. It was me. It was everyone."

"You could have told me," I said, still looking down to hide the tears.

"What?"

"You could have told me." I raised my head, and I didn't care if he saw. "You could have told me you needed help."

His ghostly face recoiled. "I was trying to . . ."

"To protect me," I said. "I know. I just wish you'd told me the truth. I could have handled it. I could have helped."

I looked at his stricken face, regretted what I'd said, but knew I'd had to say it.

"The truth," he said. "You want to know the truth."

I nodded, though the way he said it I was no longer sure.

"The truth," he said again. His eyes were on my face, but they were no longer on me. "I'll tell you the truth."

I waited.

"The truth is . . ." He drew a deep breath, and his eyes locked on mine. "I was a father. Once. I had a son. Just before you arrived in camp."

Now it was my turn to be shocked. "What happened to him?"

His eyes rolled away. I saw the tears sparkling in their corners.

"He gave up," he said. "And then he died. He was about your age. A couple of years older."

"He killed himself?"

"He gave himself to the Skaldi. I couldn't stop him."

I stared at him, speechless. "How?" was all I could say.

"It was how we found you," he said. "You and Aleka and Yov. He had—wandered off. Disappeared. We had fought. I didn't realize the depths of his despair."

Tears flowed freely down his wasted cheeks.

"We went to find him," he said. "And found only this."

His bony fingers unclenched, and I saw the red-handled

pocketknife resting in his palm. Its letters had been wiped clean of last night's filth, but I knew this was the blade I'd used against the Skaldi.

"His knife was in your hand when you came to us," Laman Genn spoke through his tears. "The Skaldi that destroyed your colony must have used his body to travel to you. It was the same creature that attacked you and Yov. The same creature that stole your memory."

My mind moved at lightning speed again. I remembered what Aleka had told me: Laman had injured his hip trying to save a child. But he had failed. What she hadn't told me, what she possibly hadn't known, was that the child he'd failed to save was his own.

"So what was I?" I said. I tried to keep my voice soft, but I knew my words might wound. "Another experiment? Or a replacement?"

"No," he said vehemently. "A second chance. A chance to—save you. To teach you. All the things I couldn't teach him." His eyes pleaded with me, or with someone else, for understanding. "You were a blessing to me, Querry. A chance to atone for the sins of the past. You were so much like him. It was a foolish hope, but I felt the creature had left a part of him in you. A part I could still reach. One so seldom gets a second chance. And when one does . . ."

It usually goes the same way as the first, I thought, but didn't say.

"I hope you can forgive me," he said. "I know I was never

a true father to you. But my wound was so raw when you came to us. If it was true you carried a trace of my son, it was also possible you shared in his despair. That you might give up as he had. You were too important to the colony to let that happen. I needed to protect you, to—heal you. To keep you alive, to keep him alive. Even if that was only a memory."

The hand that held the knife groped in the dust for mine. I took it, felt through my bandages the ice his skin had become. I squeezed gingerly, hoping he could still feel my touch.

"His name," I said. "Was it Matay?"

He nodded. "In one of the old languages it means 'gift from God.'"

A spasm stiffened his body. I rose to one knee to find Tyris.

"Don't," he whispered.

I sat again and gripped his hand. The knife's plastic handle felt as cold as the flesh that held it.

We stayed like that for a long time, while the sun marched across the sky, and his breath became a rumor and his face turned to chalk. I didn't know if he realized whose hand he was holding, or if he cared. He was silent for so long I had decided he would speak no more when I saw his lips move and heard his voice emerge in an almost noiseless mutter.

I leaned close to hear.

". . . never left you," he said. "Petra followed you all the way. We stayed close, and she called us when the time came."

"She was willing to die for me," I said.

"Yes."

"And Korah."

"We all were."

"Even you."

He nodded.

"Why?"

His eyes found my face. Whether he could see me anymore I couldn't tell.

"We waited," he said. "At the nest. Watched. I wanted them all to see. Aleka too. To see and believe."

My eyes opened in wonder at his final stratagem. "You let me leave camp."

He nodded again.

"You let the Skaldi attack me."

He had no strength left to nod, but his lips parted in a gentle smile.

"What if I'd failed?"

His dying eyes showed no doubt. "I knew what we would see. And I knew, once they'd seen, they would follow you. No matter what happened to me."

I was staggered, but not by the risk he'd taken with my life. By his faith.

"It was luck, Laman," I said. "Just luck."

"There is no luck left in this world," he whispered. "There's only power, though we may not understand its source." With his free hand he reached up to touch my cheek. "You can't choose the life you're given, Querry. But you can choose the kind of man you want to be."

I nodded fiercely, my tears falling on his face. They blurred my vision, erased the whole world. I could no longer see the man whose hand I held. All I could see were the sons who had come before, the three sons of Laman Genn. His own son, seeking forgetfulness in the Skaldi's pitiless embrace. My brother, taken by the monster that had tried to destroy us all. And me, the one son who had lived. The one who'd been given a future, even though I'd forgotten my past.

I closed my hands over Laman Genn's, brought them to his heart. I felt his restless spirit stir.

"Dad," I said without thinking. "Tell me . . ."

But his eyes had closed forever.

20
LAST

We laid Laman Genn to rest on a day like any other.

His grave faced the river, close enough to hear its trickle as we stood by the gravesite, far enough to keep it from washing away on one of those rare days when storms caused the water to overflow the banks. I had suggested the spot. I'm not sure why. We'd situated the other graves on higher ground, but something about the river appealed to me. I thought it was a more peaceful place, I guess.

We'd worked all night to bury the others. The row of graves seemed endless, but little rested inside: the bodies we'd brought back from the nest, the occasional intact uniform top of Araz's followers. Wali removed a twisted nugget of gold from his pack, the remains of a ring he'd given Korah, and buried it in memory of her. Aleka had found it in the bomb shelter the night after Korah died. In place of Petra's body we planted a stick bearing a patch of uniform. The way it flickered in the wind reminded us of her blinking. That made us smile.

Yov's grave was as empty as the rest. Aleka stayed by it a long time. I put a hand on her shoulder, felt the silent grief wracking her body. Then I left her and went to help the others prepare for the burial of the man who'd led us for so many years.

We worked methodically but quickly. With the nest gone, we stayed by the riverbank all night and morning, digging with cups and shovels until dark, resuming our work as soon as the sun cleared the horizon. When our skin began to blister we wrapped his body in canvas and laid it in the shade, but we knew we had to get it in the ground before long. We also decided to erect a headstone, something the old woman who'd survived it all said they'd done in days long past. While the colony's remaining adults pried a slab from the riverbed and used a hammer and stake to chip it into a roughly rectangular form, while the little kids played in peace by the waterside, it fell to me to come up with something we could carve into the grave marker.

Aleka had suggested me as the writer. A few words to honor him, she'd said. To remember him. A line or two for anyone who might happen upon the grave, from our colony or another, to read if they could and reflect on the life he'd lived and lost. At first I objected, telling her it seemed wrong for me to do it, the one who'd known him a shorter time than anyone in camp. But the others insisted, and I couldn't tell them no.

So I spent the morning hours by the riverbank, at the spot where he'd breathed his last. Not that I expected to find any inspiration there. The mark of his body on the ground, the semicircles of my heels, were all that remained of our final interview. Wind and water would remove those signs too in no time. And we'd move on as well, in search of something none of us could name. If ever we returned to lay dried weeds on his grave or to check how the inscription had weathered, we'd find the place exactly as it was now, unchanged except for the disappearance of the little things, the marks and scratches that commemorated our passage across the land.

Now that the secret had leaked and the man who'd kept it from me was gone, I'd asked the members of his camp about his son. From Soon and Tyris and Nekane, I heard stories of a Laman far different from the man I'd known. They described this younger Laman as tough but compassionate: a commander who used to laugh, to tease the little kids, to forgive people's faults and run his colony more like a family than a boot camp. Next they told me about Laman's wife, a woman they called Asheh, who had died giving birth to Matay. After her death, they said, Laman Genn had changed. They told me how from the time Matay could walk, Laman had drilled his son morning and night, kept him from joining the other kids in play. Kept him from everyone, really. They spoke of midnight battles in Matay's tent, two shadows confronting each other across the canvas screen, overheard reprimands and accusations. Nessa described Matay to me: aloof, alone. A boy in a man's uniform, the perfect soldier. Forced to relive a past he'd never known. And when he couldn't take it anymore and sought oblivion with the Skaldi, it was as if Laman Genn's last dream had died with him.

But I knew, in a way the others could understand but never truly feel, that a part of Matay had survived. I knew what it felt like to be the man's son, even if he wasn't really my father. I knew the dream he'd died to preserve.

I knew because the dream was me.

So I wrote what seemed to me needed to be written. I hadn't written a word in all the time I could remember, and the letters came slowly, but they came. I wrote them in the dust with Matay's pocketknife, then erased them and wrote them in my thoughts. I told them to Nekane, one of the few left in camp who could read and write, and she nodded in approval. I kept them in my mind for the time to come.

Which led to me standing by his grave in the late afternoon sun, watching as his shrouded form descended into the hole we'd dug. What was left of our colony watched with me, sixteen out of the fifty-one I'd woken to six months ago. The headstone stood in place, a chipped and angular piece of rock sticking from the ground like the foundation of a wall waiting to be built. I'd draped a piece of cloth across the inscription, so only Nekane and I knew what she'd carved there. Aside from that, we performed no ceremony, no dressing this burial up to look different from any of the other funerals we'd held the day before. We didn't have the means, and besides, I didn't think he'd want it to be that way.

When the ropes that had borne his body during its final descent were pulled back up and coiled on the ground, Aleka took her place beside the headstone and spoke a few words.

"Laman wouldn't have wanted us to give up," she said. "He would have wanted us to go on without him. His only wish all these years was for his people to survive, to triumph. He knew there would be sorrows, losses we'd have to endure, sacrifices we'd have to make. He denied himself so much for the future of this colony. That we're standing here today is proof he succeeded."

I smiled a little to myself when I heard that. Not because it was untrue. But because it was unfinished.

"Querry?" she said, and stepped away from the stone.

I took her place and felt everyone's eyes on me. I wondered if this was how Laman had felt the many years he'd been the center of attention, the focus of his colony's hopes and dreams. Maybe Matay had felt this way too. Exposed. Unsure. With nothing to say, and so much that needed to be said.

So I tried to keep my words to a minimum.

"Um," I started. That was one word I could have done without. "The thing about Laman was . . ." I swallowed. "He loved us. That's all. I don't think I realized that until he was gone. I hope he knows I realize it now."

My wrapped hands shook as I reached for the strip of cloth that masked the headstone. I fumbled with the knot I'd tied, took what seemed minutes before I got it undone. It fluttered into the hole where his body lay.

Nekane had carved his name in bold, uneven letters: *LAMAN GENN.* Beneath that she'd cut the words: *AGED 52 YEARS. BELOVED LEADER OF Survival Colony 9.* And then a single word, the only word I'd written: *FATHER.*

It's enough, I thought.

The smiles and nods of the people around me told me they agreed.

One by one, the survivors stepped forward to say their good-byes. Wali placed his mess tin in the grave, the one Laman had chewed him out for burning. Aleka saluted, her eyes fixed on the late-day sparkle of the river. Nekane lowered the crutch she'd carved for him in his final days. Those who had no gift to give scooped a fistful of dirt from the pile beside the grave, sprinkled or tossed it onto his body. Keely knelt and used both hands to gather his offering. The old woman chattered away about what a shame it was that Laman hadn't kept a collection jar. That, she said, would have been the best way to commemorate his life. She still fondled her husband's, the one she'd saved all this time. Neither Laman's commands nor Araz's threats had been enough to pry it from her.

I was last to approach the grave. I knelt beside it and bowed my head. In my mind I saw all the people who were gone. Laman, Petra, Mika, Danis. Korah. Araz and Kelmen and Kin. Asheh. Matay. People I hadn't known. The older brother I would never know. All of them, like the world before us, a world we'd lost before we had it, had lapsed into memory. When the old woman died, her world would be utterly lost too. And if none of us made it, then all memory would come to an end.

A sob shook my chest as the grief of all the things we'd left behind swept over me. I covered my face with my hands, squeezed my eyes shut, but the tears wouldn't stop. I sensed the others standing silently around me, witnesses to my sorrow. Then I felt hands on my shoulders and saw that Aleka had knelt beside me. In moments the others joined us, forming a circle of linked arms and bowed heads around the grave. The tears none of us had had time to shed flowed freely now, and I felt as if my tears had joined a river of tears. As if I was truly a part of Survival Colony 9 at last, and I was crying with it for all its lost children.

We stayed like that a long time, while the sun wheeled overhead. Gradually our tears dwindled into the sound of the murmuring river, the sighing wind. Deep down I felt the hole within me, the part I'd never get back. I knew none of them could fill that hole. Not Laman, or Aleka, or Korah, or Keely, or any of the others. The only thing they could do was exactly what they'd done: be there. Live with me, live for me.

Fight for me. Even die for me. If that wasn't enough, then I had a much bigger problem than not knowing who I was. If that wasn't enough, then whoever I was wasn't a person I wanted to be.

We said a final prayer for our family, then left the grave.

We stayed by the river for three days. No sign of Skaldi disturbed us, no threat of rupture arose within our ranks. We rested by the river to restore our souls, to let the memories soften a little under the quiet lapping of the water and the twinkles of sunlight on its surface. Some found solace sitting by Laman's grave, others found it playing with the little kids, who now nearly outnumbered the rest of us. At night we lit campfires and spent the time sitting together, sometimes talking, mostly gazing around the circle in silent thanks for those who remained.

I spent a lot of those three days by the river at the spot where he'd died. Skipping stones, watching their trails punctuate the water like an arc of stars. I remembered playing that game, connect-the-dots, with the little kids when Laman first assigned me to watch them. It was a way to keep them busy, a way to keep them from worrying about what was going on. I'd scratch holes in the dust, then they'd use their fingers or a stick to draw lines from hole to hole. I was no artist, and the drawings that emerged didn't look like much of anything: a lopsided tent, a crook-eared bunny, a person with stick-figure arms and gargantuan head. Half the time the kids would connect the dots in the wrong order and it wouldn't look like anything at all. Or they'd trample the drawing in their eagerness to finish it and end up with something that was part drawing, part footprint, part smudge. They didn't seem to care, though. Kids that age, they're not looking for answers. They don't even know which questions to ask. They're just drawing lines in the dirt, making it up as they go along.

I wished I could be like that. I wished I didn't know how much I didn't know.

But I did know I'd come too far to go back.

And because I knew that, I also knew this hiatus couldn't last. I knew, if not today then tomorrow, if not tomorrow then the next day, we would have to leave this place behind. The canned goods wouldn't last forever, and there was hunger to think of, the hunt to feed our bellies. More than that, there was the hunger that came from years of running, the fear of staying put, the hope of finding something better over the next rise. Years of running hadn't fulfilled our need, but that hadn't stopped us from searching. Deep down, in our blood, in our history, we were an unsettled people, always on the move, always on the lookout for more. Our restlessness had doomed us in the past, but it was all we knew that might save us in the future.

And so we couldn't stay, because we had to go. It was as simple as that.

Maybe that was why it was so easy, on the third night,

to look around the campfire and see reflected in each other's eyes the decision we had all made.

The day of our departure dawned pale and drab as always. People rose, bundled their packs, secured the shoulder straps. The little kids played hide and seek behind the few boulders and scatterings of scrub brush this place afforded them. I heard Keely shout, "Ready or not, here I come!" Aleka circulated through camp, silently approving our work. I watched her slim figure pass among the survivors, gray as a shadow, gray as a stone. Over the past three days, I'd seen a surprising number of items we were supposed to have disposed of coming out of packs—the slippers, the bunny book, the doll's head—but when I asked her about it, she just smiled and walked away.

She and I hadn't spent much time together since Laman's funeral. Unofficially, she was now the leader of Survival Colony 9, and she had better things to do than chase after me. We'd kept our relationship quiet, maybe waiting for the right moment to go public, maybe giving it time to sink in. Good news arrived so seldom in this world, it made sense to savor what little we had.

But there were still lots of questions I wanted to ask her. About my past. The power that protected me. My father. My brother. Myself. She probably couldn't answer all of them. Still, it felt good to know that I had someone to ask.

Now she came over to my spot, where I lay fully dressed but still covered by a blanket, enjoying a few final moments of laziness, or rest, or remembrance.

"Ready to go?" she asked.

"In a minute."

"You know what today is."

I shook my head.

"We don't keep track of them as well as we should," she said. "But I wanted you to know I haven't forgotten."

She handed me a cloth-bound package. I plucked at the twine that held it together, peeled back the wrapping. She watched, the ghost of a smile touching her lips.

The package contained a book. But unlike the bunny book, this one appeared homemade. Its cardboard cover was charred and wrinkled, smelling both musty and pungent. Loops of string loosely bound the whole. When I opened to the first page, I saw a picture of a baby, a charcoal drawing. Thumbprints smeared the image and the edges of the page had been eaten by time, but I had no doubt who it was. Its huge, soft eyes stared back at me across the years, years I couldn't remember, years I might never get back.

I flipped through the rest of the crumbling pages. They were all blank.

"I wasn't able to keep it up," she said apologetically. "But happy birthday, Querry."

She brushed hair from my eyes. It seemed as if she was about to say something more, but she only smiled. Then she turned and walked off to supervise the others.

I tucked the book away with Matay's pocketknife and lay

on my back, hands behind my head, staring into the wide open sky.

How much memory, I wondered, does it take to make a life? The oldest member of our colony had over seventy years worth, the youngest member fewer than six. I owned no more than a tenth of his memories. But the ones I did have, were they enough? Me and Laman playing catch. Me and Korah sitting by the pool. Me and Aleka daring a rescue. Me and Keely marching through the dead of night. I remembered loss, and fear, and pain, and some small amount of joy. I remembered others. I remembered me.

And I remembered what Laman had told me, what he'd told all of us. *Life*, he'd said that day in the compound, *isn't a penance for the past. Life isn't about looking back. It's about looking ahead.*

So much had changed since then, I could hardly believe he'd said it just over a week ago. I hadn't remembered that today was my fifteenth birthday, but it seemed like a good day to begin to live the lesson he himself couldn't always live.

What I would find in the days ahead I couldn't guess. Maybe I'd find the world of dust and ruin endless, the monsters we'd struggled to slay in pursuit of us still. I might find that my memory had vanished for good. Or, worst of all, I might find that there was nothing left to find.

But I had found a mother. I had found a family. I had found their faith, and maybe, in time, I would find the strength to make it mine. I might find there was still life, and hope, and beauty in the world. I might find a friend. I might even find myself.

So I'd go with the survivors of Survival Colony 9, be with them, live with them, fight with them. I'd let no enemy steal what was best about us, the love that made us strong. I'd do what I could to make sure what we had lasted. Though if it came to that, I'd die with them, too.

But I wouldn't lead them. I wouldn't pretend I had all the answers. I'd find another way, my own way. I'd be who I was. Whoever I was.

Querry.

That was the name my mother had given me, the name of the child in the baby book. But I had another name too, and I'd carry it in honor of the man who had willed it to me.

Querry Genn.

I tried the name on my tongue. For the first time, it sounded right.

"My name is Querry Genn," I said to the stillness of the newborn world.

Then I rose to meet the dawn.